Until We Meet Again
Bailey Thomas

Bailey Thomas Books, LLC

The Unfinished Love Series – Book 2

Fate: an inevitable and often adverse outcome, condition, or end.
(*Merriam-Webster*)

Contents

1

Vigilante

Have you ever been so grossed out that your insides began to contract because of how unappealing something was? I was specifically referring to a moment when you felt so sick you wished your senses would suddenly fail. Well, that was how I felt when I saw my best friend, Avery, and my brother, Graham, kissing. I may have been overreacting and exaggerating a tad, but they had been together for over two years now, and I still hadn't gotten used to the sight of them being affectionate with each other. Avery was my best friend first, so my brother should have been thanking me every day for even bringing her into his life, but instead, my repayment for being Cupid was watching them cuddle and kiss every second they could. I thought the honeymoon phase would have been over by now, but I was starting to think that their relationship would permanently stay in a state of endless affection.

I began grabbing my stomach and making obnoxious gagging sounds, which doubled as a way to get them to stop kissing, and as a tactic to remind them that I was still in the room. Strands of hair got stuck on my tongue as my open mouth pretended to hurl. They tasted like bitter shampoo, but I couldn't put a stop to my performance. I had to make my presence known. Sometimes, I thought Avery and Graham got so lost in each other's eyes that the whole world around them would disappear, including anyone in close proximity to them. Therefore, my over-the-top performance of acting like I was going to be sick at any moment was a flawless tactic for bringing them both back down to earth and reminding them that they weren't the only two people left on the planet.

"You ever heard of *The Boy Who Cried Wolf*?" my brother called out to me. "One day you are actually going to be sick, but nobody will believe you because of how often you fake it."

"You ever heard of a room?" I shouted back at him. "Go get one."

In return for my snappy comment, he simply rolled his eyes at me—but at least I got him to give his lips a break.

Graham was my only sibling so naturally I was very protective of him, even though he was older than me. There was plenty of sibling love to go around with it just being the two of us, but it also meant there was a lot of banter. We probably hugged and fought every day. There was no mistaking that we were siblings by the way we acted toward one another, but we also looked alike. Our parents' light brown hair and hazel-eyed genetics perfectly transitioned over to us. We both possessed freckles too, but mine were definitely more prominent than his, which was a trait that slightly separated us.

Even though I often messed with my brother about restraining his affectionate acts to the privacy of his own room, it wasn't really that big of an ask considering he lived in an apartment a few floors away. Avery and I lived together with our other best friend, Hannah, who completed our friendship trio. Although Avery and I had been best friends since high school, Hannah seamlessly fit into our dynamic when we had met her a few years ago at the complex we resided in now. She was the best thing to come out of living at the Exe Apartments.

The apartment building itself perfectly resembled the fast-paced life and exciting party scene that the surrounding city of Las Vegas had to offer, but on a smaller scale. Avery and I signed a lease on the spot when we heard about the extravagant pool parties the complex hosted. In hindsight, our young, twenty-two-year-old brains put too much emphasis on the amenities offered rather than the practicality of the actual living situation, but we definitely ended up paying the price for it in the end—well, rather Avery paid the price for it in the end.

"What's for dinner?" I groaned as Graham slowly removed himself from the couch and started heading toward the kitchen. Since I had interrupted their little romantic session, the next order of priority was eating. The clock had just hit 6 p.m., and I was ready for some food to hit my stomach.

"I don't know. I was thinking of searing some scallops," Graham answered. "Unless you haven't finished recovering from being sick."

That time, it was my turn to roll my eyes at him, but having a brother who was also a head chef at a fancy steakhouse was definitely a perk to being related to him. I didn't mind my annoying older brother living in the same complex as me when he consistently made dinners that would make anyone's taste buds do a happy dance.

"It's just going to be us three tonight," Avery chimed in, removing herself from the couch since her boyfriend's presence was no longer there. She joined me at the kitchen table, giving herself a great view to watch Graham cook. "Hannah is working tonight."

"Oh my gosh, I told her to take a break. It's a month before her wedding," I explained.

"She said this was going to be her last gig for a while," Avery pointed out. "Then, it's full wedding mode."

Technically, I was Hannah's boss. I started my own company matchmaking wealthy families to high-quality nannies. Hannah was one of the nannies in the network. She was actually one of my best employees, but with her wedding coming up shortly, I wanted her to focus on making sure her special day went as smoothly as possible rather than watching kids.

"Speaking of her wedding," Avery continued. "Have you found a date yet?"

I didn't mind being the single one in the friend group. After seeing the men Avery had dealt with, I considered myself lucky to be single. However, not having a boyfriend had its downfalls, especially during wedding season.

"I was thinking of just going alone," I admitted casually.

"Paige Jensen!" Avery shouted. "You can't go to Hannah's wedding alone."

"And why not?" I fired back.

"She specifically saved a seat at your assigned table for your plus-one. Do you really want Hannah to have an empty chair at her reception?" she reasoned. "She would freak out."

It obviously wouldn't have been ideal for there to be nobody seated next to me, but Hannah had way too much faith in my ability to find a guy to bring. I couldn't remember the last time I had been on a date, let alone had a serious boyfriend. Avery's love life and history with toxic relationships was enough to keep both of us busy. I didn't have the time nor desire to find a man of my own.

"I can ask one of the chefs at the restaurant to go with you," Graham chimed in. "I'm sure one of them would be willing to accompany you."

"Thanks, but no thanks," I answered. "I don't want my brother picking out a date for me."

"She's already being set up by Hannah, anyway," Avery directed toward Graham.

"Oh really?" he questioned.

"Yeah, Paige has a blind date tomorrow," Avery alerted.

"Thanks for the reminder," I groaned.

"The wedding is only a month away, and Hannah is counting on you to bring someone," Avery scolded.

At times, I wished we were back in Michigan where I could have easily asked some random guy I went to high school with to give up a Saturday afternoon for me, but unfortunately I didn't have the same friendships in Las Vegas as I did back home. Leaving our hometown and moving to Nevada right out of college was definitely an adventure that strengthened Avery and I's bond and allowed us to meet Hannah, but I was never able to recreate the same friendships that I had growing up. I had made some friends along the way, but recently my social life had taken a backseat as running a business took a lot more time out of my schedule than I would have originally imagined.

"If the blind date doesn't go well and you don't find a date in the next few weeks, I'm signing you up for one of those dating apps and picking a guy for you off there," Avery threatened.

"Ew, gross," I countered. "Have you seen the men on there?"

"She'd better not have," Graham piped up.

Avery blushed, knowing full well that she didn't even notice any other guy but him.

"There's like murderers and serial killers on the apps now," I responded.

"I'm pretty sure murderers and serial killers are the same thing," Avery said, totally missing the point.

"There's definitely a difference," I stated. "And, I think we've had enough of finding a guy that ends up being a criminal."

Avery returned my comment with an awkward chuckle. It had been more than two years since Kyle Kingsley had entered our lives, but it was still a sensitive topic.

"I'm sure Paige will give her full effort into the blind date tomorrow," Graham interjected, trying to add lightness and positivity back into the conversation.

"I'll do my very best," I let out, even though the odds were not in my favor.

I was excited to celebrate Hannah's special day, however, the stress of finding a date was starting to weigh on me. If I could go back in time, I would have told her to not give me a plus-one. On second thought, if I could actually turn back the clocks, I would probably never have toured the Exe Apartments. In fact, I may not have even agreed to make the move to the state where Kyle Kingsley lived if I had known what I knew now. The mere thought of him was enough to make my blood boil.

Kyle was a snake who used to double as the Exe's pool security guard. He was never that cute to begin with, but he somehow caught the attention of my best friend. From the start, I knew there was something off about him, however, I ignored my instincts because I wanted Avery to have a fair shot at finding love without me getting in the way. She had just gotten out of a relationship with her college sweetheart, Ethan Wiley, and was ready to put her heart back out there again. I was happy to see her try dating again, but she managed to fall for someone who made her cheating ex look like a decent human being.

At the time, Avery had a skewed view of love. Her parents had won the lottery when she was in high school, and abandoned her to travel the world with their riches, leaving her in the hands of her horrible aunt. As soon as Avery turned eighteen, her Aunt Joan kicked her out of the house, and she finished out her senior year living with me and my family. We were pretty certain her aunt had only taken her in because her parents had bribed her, considering Aunt Joan was not capable of, or willing, to take care of anyone else but herself.

I enjoyed having my best friend live with me. It was probably every teenager's dream come true. Having Avery there was like having a permanent sleepover buddy. Little did I know, she was slowly developing a crush on my brother. Aside from his culinary skills, I didn't know what she saw in him, but they both ended up happily together about five years later. Too bad Avery had to get her heart, spirit, and face broken before she got to end up with her Prince Charming.

Kyle Kingsley had this sort of dual personality. A part of him was charismatic, outgoing, and friendly, but that side of him only came out when he was manipulating my best friend. Avery fell for his charm, even after he left her at a bar, flirted with girls in front of her, and put her in uncomfortable and unsafe positions. I never knew what it was about Kyle, but he had some sort of trance on Avery that always kept her going back for more. He expressed never wanting anything serious with her, but that didn't stop Avery. She was relentless in her pursuit of him, hoping that after spending enough time with her, Kyle would eventually fall for her in the end—however, that couldn't have been farther from what had actually happened.

Instead of their love story ending in a white dress and church bells, it ended with a hospital gown and police sirens. Kyle and his brothers decided that it would be a great idea to break into our apartment and steal the lottery winnings that they thought Avery's parents had given her a portion of. What they didn't know was that her father also had a gambling addiction, and the $17 million that he had won on a lottery ticket was quickly squandered away in a few casinos on a trip to Vegas. There was no money left, but of course, Kyle didn't know that. He and his brothers beat up my best friend while she was tied to a chair, demanding she tell them where the hidden funds were. They eventually left once they figured out there was no money, but the damage they had done was permanent. Good thing my brother was there to piece back Avery's shattered spirit and broken heart. Somehow, every part of Avery's soul was crushed and ripped apart, except for the trauma bond that she still had with Kyle. I fully believed that any remaining tie to him at this point had been severed, but she still never gave up Kyle or his brothers to the police. I swore that if I ever saw Kyle again, I would give him the revenge he deserved for putting my best friend through all that. However, it had been over two years since the incident, and there hadn't been a single sign of him. I always kept my guard up, though, because I figured he would pop up into our lives when we least expected it, but I really hoped my suspicions were just the side effects of extreme paranoia and that we actually had nothing to worry about. But Kyle Kingsley was a snake, and if there was ever a crack in Avery's life, I was sure he would find some way to take the opportunity to slither back into it. Yet, this time, he would be met by me, an infuriated best friend full of vengeance.

"Paige," Graham remarked from across the kitchen, "how many scallops do you want?"

The kitchen smelled delicious, but suddenly my nagging stomach that was bothering me a second ago was no longer an issue. The thought of Kyle had consumed me and suppressed my hunger.

"Just a few," I responded back. "I'm not that hungry anymore."

"Really?" Avery questioned. "I thought you were starving."

"She must be imagining us kissing again," Graham joked.

I actually wished that the unsettling feeling in my stomach was due to my brother and best friend's overuse of public displays of affection, but that time, I was thinking about much worse. The image of Kyle Kingsley's face popped into my head, and it truly did take everything in me to keep from throwing up.

2

Love is Not Blind

"This is going to be the best girls' night ever!" Hannah shrieked as she leaned as close to my mirror as possible to apply her mascara. My bathroom wasn't big enough for Avery, Hannah, and I to be crammed inside it, so her elbow almost hit me in the process. It would have been a disaster if she had actually made contact, as my eye would have then matched her black leather jacket. It was her favorite article of clothing to wear, as it really made her red hair pop. I had borrowed it from her a few times, but it definitely looked better on her.

"I don't think it counts as a girls' night when we are meeting a guy at the bar," I moaned as I was putting the finishing touches on Avery's makeup.

"I think it adds to the fun," Avery agreed, moving her head toward Hannah and almost forcing me to mess up. She was very close to having blush end up in her hair.

"Yeah, because you aren't the one being set up," I returned, holding her head still again.

All three of us were crammed in my bathroom, preparing for a girls' night out. I loved when we all got ready together, even though we each had our own bedroom and bathroom in the unit. We got to share outfits, makeup, and hair tools, but mirror space was in short supply. My bathroom was clearly only made for one person. I was pretty sure Hannah had already accidentally elbowed me in the face roughly five times in the past hour.

"I love the idea of a blind date," Hannah added. "I think it's mysterious."

"I think it's dumb," I returned sharply. "Blind dates never work."

"Maybe this one will," Avery blurted out in a hopeful tone.

"Well, we will never know if I can't finish your makeup because you won't hold still," I directed, holding her chin to prevent her face from moving.

Hannah and I had an exquisite eye for shades, colors, and palettes. We were most likely celebrity makeup artists in our past lives. I grew up watching tutorials in my free time and trying to mimic what I saw in the videos. After roughly ten years of practice, I could almost consider my skills on a professional level.

I loved pulling a cute dress out of my closet and then tailoring my makeup to it. For this outing, I chose a simple black top accompanied by my favorite pair of jeans. It was my typical outfit for going out to the bars, but I never got tired of it. The outfit was a timeless look. Avery also decided on a similar outfit, but chose a navy blouse instead. She had great style, but most likely because she always borrowed from my closet.

It had only taken me about an hour to get fully ready and finish my own makeup routine, but I couldn't put my brushes down yet. Before we went out for our girls' night, I had to factor in the time it took to do Avery's makeup, too. She needed all the help she could get since she didn't even know the difference between lip gloss and lip tint. I was basically her personal makeup artist, but I didn't mind. I liked the extra practice, and it allowed me the opportunity to make my best friend feel beautiful. I didn't have a sister growing up, but Avery was basically family. Graham never let me exercise my beautician skills on him, but Avery was always a willing participant.

"The blind date is nothing serious. It's just so you have a date to my wedding," Hannah explained. "After that, you never have to see him again."

"Trust me," I began. "You won't have to worry about that."

"I don't know. You could end up really liking him," Avery theorized.

"I don't even have time for a relationship right now," I said. "My business has taken over most of my time."

"So, hire an assistant," Avery encouraged. "You've taken on so much responsibility lately. I think it's time you give yourself a break and get some help."

Avery wasn't entirely wrong. My company was in a good enough place where I could hire an extra person to take a load off my plate, but throwing myself into my work was also an escape for me. I didn't have to worry about dating when I was so engrossed with my career.

Before owning a company, "social butterfly" was my middle name. I loved being in every social circle, making new friends every weekend, and flirting with most of the guys I met. It was fun for me, but nothing compared to the fulfillment I got from doing a great job at work. I loved being a nanny, and starting a business from it was my pride and joy. My social life took a backseat when my career took off, and I never put it back into the forefront of my life. I figured Hannah and Avery were all I really needed, but they were starting to form their own lives with their significant others, and I was still the single friend.

"At least just think about it," Avery continued on. "I know you love your job, but I also want to see you happy."

"Thanks," I answered, "I guess I could look into getting an assistant."

"Yeah, and don't even worry about the blind date tonight," Avery stated. "Just let your hair down and have a great time. You will have Hannah and I there the entire time."

"Absolutely! Just be yourself," Hannah encouraged. "We will have a great night!"

I was truly excited to go out together, despite knowing a guy was waiting to meet me. It was one of the last weekends before Hannah Livingston would become Hannah Stockton. I was happy for her to marry the love of her life in less than a month, but I hoped it wouldn't hinder our girl time. Hanging out together was something that I always looked forward to, and I was nervous that Hannah's new relationship status would limit the amount of nights we would have left together.

"You have to at least tell me his name," I begged Hannah.

"Don't tell her," Avery butted in, whipping her head toward Hannah and almost making me smear lipstick across her face, "or else she will look him up and judge him before she even gets to know him."

"Well, how am I supposed to know what to call him?" I objected, adjusting Avery's head forward again. It was going to take me double the time to do her makeup if she was going to be constantly moving.

"I'll tell you his name once we get there," Hannah promised.

"Fine," I groaned.

I returned my attention to the task at hand and decided to pick a lip shade that would accentuate Avery's darker features. Although we were joined at the hip and basically sisters, our physical features were complete opposites. Her chestnut hair and chocolate eyes made it obvious that she was not a Jensen. Graham and I looked identical with our freckles and sandy brown hair, but Avery stood out from us. She used to be really self-conscious about her looks, but I always thought she was really pretty.

"Where did you even meet this guy?" I asked, trying to gather as much information about him as possible since I was deprived of his name.

"He works at the Exe," Hannah responded nonchalantly.

"Oh, absolutely not!" I responded. "That's it. I am not going. I refuse."

I set down the lipstick, deciding not to complete Avery's look or go out with the girls anymore. After Avery's disastrous history with Kyle Kingsley, I swore I would never get involved with someone who worked at the complex. The Exe Apartments were for living and fun pool parties, not for finding a guy. Granted, Hannah's fiancé, Elliot, was also a former apartment employee, so I guess I had a fifty-fifty shot of either being tied to a chair, robbed, and beaten up for money that didn't even exist, or engaged.

"I'm just kidding," Hannah laughed hysterically. "He was my manager when I was a waitress a couple of years ago. He's a really nice guy."

A rush of air left my body when I let out the biggest exhale. I was not interested in taking a gamble of going out with someone who worked in the building.

"See, Paige," Avery inserted. "He's nice, and he knows how to manage people. I hear wedding bells already."

I rolled my eyes at her and purposely pressed a little harder than usual when applying her lip gloss.

"Hey!" Avery shouted, "Don't take your frustrations out on me. If you would have just found a wedding date on your own, then Hannah wouldn't have to set you up with her former coworker."

Avery had a point. I had waited until the last minute, hoping either Avery or Hannah would forget that I didn't have a plus-one, but I had severely underestimated their memory. Ever since I was notified that I was supposed to bring a date, both of them had been hounding me about it by constantly asking who I was bringing. I figured their nagging would eventually subside, but Hannah's wedding was almost here, and I was no closer to finding someone to bring with me.

"Don't worry. He's not weird or anything," Hannah noted. "You guys might even be friends afterwards."

"Yeah, sure," I answered sarcastically, knowing I had no intention of talking to this guy after tonight.

I completed the last steps of Avery's makeup routine by spraying a few spritzes of setting spray. Once she opened her eyes and checked herself out in the mirror, a giant smile emerged. Seeing her reaction each time always made everything worth it.

"If he is weird or annoys me," I began while packing up my makeup kit, "I'm leaving immediately."

"I'm sure Hannah wouldn't set you up with a creep," Avery assumed.

"Of course not," Hannah exclaimed as she finished getting ready. "He's a total catch."

"Then, why didn't you date him?" I questioned, wondering how Hannah was able to speak so highly of this man, but never actually dated him herself.

"Because I don't date people I work with," Hannah shared, winking at Avery.

I could tell Avery attempted to blush, but I had already caked her face with foundation, so it wasn't noticeable.

Graham was the head chef at a steakhouse called Iron Nine, and Avery was the Chief Marketing Officer of the restaurant, so technically they worked together. Avery was never a stranger to mixing business with pleasure. Apparently, guys who either worked with her or worked where she lived were her type. If I had a boyfriend, he would have to be an astronaut because I wouldn't want to be with someone who worked on the same planet as me. In my eyes, personal and professional life needed to stay far away from each other.

"Ready to go?" Avery called out to us, still admiring herself in the mirror.

"Let's do this!" Hannah eagerly answered as she left the bathroom. "To the bars!"

Avery followed closely behind her, eager for a girls' night out and to leave the crammed space.

"This guy better be hot," I muttered, following them both out of the bathroom.

I wasn't looking forward to going on a blind date. My expectations were extremely low. I just hoped he would at least be good-looking. It would be way easier to endure a night with a guy who looked halfway decent.

"You think everyone is hot," Avery responded while we all grabbed our purses and packed them with the necessities. For me, that just included a wallet and a few lip glosses, but Avery liked to pack her purse as if the world was ending and she needed the items inside of it to survive.

"I don't think everyone is hot," I quickly answered.

I wasn't necessarily picky on physical appearance, but I could easily bring up someone who I thought was conventionally unattractive, however, everyone was in such a great mood that I didn't feel the need to bring up Kyle.

"What is your type, anyway?" Hannah politely asked.

"Tall, dark, and handsome," Avery answered for me. "Successful. Funny. Outgoing."

Avery continued to list off traits that although I would love to have in a guy, they weren't necessarily on the top of my mind.

"Probably just someone who lets me be myself," I eventually responded. "I want to be with someone who brings out the best version of me, and appreciates all my flaws and quirks."

Avery and Hannah exchanged quiet glances, presumably surprised that I actually had a thought-out answer. Recently, I had been so focused on work that I hadn't expressed an interest in dating, however, that didn't mean I didn't know what I wanted.

"Well, maybe you will find that tonight," Hannah said with a wink.

"Oh, I can't wait for this blind date!" Avery exclaimed, excited for me. "Could you imagine Paige Jensen in love?"

"Alright, let's not get our hopes up," I interjected. "I'm just trying to find a wedding date, not a husband."

"But what if it's meant to be?" Avery proposed.

"If it's meant to be, it will be," I responded, trying to set realistic expectations.

If my fate was to end up with this blind date, then so be it. I wasn't one to mess with destiny. As much as Hannah and Avery hoped I'd end up with the mysterious man and live happily ever after, I didn't think that was in the cards for me. My fate might have led me to the blind date, and maybe he'd even come with me to the wedding, but I knew I still had some say in the matter. I wasn't going to force anything, but if we were truly meant to be, we'd find our way. Until then, I was going to keep my head high, my heart open, and my future in my own hands.

3

The Name Game

It was the beginning of August, and therefore, the heat was enough to fry an egg on the pavement, even at ten o'clock at night. It was so hot that I figured all the hard work I had done getting Avery ready would be for nothing, as I was certain that if we were outside for any longer, her makeup would melt off. I figured the bouncer would have put in a little more effort while checking identifications because his all-black attire was surely baking him like an oven, but he continued to work at a snail's pace.

My feet hurt from standing in line, even though we had only been waiting to get into the bar for a few minutes. I believed the discomfort from being so hot had intensified every feeling I was having, making me believe my ankles would collapse at any moment. The only thing keeping me from taking my heels off was the smoldering sidewalk beneath me.

Hannah had removed her leather jacket, and Avery was fanning herself while we waited. The line was slow-moving, but there were only a few more people ahead of us. I made a mental note that the first drink that I'd order would be an ice-cold water, and it would probably take some persuading to prevent me from dumping the entire thing onto my head. Las Vegas summers were unforgiving, and this was another ruthless night.

"Please tell me your wedding is indoors," Avery begged, deciding to throw her hair into a ponytail.

"Inside and well air-conditioned," Hannah confirmed as she wiped a bead of sweat that was dripping down her forehead.

"Good, I don't think I'd survive being outside during the day," Avery insisted.

"Outdoor weddings in Las Vegas should be illegal," Hannah added.

"So should waiting in line outside a bar," I spoke up, checking how far we were from the front.

I noticed the line was briefly held up as someone was arguing with the bouncer.

"I think there is an ice cream shop down the street," I pointed out. "We could easily move our girls' night to somewhere cooler."

"Nice try, Paige," Avery relayed, "but we are not going anywhere until you meet your potential wedding date. Hannah's wedding is around the corner, and you still do not have a plus-one."

I let out a distasteful grunt and took a few steps forward as the line was beginning to move again.

"And what if I don't find anyone by then?" I asked, revealing an actual concern of mine.

I appreciated Hannah giving me the opportunity to bring a date, but at that point, I would have rather attended her special day alone. I didn't believe there was enough time to find someone I could tolerate enough to bring to such an intimate event.

"Well, I totally understand if you can't find anyone," Hannah shared, although I could tell she was a bit disappointed. "I just wanted to make sure you had fun at my wedding."

I was relieved to know that Hannah didn't view my inability to find a date as that big of a deal, however, I still felt bad that she had gone through the trouble of reserving a spot at her reception for me to bring someone.

"I'll still look around," I remarked, not wanting to let her down. "I have about a month left."

"Exactly," Avery chimed in. "There is still plenty of time to find a date, and tonight could be the night!"

Hannah's smile returned to her face, and I knew there was no way that I could show up to her special day by myself. Avery was right—Hannah was really counting on me to bring someone, and I didn't want to let her down.

"Can I at least know the name of who I am meeting now?" I asked.

My blind date was one of the last things I wanted to think about, but at least it took my mind off the relentless heat.

Avery and Hannah looked at each other as if they were deciding whether or not now was a good enough time to tell me.

"Come on," I begged. "You told me you would tell me when we got to the bar, and we are basically here."

"Ugh, fine," Avery said, nodding in Hannah's direction to give her the approval to disclose.

"His name is Reid," Hannah eventually revealed.

"Reid?" I repeated. "Like, 'read' a book?"

"Yup, just like that," Hannah stated proudly.

"Oh, great," I responded unenthusiastically.

"See, I knew you would judge him," Avery pointed out. "This is why we waited to tell you his name."

"I'm not judging him," I relayed, even though I had already made assumptions in my head based on one piece of information about him. "But, I bet I could guess his entire life based on his name."

I took a few more steps in line as it continued to move, and I was happy to notice that we were next.

"Give it your best shot," Hannah encouraged.

"Hm," I began, really thinking hard about it. "Reid sounds like he has a great credit score, loves long walks on the beach, prefers to have his mother live within a five-mile radius of him, and separates his whites and colors when doing laundry."

Avery and Hannah couldn't keep from laughing at my general description of my blind date. I appreciated their laughter as it was meant to be a joke, however, I'd like to see someone else come up with a better description of someone named Reid. I bet I was pretty close.

"IDs," I heard the bouncer grumble in a thundering voice.

We had finally made it to the front of the line, and all three of us scrambled into our purses to hand our IDs to him as quickly as possible. We all wanted to get out of the extreme heat, and we were over waiting in line for a subpar bar. Lucky's Tavern was our go-to spot for girls' night because it had a very casual atmosphere with games and cheap drinks, but it was far from being a main attraction in the city.

We handed the bouncer our identifications, but he only briefly looked at them before handing them back to us. A part of me was offended that I didn't look near twenty-one anymore, but I was also eager to get inside.

"Enjoy your night, ladies," the bouncer exclaimed as he let us inside.

Hannah, Avery, and I rushed through the doors, but as soon as we entered into Lucky's Tavern, the droplets of sweat that had populated my exposed arms immediately froze. The bar completely overcompensated for the extreme temperature outside and decided to blast the air conditioning. Hannah immediately put her leather jacket back on, and Avery let her hair back down.

"Did we just enter the Tundra?" Avery exclaimed, shivering. "It's freezing in here!"

Hannah offered her jacket up to Avery, but she politely declined. I was sure Avery knew that if she took the leather jacket, then Hannah would end up cold next.

"It's nothing a few drinks can't fix!" I announced, leading the girls to the bar.

My body was drained from using all of its energy to cool itself down and then suddenly switching gears and trying to warm itself back up, but I would have chosen the freezing bar over the ninety degree weather any day.

"Is Reid here yet?" Avery asked Hannah.

Hannah appeared to be scanning the place for my blind date, even though he could have easily been inside undetected. A part of why we loved Lucky's Tavern so much was because of how large it was. It was easy to avoid people in such a huge building.

"Doesn't seem like he's here yet," Hannah proclaimed. "I'm going to call him and find out where he is."

"Let's call him in the restroom," Avery suggested. "It will be quieter in there, and I want to check my makeup. I may have sweated some of it off."

Avery and Hannah began walking in the direction of the bathroom.

"Paige, are you coming with us?" Avery questioned.

"No, I'm going to stay here," I responded. "I'll grab us some drinks."

"Nothing too strong for me," Hannah shouted over the music. "I'm driving us home."

"Got it," I said, as Avery and Hannah headed off to get a hold of Reid.

I used my last few minutes alone before my date showed up to order us all drinks. I wasn't against meeting Reid, but I was a little anxious to meet someone new. It had been a while since I had gone on any sort of date, let alone a blind one.

"Can I get three hot chocolates?" I asked the bartender who was wiping down a few glasses.

My initial idea of ordering an ice water turned into requesting a beverage that was mostly consumed in the heart of winter, but that is what it felt like inside.

The bartender paused his cleaning duties and looked at me quizzically.

"It's August," he declared. "We don't serve hot chocolate in the summer."

"But you have the ingredients to make it, don't you?" I returned.

The bartender raised an eyebrow at me, probably confused as to why I would even think to order a hot chocolate.

"I do, but we are not currently serving it," he answered with a little more force.

"Oh, come on. I'm sure it will only take a few minutes to make," I pleaded. "Please."

I gave him the look of a damsel in distress who had one simple request to make all of her dreams come true.

The bartender looked back at me, and we were having a mini staring contest. Little did he know, I grew up with a brother who challenged me to these my entire life, so I could have stayed there all night.

"Pretty please," I added, folding my hands and begging him to accept my order. I pouted my lip to add even more of a dramatic effect.

"Okay, okay, fine," the bartender eventually said. "But I am not refilling them."

"Fine with me," I answered with a giant grin.

"Three hot chocolates," he exclaimed, repeating the order out loud.

"Actually, make that four," someone behind me shouted.

I turned to find a man about my age trying to tack on to my order. He was well over six feet tall with a hair color that was too blonde for my preference. I appreciated his body composition as it was clear that he worked out, but his sense of style was severely lacking. He was wearing a Hawaiian shirt that I found completely horrendous. I questioned his outfit decisions, but then again, I was at the bar ordering a hot chocolate when it was almost a hundred degrees outside.

The bartender rolled his eyes, but since he didn't shoot down the guy's order, I assumed he was okay with making an extra cup.

"It's so cold in here," the man relayed. "Hot chocolate is definitely the way to go."

"Mhm," I muttered, offering a fake smile and hoping my short answer would hint to the guy that I was not interested in carrying on a conversation with him.

"Do you come to Lucky's often?" the man questioned. "I find it to be the hidden gem of Vegas."

I admired his willingness to want to continue talking to me, but I only had a few minutes of alone time before my night would be consumed by trying to get to know my potential wedding date, and I didn't want to spend it exchanging words with a stranger.

"Yeah, it's a great spot," I agreed, casually.

I didn't want to look the guy in the eyes and make it seem like I was inviting him to more conversation, so I kept my focus on the bartender who was preparing four hot chocolates.

"Are you having a bad day or is my shirt just that bad to look at?" the guy offered up as a joke, followed by a slight chuckle.

"Both," I answered harshly.

My sudden honesty caught him off guard, and his smile began to fade.

Fortunately, the awkward moment was interrupted by the bartender who slid four cups of hot chocolate across the counter. I corralled three of them, leaving one for the guy next to me.

"It's on the house as long as neither one of you bother me again," the bartender proclaimed.

"You won't hear a peep from me," I responded with a wink.

I felt the heat radiating from the cup, and I instantly felt warmer. It was so tempting to drink as the smell of chocolate hit my nose, but I decided to let it cool before I consumed any of it.

"Cheers, I guess," the guy said in a saddened tone as he raised the fourth hot chocolate in the air.

"Cheers," I began, feeling bad for crushing his energetic spirit, "and sorry about earlier."

"It's okay," he answered sincerely. "We all have bad days...and bad shirts."

He awkwardly chuckled again, looking down at his Hawaiian button-down.

"Well, I am not having a bad day...yet," I shared. "But in a few minutes I probably will. I'm meeting a blind date here shortly."

The man took a seat at the bar next to me, letting out a giant sigh of relief.

"Oh phew," he sighed deeply, "so it's not my shirt that's bothering you."

"Well, your shirt is ugly," I confirmed.

I let out a giggle at my own comment, and the man took that as a green light to laugh with me. I continued to poke fun at his wardrobe until a huge wave of realization came over me. I immediately stopped any laughter and put on a straight face.

"Your name wouldn't happen to be Reid, would it?" I asked nervously.

"Ha, no. My name is Michael," he introduced with an outstretched hand.

"Paige," I returned gently, shaking his hand.

"I assume Reid would be the name of your blind date," he uttered.

"Yeah, one of my best friends is getting married, and I unfortunately do not have a date to her wedding yet," I shared.

"Ah, so this Reid guy is supposed to be your plus-one?" Michael concluded.

"We'll see," I said. "I just hope he's not weird."

"Right," Michael agreed. "Imagine him showing up in like a Hawaiian shirt or something."

"That would be an immediate deal breaker," I noted sarcastically.

Michael continued to take all of my beatings against him about his shirt.

"Actually, Reid has great credit and separates his whites from his colors when doing laundry," I pointed out in a playful tone.

"Uh, how do you know that about him already?" he asked.

"I don't. It's an inside joke with my friends who are still in the bathroom," I informed him, staring at the untouched extra cups of hot chocolate.

"Ah, I figured you came here with your friends, but I didn't want to say anything just in case you really liked hot chocolate," Michael smiled, staring at the other two cups. "So, what's the inside joke?"

"It's nothing," I muttered.

"Oh, come on," Michael pleaded. "I'm interested now."

"Um, well, basically I do this thing where I make assumptions about people based on their first name," I shared.

"So, in your mind, a guy named Reid pays his credit card bill on time and has great laundry habits?" Michael summarized.

"Pretty much," I agreed, slightly embarrassed.

"Oh, I like this game," Michael exclaimed. "What do you assume about me based on my name?"

"Uh, well, I'm not too sure," I admitted shyly.

I wasn't prepared to be put on the spot.

"It can't be too hard," he started. "Michael is a pretty common name."

"Well, I guess I would assume that you are a family man," I hesitantly shared.

"I think you can do better than that, Paige," Michael teased.

His playful personality put me at ease a little bit, so I decided to give it my best shot.

"Based on your name, I would guess that you're mysterious. You are very picky about who you share your true self with. Some are fortunate enough to get to know the real you, but most only get to know the version of yourself that you decide to portray," I explained. "Oh, and I would assume that you dip your fries in ranch over ketchup."

"Wow. You're almost completely spot on." Michael stared blankly back at me. "But, I prefer ketchup over ranch."

I enjoyed the playful banter, but I didn't ignore the fact that the portion I had gotten right about him was the part about his mysterious personality.

"Okay, my turn," Michael said.

"Wait, what?" I uttered, not expecting the game to be reversed on me.

"I want to play, too," Michael expressed, evidently pondering on what assumptions he could make about me based on my name.

I hesitantly waited for him to reveal his answer. I had never been on the other side of the game before, so I was a little nervous.

"I think you love your friends," Michael eventually stated.

I was relieved that my nerves had been for nothing as he clearly played it safe, but there was no fun in his average response.

"Too easy," I pointed out. "Come on, I went all out with you. Give it to me straight."

Michael chuckled, rubbing his hands together as if he was conjuring up the perfect answer.

"Well then, Paige," he started. "I would assume that you put up this hard exterior wall that is supposed to protect yourself, but actually ends up scaring off most guys. So, you probably haven't been out with a guy in a while, which is partly why you are nervous for this blind date."

My face was emotionless as I tried to process Michael's assumptions about me.

"Oh, and the color orange freaks you out," Michael added.

"Orange does not bother me," I fired back.

"Hm, I guess I must've only gotten the first part right then," he boasted.

I was speechless, not knowing how I got myself into this position. A random guy at Lucky's Tavern was telling me about myself, and I didn't even have the ability to deny it.

"Well, Paige," Michael started as he removed himself from the seat next to me. "I'll let you enjoy your alone time before Reid shows up. I hope you enjoy your blind date. Maybe I'll see you again sometime."

"Yeah, maybe," I answered, still trying to process the last five minutes.

"Give Reid a chance and don't scare him off," Michael offered as parting words. "You can be intimidating to talk to."

He grabbed his cup of hot chocolate and disappeared through the crowd of people packed inside the bar. As soon as I had completely lost sight of him, Avery and Hannah reappeared beside me.

"Reid is running a little late, but he said he would be here in no more than fifteen minutes," Hannah explained. "He apologizes for making you wait."

"It's fine," I answered in a polite tone. "I'm sure he just got caught up in traffic or something."

Avery grabbed one of the cups of hot chocolate and smelled it.

"Did you put something in these drinks to make you act nicer?" Avery asked.

"No," I objected fiercely. "I just didn't want to come off as...intimidating."

"That's probably a good idea because I am not even trying to date you and you scare me," Hannah cried out.

Avery and Hannah laughed, not knowing that a random man's comment had stuck with me more than I thought it would. I knew I had a hard exterior, but I didn't think I was scaring guys off. Maybe that's why I hadn't been asked out or approached at a bar recently. However, it made me curious as to why Michael didn't seem too scared of me.

"Do you think the bartender could get me a straw so that I don't have to drink it through the lid?" Hannah asked aloud.

"Um, let's not bother the bartender anymore," I responded, well aware that I had already angered him enough.

"Hm, okay," Hannah agreed. "Dance floor then? We can dance the night away while we wait for Reid."

"I'll race you there," I commented, grabbing my hot chocolate and hopping off the barstool.

Avery, Hannah, and I skipped to the dance floor, which was in the opposite direction of where Michael had disappeared to. I really wanted to ask him what he meant by his comment and inquire about why I didn't scare him off like I apparently did to everyone else. Lucky's was a large bar, but I was sure I would run into him again tonight. It was hard to hide in a Hawaiian shirt.

4

Bullseye

Girls' night out turned into me wishing I had stayed in. I only got to enjoy a few minutes with my best friends on the dance floor of Lucky's Tavern before Reid arrived. He didn't look as nerdy as I had pictured him, as he looked like a regular guy. He wasn't much taller than me and he smelled kind of like gasoline, but I figured he just stopped to fill up his car before heading over to the bar. Reid had a similar hair color and texture to Avery's—dark brown and mostly straight. The bar was pretty dark so I couldn't tell his exact eye color, but it seemed slightly lighter than his hair.

In my mind, being on the dance floor was a great icebreaker for meeting a blind date, since I couldn't really hear him when he talked anyway, and I still got to hang out with my friends. Unfortunately, it didn't take long for Hannah and Avery to suggest that he and I get to know each other by ourselves. After almost being able to endure the entire date without having to really talk to him, we eventually left the dance floor and found a quieter spot to chat.

We managed to find a few open barstools still in view of the dance floor, which worked out in my favor in case I needed to call Hannah or Avery over to save me. However, judging by how the spinning stool gave Reid trouble, it was safe to assume that his struggles with sitting down on a stool meant that he wasn't someone that I should be fearful of.

"I'm so happy for Hannah," Reid began, forcing conversation once he finally conquered his seating battle. "She seems so happy with Elliot."

"They appear to be a good fit," I answered casually.

"I don't know if she told you or not, but Hannah and I used to work together," he shouted over the music. "I was her manager."

"Yeah, she mentioned it," I affirmed.

"I was also a manager when I lived back in Utah," Reid continued. "I moved to Vegas about seven years ago."

I wasn't really sure how to respond, so I just nodded my head and smiled. The date was already awkward enough, and the conversation was adding to it.

"So, what do you do for work?" Reid asked kindly.

"I run my own nanny matchmaking business," I returned, tired of the boring date questions. "How about you?"

I wasn't really listening to his response because out of the corner of my eye, I saw a couple of people playing darts. I used the term "playing" loosely, as they were basically just chucking the dart at the wall and cheering if it happened to come close to the vicinity of the board. In my college days, I spent a lot of time around the bars, so I was no stranger to games such as corn hole, billiards, and even darts. I used to pretend that I didn't know how to play and make absolutely ridiculous bets so that people would be tempted to put a wager on the game. As soon as we started playing, I would drop the innocent girl act and actually show off my skills.

"Hey, have you ever played darts before?" I asked Reid, totally interrupting him mid-sentence.

In the past, I had hustled enough money to pay for an entire semester of college. I hadn't used my scheming tactic in a while, but I was tempted to see if I still had it.

"Um, no, why?" Reid asked.

"Well, today is your lucky day," I said as I leaped off the barstool.

Reid attempted to mimic my motions, but his feet almost missed the ground, and he stumbled before standing up.

I was unamused by his inability to properly work a barstool, but I dragged him over to the crowded area.

There was a sea of people surrounding the game that was currently in progress. I didn't know how it was entertaining in the slightest as the players were clearly amateurs. Sounds of darts completely missing the board and smacking the wall were normal occurrences.

"I've got next!" I shouted through the crowd.

"Sorry, sweetie," a severely unshaved man replied next to me. "We are already next."

He pointed toward the group of similarly hairy men around him.

"Okay, well, then can I play after you?" I questioned.

The group of men responded to my question with boisterous laughter.

"This isn't regular darts, honey," another gentleman in the group called out. "This is Money Darts."

"What is Money Darts?" I asked him.

"Ah, sweetie," the initial gentleman who I spoke with answered, "If you have to ask, then you can't play."

His friends followed his response with more laughs.

Instead of asking them, I should have just watched the game as it was easy to pick up on what Money Darts was. There were differing amounts of cash taped to the dartboard. The higher bills were toward the center, and the lower ones were stuck to the outsides. Everyone who played had to put money on the board, and only those who could actually aim and hit the bills could take home whatever amount their dart landed on. The center was covered with money. Clearly, nobody had even come close to a bullseye.

"Alright, who's next!" an older gentleman who seemed to be running the game called out after the current contestant had finished. There was still plenty of cash on the board, so it must've been an unsuccessful game. "The entry fee is now thirty dollars, and half of it must go to the center!"

The group of men next to me, who claimed they were next, decided against competing when they heard the new entry fee. Apparently, they weren't too fond of the increased price.

"I'll go next!" I yelled.

The older gentleman who was hosting the game pointed at me, so I took the opportunity to step into the center and collect my darts. I paid the admission fee and watched as my crisp bills were being stuck onto a dartboard. I was only allocated five darts, which was more than enough to win my money back if I hit the center. However, I had a larger strategy at hand, so instead, I launched two of them into the wall, yards away from the board, and winning no money.

"Three darts left," the host explained politely. "Try to aim for the center."

"Ten dollars she won't even hit the board!" one of the guys in the hairy group shouted.

"Care to make it twenty?" I fired back at him.

The crowd got quieter as a live bet was happening. They all stared at the man, anticipating if he would take my counteroffer. All the attention on him must have gotten to his head as he decided to up the antics.

"Fifty dollars you won't even hit the board!" he returned, fishing into his wallet and waving his money in the air.

"Deal!" I called out, grabbing more money out of my purse and slamming it down on the high-top table near the host.

The crowd roared as Money Darts had just gotten more interesting.

I had three darts left to hit the board, but I was aiming for more than just that. One-by-one I fired my last three darts, right after the other. First, I hit the three twenties that were stacked on top of each other in the inner circle of the board, near the center. My second dart was even closer to the bullseye, winning me what looked like over a hundred dollars. I saved my best shot for last, as I used the third dart to win all the money in the middle.

Almost everyone cheered as I hit the center of the board and hustled the man out of his money.

"Can I play again?" I asked the host, who was standing there stunned.

"Uh, sure," he answered hesitantly.

I gave him another thirty dollars in exchange for five more darts and hit the rest of the large remaining amounts of cash on the board. By the time I was done, there were only a few straggling singles left near the outer edges of the board.

"Anyone else want to play?" I asked the crowd once I was finished, even though there was barely any cash left over.

I peered around the people surrounding me, but nobody took me up on my offer. Even if someone had managed to claim the remaining money, it wouldn't have been enough to cover the thirty-dollar entry fee.

"I'll play," someone shouted, pushing past the gathered crowd to get to the front.

Unfortunately, another innocent victim was about to lose their money. I had almost decided to call it a night, as it was getting pretty late and my purse was already stuffed with cash, however, the blue shirt covered with flamingos and palm trees that draped across the man who approached the dartboard made me decide to play one more game.

"You, again," I muttered when he handed me the darts he had pulled off the board.

"I couldn't stay away," he playfully returned. "How's your blind date going?"

I looked in the corner where I had left Reid and saw him swirling around on the barstool that he was sitting on. It appeared as though he had finally learned how it had worked and was enjoying the benefits of the chair's ability to spin.

"I've been on better ones," I responded.

"I don't know," Michael continued on, "It's hard to top a date where you leave with more money than you came with."

He stared at my overflowing purse, and it was obvious that he had been watching me hustle guys out of their money.

"Yeah, I've been pretty successful tonight. It's not too intimidating for you, is it?" I teased.

"Not even in the slightest," Michael returned. "In fact, it's so not intimidating that I figured we'd make this game a little more interesting."

"I'm listening," I said.

"One dart," Michael began. "Closest one to the center wins."

"Sounds easy enough," I noted confidently.

"Loser gets the winner another hot chocolate," Michael explained.

"Ha, you really think the bartender is going to make another one?" I questioned.

"I don't know. That's for you to find out when you order me one," he proclaimed.

The cockiness was oozing from his body, and I made it my mission to beat him.

"Ladies first," Michael offered, gesturing toward the board and stepping out of the way.

His smugness was fueling my fire and my competitive spirit took over.

I set the extra darts on an empty nearby table and kept one in my hand. I stood in front of the dartboard, aligning my elbow with the center and imagining a straight line from my arm to the bullseye. I shut one eye and used all my focus on aiming the dart at the exact spot I wanted it to go. In one motion, I brought the dart toward me, and like a catapult, I extended my arm forward and released the dart at the end of the movement. It flew through the air smoothly, and it landed with a loud thud against the board. The bystanders around me clapped as they observed where it had landed—almost a perfect bullseye. The position of my dart only gave Michael a few centimeters of space for which he could actually beat me. It was unlikely that his dart would even make it close to that, but it wasn't impossible.

"Your turn," I proudly boasted.

"Cute shot," Michael called out. "I can't wait for this hot chocolate."

He still remained confident even after seeing my near-perfect shot. It made me feel uneasy as someone who was still that cocky after watching me barely hit a bullseye was unnerving. I had almost come to think that it was my turn to be hustled.

Michael took my place in front of the board and stood in a stance that had mimicked mine. Even the way he gripped the dart and lined it up to the board was similar to me. He began aiming the dart at the center and cocking his arm backward.

"I like my hot chocolate with extra marshmallows," he snickered at me before eventually firing the dart like a bullet through the air.

When the dart landed, the audience audibly gasped, and I was almost too afraid to look. By the way everyone was covering their mouths, I was certain he had beaten me.

I slowly turned my head to see where it had landed, but when I looked at the board, my dart was the only one there. My eyes were frantically searching for where it had landed until I followed the crowd's eyes to a man who was frozen in fear. Michael's dart had hit the wall right behind Reid, nearly missing his head by a few inches.

"I'm so sorry!" Michael called out, rushing over to Reid.

The dart was nowhere near me, yet my heart was racing as if it was. I was stunned with how close he was to hitting him.

Since he was my blind date, I figured it was best that I also check on him, so I ran over to Reid to ensure that he hadn't suffered a heart attack.

"Reid, are you okay?" I shouted when I made it over to him.

"Reid? Like as in he separates his laundry, Reid?" Michael questioned.

"Huh?" Reid asked, confused.

"Yes, that Reid," I stated. "You almost killed my blind date."

"I almost made your blind date, blind." Michael laughed at his own joke, and I honestly found the whole thing funny too, but I didn't want Reid to feel embarrassed.

"Are you sure you're okay?" I repeated to Reid.

"Yeah, I'm fine," he answered shakily. "It just scared me."

After a few minutes of forcing him to take some deep breaths, he eventually calmed down, but the darts game was shut down as one of the managers heard of the incident and took the darts away for the night.

"Can I get you a water or anything?" Michael offered. "I'm headed to the bar anyway."

The amazing feeling of winning the darts game suddenly consumed my body as I remembered that Michael now owed me a hot chocolate.

"No, I'm alright. Thanks, though," Reid declined.

Michael and I backed away from Reid once we were certain he was fine in order to give him some space.

"Nice aim," I sarcastically commented.

"If your blind date was the target, I would have won," Michael pointed out.

"Too bad he wasn't," I exclaimed.

"Well, I could get you that hot chocolate now, or we could do a raincheck so I can see you again," Michael proposed.

"Hm, I think I'll take that hot chocolate now," I said. "Send my best wishes to the bartender. I'm sure he will be overjoyed to know that you are bothering him again."

"Wow, I'm that horrible that you don't want to see me again?" Michael joked.

"It's the Hawaiian shirt," I sarcastically let out.

"Fair enough," Michael asserted, turning to head to the bar for losing a bet.

I took pride in hustling a bunch of guys out of their money simply because they decided to underestimate me and my ability to throw a dart at the wall, but nothing compared to the feeling of watching Michael take the walk of shame to the bar to order me another hot chocolate. I pleasantly watched his Hawaiian shirt get lost in the crowd of people—this was going to be the best hot chocolate I'd ever have.

"Hey love birds," I heard Hannah shout behind me.

"How's the date going?" Avery asked.

At the sounds of their voices, I took a few steps away from the scene of the crime. I didn't want Hannah or Avery to have any suspicions of what had occurred in the last few minutes. I was supposed to be getting to know my potential wedding date, but I instead had honestly forgotten he existed until he almost took a dart to the face. I felt bad that I had basically ignored him the entire night, but Reid didn't seem to mind as he quickly hopped out of the barstool he was sitting on and cheerfully joined me by my side as Avery and Hannah approached us.

"We've been having a great time so far," Reid answered. "Except for the darts."

"Oh, I am so glad to hear you guys have been getting along!" Hannah responded.

I shot a few glares at Reid as it was my intention to keep the conversation as far away from darts as possible, but it seemed as though Hannah had assumed that we were playing the game together instead of him watching me sucker guys out of their money.

"So...maybe you guys will see each other again?" Avery chimed in.

"Like maybe at my wedding?" Hannah said in a hopeful tone.

"It's up to her, but I'd love to accompany Paige to your wedding," Reid offered kindly.

I was glad that I hadn't completely ruined his night by using our date to win bets, but I also felt bad for him. I wondered what kind of dates he had been on in the past that made him think that this was a good one.

"We'll stay in touch, Reid," I responded, not wanting to give him a direct answer. "It was nice getting to know you, though."

I smiled at him to make it appear as though I enjoyed his company as much as he enjoyed mine, but I was honestly looking forward to not having him be my plus-one. He was nice and all, but Reid was so boring. I would have rather attended the reception with a life-sized blow-up doll than him.

"Well, we were just coming over here because it's getting late and we are about to head home," Avery announced.

"Wow, it is almost 1 a.m.," Reid concluded after looking at his watch. "I can't remember the last time I stayed out this late, but time flies when you're having fun!"

His cringey comment was too much for me to force a smile at, but the awkward side hug that he gave me afterward was enough to make me want to crawl out of my skin.

"Well, are you ready to go?" Avery directed toward me.

"Actually, I think I am going to stay out a little longer," I answered.

"You sure?" Avery asked. "Are you going to be okay by yourself?"

"Reid will take me home after," I shared, putting my arm around him.

It took every fiber in my being to prevent myself from pulling my arm away.

Hannah's eyes lit up at the tiny ounce of physical touch.

"Oh, okay. You two have fun then," Hannah noted with a wink. "Don't let us get in the way of your date."

Hannah's naive nature was on full display tonight. I was sure Avery had caught on to the fact that I was not feeling Reid, but she seemed to shrug off her suspicions in order to let Hannah enjoy the idea that I actually liked him.

"Call me if you need anything," Avery whispered in my ear as she gave me a hug.

I nodded to let her know that I had heard her.

"Can't wait to hear all about it tomorrow," Hannah screeched when it was her turn to give me an embrace.

"I'll see you guys tomorrow," I relayed.

Reid frantically waved at my friends as they headed toward the door, not knowing that the rest of the night wasn't going to be centered around getting to know each other more.

"I'm so glad you decided to stay out with me," Reid remarked, pulling me closer to him.

"Yeah, of course," I grumbled moving away from him.

I could tell why him and Hannah were friends—they both were completely clueless to their surroundings.

"So," Reid began trying to make conversation. "What's your favorite part about Lucky's?"

My eyes lit up at the sight of a steaming cup in the hands of a man in a Hawaiian shirt headed toward me. It was funny to watch him avoid the crowds of people around him in order to not spill it

"The hot chocolate," I answered back.

"They serve that here?" Reid asked quizzically.

"They sure do," I answered proudly.

5

Busy Bee

My summer routine was pretty simple. Monday through Friday I would throw myself into my work, attaching myself to my computer until the sun went down. I was usually either recruiting new nannies, helping match families to one of my employees, or occasionally handling complaints. I was sold on the name, *Paige's Perfect Pairings: A Nanny Network*, as soon as Hannah suggested it, but a majority of my time and budget was simply spent on making the city aware of my services. I was naïve to think that my company's fun and unique name was enough to sell my business, but a lot of marketing went into running my company, which was an area where I could see hiring an assistant for. One of the tasks that I was working on consisted of crafting a job posting for the open position. I was strongly considering Avery's advice to free up some of my time by adding someone to my team who could help handle my responsibilities. I wasn't looking to completely hand over the reins of my company to someone and just sit back and relax, but there was room to bring in another person.

My weekday schedule was pretty monotonous, but once I lost myself in the daily tasks of the workweek and Friday night finally came, Lucky's Tavern was where I chose to celebrate the start of another weekend. Last night was no different as I found myself in the same place as I had the previous Friday, and all the Fridays this summer before that. However, the prior weeks didn't involve me meeting a blind date, profiting two hundred and thirty-three dollars from darts, and enjoying a hot chocolate with a man who had poor taste in clothing. I couldn't help but wonder if Michael thought he was going on a tropical vacation. He dressed as though he thought Lucky's Tavern was actually Lucky's Tiki Hut.

Nevertheless, he was a lot more entertaining than Reid was. The parts of the night that included getting to know my blind date were very faint memories—most likely because I was half-asleep when talking to him. His voice was very monotone, and he barely changed his facial expressions. I couldn't remember a single fact about him, and I was very tempted to never see him again, but I had promised Hannah that I would bring someone to her wedding, and Reid was more than willing to go with me.

When Reid drove me home from the bar at around 2 a.m., I still refrained from giving him an absolute answer as to whether or not I wanted him to be my plus-one, but he was looking like my best option considering he was my only option. I'd probably end up avoiding him for most of the wedding, but at least I would have a date and it was someone who Hannah knew and was comfortable with. The last thing I wanted was for Hannah to be uncertain about one of her guests.

Though my Friday night may have slightly deviated from the previous ones, I was fully expecting to get back to my usual summer routine, as today was another Saturday afternoon spent at an Exe pool party. The infamous parties that Avery and I had solely based our apartment selection on were still fun and memorable, but they had gotten a lot less wild with each summer that passed by. Maybe I was just getting older and instead of dancing with random strangers and flirting with every guy, I usually just laid out in the sun, which made the parties seem less crazy. However, they were still fun social events that Hannah, Avery, and I still tried to attend every weekend.

There weren't a lot of Saturdays left in the year to enjoy the fun event, as Labor Day weekend was the last pool party of the year and August had already begun, but we didn't act as though the summer was winding down. Avery was being antisocial and reading a romance novel as usual, Hannah was seated in the beach chair next to me, nodding her head to the beat of the music, and I was closing my eyes, pretending to enjoy the sun, when really I was thinking about what work needed to be done the next week. I tried to refrain from thinking about my job on the weekends, but it was hard to ignore it. My career was my life.

"So should we address the elephant in the room now or later?" Hannah eventually asked, breaking the silence between us. "Or should I say, the 'Reid' in the room?"

Hannah chuckled at her own joke, but it was just another reminder as to how oblivious she was to my true feelings for her former manager. Though I did acknowledge that my acting skills were top-notch, I didn't think I was good enough to sell the idea that I had even a slight interest in Reid. But,

I guess I had Hannah fooled. I still didn't believe Avery was sold on my performance, though.

"Um, he was nice, I guess," I briefly shared, trying to find the positives. I didn't want to share my true sentiments about Reid and disappoint Hannah. She spoke really highly of her friend, and I didn't want to let her know that I couldn't share those same feelings.

"What happened after we left?" Avery inquired, probably trying to conclude if I actually did like Reid or not.

"Not much," I answered honestly.

In regards to Reid, not much did happen. Once Avery and Hannah headed home, my date and I didn't exchange too many words after that. I mostly spent the rest of the night drinking hot chocolate and listening to Michael explain to me how he managed to get the bartender to make him another drink after strict direction to never bother him again. Apparently, Michael bribed him with a tip large enough to make the bartender change his mind—a gratuity amount that Michael refused to disclose.

In exchange for the hard work he had gone through to hold up his end of the bet, I shared my secrets on my techniques for throwing darts. Unfortunately, the manager had taken away all the darts for the night because of the little incident of almost taking Reid's head off, so Michael and I used straws for practice. Thankfully, they were easily accessible as they were sitting in a cup on top of the bar. The bartender would have probably kicked us out if we had asked him for a ridiculous amount of straws, so we had to grab them in secret. Michael and I were clearly already on his last nerve.

I didn't realize how late I had stayed out until Reid eventually informed me that the bar was closing soon and that it was time to head back. It was another instance in which I forgot Reid was even present. I felt bad for ignoring him again, but he appeared as though the idea of just being out to the bars and on a date was enough for him. He seemed to enjoy being in a social atmosphere as he never complained once about my lack of attention toward him. I tried to make it up to him by making conversation in the car while he drove me home, and he didn't seem as bad when it was just him and I alone. Maybe it was because there was nothing else to do on the ride back besides sit and talk, but I actually found him tolerable in a more intimate setting. I figured he was just nervous at the start of the date and that was why he was being awkward, as he seemed pretty normal by the end of the night. I still wasn't confident that he would be someone I would hang out with after Hannah's wedding, but my opinion of him by the end of the night was definitely more favorable than at the beginning.

"So do you think you have finally found a plus-one?" Avery asked.

"Yeah, is Reid going to be your wedding date?" Hannah added on.

"He's definitely a contender," I said.

"A contender? Are you planning to go on more dates?" Avery pried. "I can set you up on the dating apps."

"I have another friend I could set you up with!" Hannah eagerly offered.

"Thanks guys, but I'm fine," I admitted. "I'm not that desperate."

"But, actually, you are," Avery joked. "The wedding is less than a month away."

I never gave a straight answer to Reid or my friends as to whether or not I was taking him as my plus-one. It was hard to invite someone I barely even knew. But, I realized I didn't have any other options, and Reid wasn't the worst guy in the world.

"I guess I'll just ask Reid to go with me," I finally admitted. "However, I don't want to ask him right now. I want to give it a few days before I bring it up to him so I don't seem too eager."

"Yay!" Hannah shrieked. "I knew you two would hit it off!"

"Don't get too excited," I warned her. "I'm just inviting him as my date. It's nothing too serious."

"Well, I'm just excited that you're finally bringing someone," Hannah relayed. "I can't wait for my wedding!"

"It's going to be an amazing day," I agreed.

"I'm proud of you for giving him a chance," Avery encouraged, knowing the decision was way outside my comfort zone.

I was also proud of myself and relieved to finally have a date, but I still would have rather attended Hannah's special day alone.

"So as my co-maids of honor," Hannah began, "are you excited to talk about me in front of everyone? How are your speeches coming along?"

"I'm almost done with mine," Avery affirmed. "I think everyone is going to love it!"

"Oh, I can't wait!" Hannah bellowed.

"And don't worry," Avery started, "I'll make sure Paige's speech is appropriate."

"What?" I questioned. "Mine is definitely going to be appropriate."

Hannah and Avery looked at me as though they didn't believe me. They had every right to share that feeling though as I did love the dramatics.

"Well, I was going to mention the tattoo Elliot got of a cat to try to impress you," I revealed, "but I'm pretty sure the wedding guests don't want to see the feline on his upper thigh."

"Yeah, please don't mention that," Avery noted.

"I mean, I did think it was kind of cute," Hannah stated, "but yeah, probably not a good idea to bring that up. In fact, I'm pretty sure I promised him that I wouldn't tell anyone about that."

"On second thought, maybe I should mention it then," I said jokingly.

I was able to get Avery to laugh, but Hannah decided to grab a nearby beach ball and chuck it at me instead. Hannah was the least violent person I knew. She was always extremely positive, so I always found it funny when she showed any slight sign of fieriness.

Although it appeared that Hannah threw the beach ball with all her force, it didn't travel that fast in the air and I ended up catching it before it hit me. I wanted to continue messing with her, so I threw it back at Hannah. I did find it difficult to launch such a light object, but I managed to bounce it off her shoulder.

I continued to laugh and revel in the fun we were having. Avery was holding her stomach from laughing so hard as she witnessed such an odd scene. I was sure it was funny to watch her two best friends chuck a beach ball at each other in the middle of the apartment's pool party. However, when I looked back over at Hannah, she had tears in her eyes.

"Oh my, Hannah, are you okay? I'm sorry for throwing it at you," I apologized.

I didn't think a beach ball was capable of causing pain, but the sight of her almost crying put an immediate end to Avery and I's laughter.

"My wedding is ruined!" Hannah cried out, holding up her ring finger in the air.

"Hannah, what's going on?" Avery inquired.

Both of us were confused by Hannah's sudden outburst.

"A bee stung me, and now my wedding is ruined!" Hannah shrieked. "How am I supposed to put my wedding ring on my finger when it is swollen!"

I raced over to her to get a better look at her finger. It truly was red and swollen, but thankfully the stinger was no longer lodged in her skin. From being a nanny, I had my fair share of treating bee stings. The swelling would obviously disappear by the time her wedding came, but Hannah was still freaking out about it. She was known for overreacting to situations, but she was also under a lot of stress with her big day coming up. Therefore, I could at least somewhat understand her sudden outburst.

"Don't worry," Avery began. "We can put some ice on it."

Hannah sniffled, holding her finger away from her as though it was infected and going to fall off.

"I need more than ice," Hannah bawled, "I need a miracle."

Avery continued to try to calm Hannah down, but she was still hysterical.

"Oh, wait!" I called out, suddenly remembering my mom's remedy. "I know a few ingredients that will quickly get rid of the swelling and redness."

"Really?" Hannah asked, finally sounding hopeful.

"Yes, my mom used it on Graham and I all the time when we would get stung," I explained. "I'll head to the store right now and grab some baking soda and vinegar."

"Baking soda and vinegar?" Hannah questioned. "Are you baking a cake or helping my finger?"

"Trust me," I claimed. "It works."

I let Avery tend to Hannah, and I left the pool to head back to apartment in order to change into some actual clothes. It was another typical day in my summer routine that ended up going awry in some way. All the previous Saturdays were spent at the pool, but none of them ended with me heading to the store to find the ingredients to heal my friend's bee sting. The weekend continued to deviate from my usual schedule, but I guess I could also say that I saved Hannah's wedding twice in one day—I found a wedding date, and now I was going to cure her bee sting.

6

A Chance Encounter

Being a nanny didn't solely involve being able to entertain kids. When I recruited for my company, I looked for people who possessed more than just the ability to keep a child alive and well. The steps to being hired included numerous in-depth interviews to ensure the candidate was capable, qualified, and a good person. I wanted to ensure that my services provided top-notch nannies, and in order to do so, it required a thorough selection process. At *Paige's Perfect Pairings: A Nanny Network*, I required all my employees to be First Aid and CPR certified. Crises couldn't be predicted or prevented, but I tried to at least hire people who were trained and prepared for different emergencies. Although caring for bee stings was not necessarily part of the qualifications, I had been in similar situations numerous times before with the kids I was watching. Thankfully, none of them had an allergic reaction that required serious medical attention, but that was how I knew my mom's baking soda and vinegar bee-sting remedy was foolproof. Not only had it worked on Graham and I growing up, but I had used it before on the children I was caring for, and it still worked like a charm.

Avery had a key to Graham's apartment, and considering he was a chef, I was sure he had the ingredients to make the concoction. But, I had always stuck to using the same brand of vinegar and baking soda that my mom had, and I didn't want to scramble through Graham's cabinets and drawers hoping that he carried the exact brands I was looking for. He was at work anyway, and I was certain the last thing he wanted was for his little sister to be scrambling through his kitchen cabinets. He was never the most organized person, so I probably wouldn't have even been able to find them to begin with. I was running out of milk for my daily lattes that I liked to consume in the mornings anyway, so I was killing two birds with one stone by being at the supermarket.

With it being the weekend, the store was a jungle of customers refilling their pantries for the week. It was like I was playing a game of dodgeball, but with shopping carts. Every time I turned a corner, there was another patron there that I had to avoid. After dodging a crying child, a service dog, and two employees, I eventually made it to the baking aisle. Baking sweet treats must have been a dying hobby as it was the most empty section in the entire store. I figured everyone must've just preferred their desserts already made. Come to think of it, as much as Graham was a beast in the kitchen when cooking delicious savory dishes, it had been a while since he had actually baked something. I contemplated grabbing some additional items in the aisle so that my brother could make me something sweet, but I didn't know what all he needed and figured he could probably create a dish with the leftover baking soda and vinegar. Surely, Hannah didn't need the entire supply to help with her bee sting.

The specific brands that I was looking for were on clear display and fully stocked on the shelves. The vinegar was easy to spot and grab, but it took a little longer before retrieving the baking soda, careful to not accidentally reach for baking powder. The wrong ingredient may have resulted in Hannah's bee sting enlarging with irritation rather than slowly healing the swelling, so I was precise when obtaining what was truly needed for my mom's miracle remedy.

I was only five minutes into the store, and I already had two of the three items that I came for, but I knew the milk would be a lot harder to secure. It was located in the very back, and although baking items may have been losing their popularity, dairy products surely weren't. I returned to my unconventional game of dodgeball and began weaving through carts and store employees, avoiding everything in my way. I slowed down when I passed the makeup aisle, contemplating restocking on a few products that I knew I was running low on, but I quickly refocused my attention to the mission at hand and redirected my cart toward the dairy section.

As expected, the aisle was packed and my game of dodging obstacles would have to come to an end as there wasn't room for another cart. I had to abandon my mostly empty cart at the start of the section and squeeze past everyone to reach the milk. The store was clearly prepared for the swarm of customers who chose to shop on the weekend as every variety of milk was fully stocked. Granted, the whole milk was running lower than the almond milk due to demand, but there was enough of everything, especially my oat milk that I happily grabbed.

The journey back to my cart was a lot easier since I was in a better mood after grabbing the last item that I came to the store for. I believed there were more people in the aisle on the way back from grabbing the milk than when I had initial entered it, as my cart didn't even come into view until I was only a few feet away from it. Thankfully, it was in the same place where I had left it. Maybe if my cart had contained some prime cuts of steak or a stack of cookies, a nearby customer might have been tempted to grab something out of it, but my baking soda and vinegar remained untouched in the cart.

My grocery list was completed in less time than I had anticipated, and I debated conducting a full shopping trip since I was already at the store. However, knowing that Hannah was most likely still freaking out back home and Avery was probably doing her best to calm her down, I figured it was best to just return to the apartment as quickly as possible. Besides, shopping on the weekends was one of the worst times to go. Every aisle was crowded with carts, customers, and kids screaming at their moms who refused to buy them candy. I was thankful that I worked a job that allowed me to stock up on groceries during the weekdays when barely anyone was there.

My cart looked like it belonged to a mad scientist, as it only contained a box of baking soda, a bottle of vinegar, and a carton of milk. I was either going to be making a crazy experiment or an even crazier drink. I reached into my basket and further separated the ingredients, placing the bee-sting remedy on one side of the cart and the milk on the other. I didn't want to risk mixing any aromas. If my latte tomorrow had any hint of an odd aftertaste, then I would know exactly where it came from.

Since the milk was on the complete opposite side of the store from the checkout lines, I had to endure another journey through the tumultuous jungle of the supermarket. My carefully separated items eventually joined back together from the shifts and turns of pushing my cart through dozens of aisles. At that point, I was certain that my latte was going to have a hint of a vinegar taste to it.

Most of the people in the store were still shopping, so the lines to check out were fairly light compared to how busy it was. The self-checkout queue was even shorter than the rest, so I wasted no time in jumping into that line. While I waited, I decided to rearrange my cart again, wanting my milk to stay as far away from the baking soda and vinegar as possible. I still had an irrational fear that the baking items were contaminating my dairy product.

"Interesting choice of ingredients," I heard a grumbling voice bellow. "Are you making a cake or creating a poison?"

I thought it was pretty intrusive for someone to not only take inventory of my shopping cart but to also judge me for it, but I wasn't as surprised by the comment when I observed the person who had made it.

"I'm making a perfume," I sarcastically let out. "I figured if I smell like spoiled milk, then random strangers won't keep coming up to me at the bar."

"You might scare off more than just strangers," Michael concluded. "I don't think you'll end up on many more dates smelling like that."

"Good," I fired back. "I could go the rest of my life without going on another one."

"Wow, no more dates?" Michael questioned. "Reid's credit score didn't win you over?"

I let out a slight laugh and pushed my cart forward as the line continued to move.

"Reid will make a great plus-one to my friend's wedding," I explained to Michael, "but after that, I think I'm going to take a break from meeting strange men."

"Am I included in that?" Michael asked.

"You're at the top of the list," I reasoned with a smile to let him know that I wasn't serious.

I forgot how intriguing it was to engage in conversation with Michael. Without the distraction of a Hawaiian shirt, I actually got to focus on his personality and his stoic presence. He seemed very confident in every word he spoke, and firm in every movement he made. Michael appeared very sure of himself, and I was curious if there was more to him than he let on. He was very mysterious and extremely hard to read. It was as if he had a hand of cards, each one with a piece of his full personality, but he only showed me the ones that he wanted me to see. Michael kept the rest of his cards close to his chest.

"I'm glad to see Reid got you home safely. I was worried about you. I figured you may have had one too many hot chocolates," Michael bantered.

"I know how to handle my drinks," I commented. "I actually could've had another."

"I think the bartender would have had a heart attack," Michael shared. "I think he died a little inside when I asked for the second round."

"Maybe we can try another bar next time," I divulged.

"Paige, are you asking me out?" Michael sarcastically gasped.

It was supposed to be a sarcastic comment. I didn't realize how flirtatious it sounded until it had already left my mouth, but it obviously seemed as though I was trying to see him again. Truthfully, I wouldn't have minded hanging out with Michael again, but I was clearly not asking him out on a date. I quickly deduced that maybe Michael had a hidden superpower in which he was able to make people around him let their guards down and feel comfortable enough to say things to him that they would have rather kept hidden. I made a mental note to watch what I said going forward, especially since he didn't reciprocate. His walls were even higher than mine.

"Maybe after I finish my dating ban, I'll consider letting you buy me another hot chocolate," I replied, trying to recover from my previous comment.

"I don't know if Reid would appreciate that," Michael jokingly pointed out.

"Reid is not my boyfriend, and he never will be," I said, realizing I fell into Michael's trap again of getting people to say whatever was on their mind.

I did find Reid on the boring side, but I didn't want to speak badly about him. I quickly pushed my cart to the self-checkout machine that had recently opened up, hoping that my latest remark about Reid would soon be forgotten. Of course, the one right next to me happened to open up at the same time, so Michael abruptly snatched it and continued on the conversation.

"What did you not like about him?" he asked.

"He's a great guy," I explained, trying to scan and pay for my three ingredients as fast as I could to escape the topic and head home. "He's just not my type."

"What is your type then?" Michael followed up.

It was a logical next question, but my brain couldn't focus on completing my transaction and coming up with the perfect answer.

"Protective," I eventually uttered, trying to give a safe answer.

I didn't want to elaborate on Reid's uninspiring personality, so I chose another trait I looked for in a guy. I didn't view it as the most thought-out answer, but it seemed to satisfy Michael since he changed the subject.

"So what are you actually planning to do with those ingredients?" Michael inquired.

"Hannah, my friend who is getting married, got stung by a bee, and baking soda and vinegar helps reduce swelling. It's a family remedy," I quickly explained as I had already finished checking out and was trying to find a way to exit the conversation and get back to the apartment. "And the milk is just for my lattes."

I inched my way slowly toward the door, indicating that I was in a hurry and it was time for me to go.

"Do you want me to walk you to your car?" Michael asked.

His cart was still half full, and although I didn't have time to wait for him, the real reason I declined his offer was because I didn't want to carry on talking about Reid or explaining what my type of guy was.

"I'm okay, thanks, though," I said. "It was nice seeing you again, Michael."

I turned to leave in order to rush back to the apartment as I couldn't imagine how Hannah's meltdown had increased since I had left.

"Wait, Paige," Michael remarked before I was out of earshot.

I could tell he was prolonging the conversation beyond its normal end, but I ended up walking back over to him concluding that Avery and Hannah could wait a few more minutes.

"I know Reid wasn't your first choice as a wedding date, but if you want, I'll go with you," Michael shared.

I let out an obnoxious laugh, shocked and surprised that Michael would even think to offer that.

I appreciated his attempt, although it was extremely unnecessary. I had already decided I was going with Reid, even if he was on the slightly boring side. In contrast to Michael, Reid was already Hannah's friend, so I figured she would be more comfortable if I brought someone she knew. Hannah had no idea who Michael was, and neither of us knew how he would behave at a big event such as a wedding. Knowing him, he would probably show up in a Hawaiian suit. Reid was the safe option, and I was perfectly fine with bringing him as my plus-one.

"Thanks, but I'll be okay," I finally responded.

"Oh, okay," Michael returned solemnly. "Just figured I'd offer."

"It's just a wedding date. It's not like it's anything that serious," I continued on, trying to restore the playful banter we began with. "Besides, I'm never going to see you again."

I finished my answer with a playful wink, and it seemed to bring out the positive side of Michael again.

"Is that a promise?" he questioned with a smirk.

"A hundred percent," I lightheartedly let out.

"Well, how about if I do see you again," Michael revealed, "then I get to be your wedding date."

"You love bets," I pointed out. "Remember what happened the last time we put a wager on something? I clearly recall it ending in you having to buy me a hot chocolate."

"Then you shouldn't be afraid to make another bet with me," Michael concluded.

I contemplated the gamble. I hadn't officially told Reid that he could be my plus-one so I wouldn't have to go back on my word, but there was something that felt off about the bet. Maybe I was just afraid of what might happen if I actually got to spend more time with Michael. He wasn't the typical guy that I was normally used to, but he was also fun and unpredictable. There was an edge about him that made me curious about what would happen if I did keep him around, as I knew it would be anything but subtle. A part of me was also hesitant because he kind of reminded me of Avery's ex. Flirty, dangerous, and charming were traits of the guy who had completely ruined her life, and I was possibly welcoming a similar guy to that into mine. However, maybe he just reminded me of Kyle because both he and Michael were blonde, and to me, all blondes looked the same. I laughed to myself as I tried to decipher different blonde men in my head, but all joking aside, I believed the core of my hesitancy was that I didn't want to end up in the same situation as my best friend. I figured the possibility of being robbed and in a hospital was low, however, my heart remained heavily guarded after seeing what had happened to her. I didn't want to also fall for a guy who would ultimately end up blinding me in the end.

"So do we have a deal?" Michael asked, interrupting my thought process.

I realized I only had a split second to decide my next move. There were numerous reasons for why I didn't want to engage in the bet that was presented before me, but I had deprived myself of fun and excitement for the past two years, and I figured now was the time to finally give myself a break.

"Fine," I eventually said, "but don't expect to see me again."

"I guess we'll see what fate has in store for us, Paige," Michael disclosed. "Until we meet again."

"Or, until we don't," I flirtatiously relayed.

"Or, until you can't resist seeing me again," Michael said.

"Good-bye Michael," I finally remarked, realizing I had an injured friend at home in desperate need of my care.

"See you later," he fired back.

Michael refused to say good-bye. It must've felt too final of a response considering he needed to run into me again in order to win the bet. He just couldn't let go of the idea that this was the last time we were going to see each other again...but honestly, neither could I.

7

Dr. Jensen

I fully expected to walk into our apartment and see our living room turned into a makeshift emergency room. From observing the way Hannah hysterically reacted to her bee sting, I figured they had rolled in a hospital bed and Avery had assumed the role of her nurse. I wouldn't have been surprised if Hannah had been claiming that her injury had spread throughout her entire body, and I would have to go back to the store to get more ingredients. If that were the case, I would have to find a different store, as I was keen to not run into Michael again. I was afraid of opening up to anyone, and being around him made me let my guard down a little. But, the biggest reason for wanting to avoid him was because I wanted to win the bet. Michael was so adamant that we would see each other again that I wanted him to be wrong for once. I figured not running into him until after Hannah's wedding would be a bruise to his ego—something he was in desperate need of.

I braced myself for the scene I was about to walk into before heading inside the apartment. If Avery was Hannah's nurse, then that would make me Hannah's doctor—the one who was in possession of the medicine. Hannah was probably begging for the remedy by now, as I did take a little longer in the store than expected. However, I had the baking soda and vinegar with me, and I was fully prepared to end all the agony.

"Dr. Paige Jensen, at your service," I emphatically announced as I opened the door to the living room. I had a grocery bag in each hand, one with the healing ingredients and one with the milk, but it didn't prevent me from bursting through the door in an animated manner. I was no stranger to the dramatics, and I wanted my entrance to match the potential chaotic scene. However, instead of rushing through the door, if I truly wanted to walk inside in a way that resembled the energy of the apartment, I should have just tip-toed in. I observed the space that the living room and kitchen occupied and noticed it was a completely sane and serene environment. Turned out, the only dramatic event happening was my three cats—Toby, Leo, and Benny—having a brawl with Hannah's cat, Tubs. And even then, that wasn't anything alarming as there seemed to be a feline wrestling match every day.

Avery and Hannah were quietly sharing a bowl of grapes at the kitchen table, and they seemed to forget why I had even gone to the store in the first place since they quizzically looked at the bags in my hands. The girl who had once been erratically crying about a bee sting on her finger was now digging her hands into a bowl of fruit.

"What took you so long?" Avery questioned with a grape in her mouth.

"Yeah, we thought you had gotten lost or something," Hannah jokingly commented.

"I got lost in the jungle of shopping carts," I returned, setting the grocery bags down on the counter. "Everyone thought today would be a great day to go shopping. The whole city was in there."

"Oh, everyone, huh?" Avery mocked.

"Did you run into anyone you knew?" Hannah inquired. "I ran into my sixth-grade teacher at the store one time."

"I didn't run into anyone nearly as exciting as running into an old teacher," I answered sarcastically, brushing off her question. I wasn't the best liar, and I definitely wasn't trying to open up a conversation about Michael. I didn't know how I was supposed to explain to Avery and Hannah that the same guy I had run into at Lucky's had also been in the checkout line, and that we had decided to never run into each other again—well, at least, I was going to try my hardest to not see him again.

"Were you magically healed while I was gone?" I asked Hannah.

I had put the milk in the fridge, but I didn't know whether to put the vinegar and baking soda in the cabinets or if Hannah was still in dire need of my help.

"I'm all better now," Hannah cheerfully noted, holding her finger up in the air.

"Turns out, Band-Aids also cure bee stings," Avery explained, staring at Hannah's finger that was carefully wrapped in a purple bandage.

"It's a miracle." I chuckled, placing the extra ingredients into the kitchen cabinet. Maybe Graham could use the items to bake me a dessert now.

Watching Avery and Hannah munch on grapes and thinking about my brother making me a cake reminded me that I was also a little famished.

However, instead of reaching for a fresh piece of fruit out of the fridge, I opted for a bag of chips in the pantry. I grabbed the salty snack and took a seat at the kitchen table with my two best friends.

I quietly listened to Avery and Hannah resume whatever conversation they were having before I busted through the front door, but I didn't feel like participating just yet. I was exhausted from the grocery store excursion, and the stress of Michael's bet was consuming all of my energy. I kept telling myself that it was in my best interest to keep a safe distance from him, but I was also beginning to think that I was only attempting to convince myself that Michael was bad news in order to protect myself. I kind of wanted him to say something wrong or commit an offense that totally turned me off from him, but even his messy blonde hair and atrocious Hawaiian shirt couldn't totally keep me away. His energy was attractive and his confidence was alluring. Honestly, it was difficult to tell whether I had a bad gut feeling about him, or the idea of dating again scared me so much to the point where I was wagering against ever seeing him again.

"So, what are our Saturday night plans?" Hannah directed toward me, shifting my thoughts away from my nerves and toward our nightly activities. "Lucky's again?"

Panic set in as going to the bar where I initially met Michael was too risky, but I couldn't explain to Avery or Hannah that I had an ongoing wager that prevented me from going to my usual places. Neither of them had met Michael before or seen me around him. They would surely look at me as if I had two heads growing out of my neck if I even tried to explain my situation. Hannah's wedding was less than a month away, and I wanted the focus to be on her special day and not my inclination to never leave the house again. There was no need to distract anyone's thoughts with insignificant bets.

"I was thinking we could just stay inside tonight," I explained casually. "Maybe a pizza and movie night?"

"Yes!" Hannah cried out. "That is such a good idea. I'm actually getting tired of going out. Wedding planning has been draining."

"Extra pepperoni?" I asked, already reaching for my phone to place an order online.

"And extra cheese!" Hannah eagerly inserted.

"Wait a second," Avery inserted. "Since neither of you have plans tonight, we should all go to Iron Nine."

"Thanks, but I've seen my brother enough this week," I explained. "I don't need to spend my Saturday night at his restaurant."

I accidentally dropped a chip in my lap, but I quickly grabbed it and ate it before anyone noticed.

"Well, you might change your mind when I tell you who is dining at the restaurant tonight," Avery teased.

"Who is it?" Hannah screeched.

She was obviously eager to know who the secret diner was, but I was pretty set on staying home. I was still curious to know who it was, but it was going to take a lot to get me to leave the apartment.

"Zane Wilder," Avery eventually relayed.

"Zane Wilder!" Hannah shrieked. "The international pop-star sensation?"

Hannah began to dance in her chair, and she started singing one of Zane's hit songs.

"Didn't he get arrested for vandalizing a local coffee shop?" I rebutted.

"Allegedly," Avery affirmed. "But it's Zane Wilder!"

Hannah ceased her mini concert at the sound of his potential criminal history.

"He damaged a coffee shop?" Hannah questioned.

"He spray-painted one of their walls," I claimed.

"Allegedly," Avery reminded us.

Clearly, Avery was really excited to meet the criminal celebrity, but even a man as talented and good-looking as Zane Wilder wasn't enough to make me enter the public world and risk running into Michael.

"Thanks for the invite, but pizza and a movie still sounds better to me," I proclaimed, resuming my online pizza order that I hadn't completed yet.

"Graham can get us a table right next to his," Avery continued sharing. "We will have a direct view of him."

I still wasn't sold on spending my night at Iron Nine, but I could tell Hannah was contemplating her options.

"Hm, Zane Wilder or extra cheesy pizza," Hannah said out loud.

"Maybe he will notice Paige and she could take him to your wedding," Avery insisted, trying to persuade us.

"Oh, that would be perfect!" Hannah cried out.

"But, then, there would be a ton of paparazzi and people trying to get into your wedding," I countered. "That would take away from your special day."

"Good point," Hannah noted.

"Graham will make your favorite appetizer," Avery tempted again, trying to sway Hannah back to the side of going out.

"Nothing beats pizza," I relayed, trying to get Hannah to stay in with me. "And it might be hard to eat a shrimp cocktail with your injured finger."

I stared at the purple Band-Aid around Hannah's ring finger.

"You're right!" Hannah called out. "I can't leave the house with an injured finger."

Hannah's overreaction to her bee sting was starting to emerge again.

"And don't forget," I added, "he's a criminal."

"Allegedly!" Avery shouted.

I licked the cheese dust off my fingers, and closed the bag of chips.

"I think it's best that I stay home then," Hannah decided.

I gave Avery a playful wink as I managed to get Hannah to watch movies with me.

"Next time a famous person comes to the restaurant," Avery lightheartedly remarked, "I am not telling either one of you."

"You don't need to tell me unless it's the person who invented pizza," I stated, completing my online order.

"I'm pretty sure that person is dead," Avery assumed.

"Well, then, I guess you won't have to alert me of any famous diners," I relayed.

I got up from the kitchen table and walked over to the pantry. There was an empty space where the chips originally were, so I placed the bag back in its usual spot. I contemplated eating a candy bar as well, but I didn't want to ruin my dinner. Eating pizza was about to be the highlight of my night.

"Your loss," Avery continued to harp on the fact that we had declined to meet Zane Wilder. "By staying inside, you could be missing out on running into someone who could turn your world upside down."

"That's the point," I whispered to myself.

I was looking forward to a quiet night inside. It was just going to be me, Hannah, a cheesy pizza, and an even cheesier romance movie. All that was enough to get my mind off work, a wedding date—and even Michael.

8

The Heart Wants What it Wants

"Do you think they make romance movies where the guy and the girl don't end up together?" I asked once the final credits appeared on the television screen.

"It probably wouldn't make for a very good movie if it didn't have a happy ending," Hannah reasoned.

"I guess," I responded, "but I think it would be more realistic if the guy decided to just never speak to the girl ever again."

"Why do you say that?" Hannah asked innocently. "Elliot would never do that to me, or anyone else."

"That's because you and your fiancé are inseparable," I pointed out.

Hannah and Elliot were always together, and if he wasn't out of town for work, he would probably be watching romance movies with us.

"Well, I also don't think it's realistic to just never speak to someone again," Hannah shared. "You can't just avoid someone forever...they always come back."

"I beg to differ," I added, since I was currently in the position of trying to not see Michael again.

At first, the idea of staying at home for a few more weeks until Hannah's wedding sounded easy. I figured it would be an opportunity to focus on my work since I was going to become a prisoner to the apartment, only leaving during odd hours of the day. Yet, I had a solid summer routine that would need to be severely adjusted in order to avoid him. There was no way I could go to Lucky's on Fridays anymore, or to the grocery store during peak hours. I would have to find a new place to hang out on the weekends, and a new supermarket to shop at.

"I think the idea of staying inside and never leaving the apartment until your wedding sounds like the ideal life," I shared. "No public interactions, and no unnecessary stressors."

"Just romance movies and pizza," Hannah added on.

"Exactly," I agreed. "Good food and good television."

"And hanging out with the cats," Hannah shared. "Can't forget about them."

"Of course not," I affirmed.

Hannah and I initially bonded over our pets when we first met. Our lives revolved around our cats back then, and to this day, they still did. I adopted Toby and Leo when I found them in my high school dumpster while I was digging in it to find my retainer that I had accidentally thrown away. They were always very calm and low maintenance pets, only wrestling each other occasionally. Benny was added to the mix when Avery gifted him to me on my birthday a few years ago. He was a lot more work as he was the troublemaker of the bunch, but Hannah's cat, Tubs, kept him occupied. Tubs was also a super energetic cat, and he usually liked to run around the apartment chasing Benny all over the place.

"It would be hard to not leave the apartment with all the wedding stuff I have going on right now," Hannah commented. "It's nice to be able to take these few weeks off of work so I can focus on it, but unfortunately, I don't think it's possible for me to avoid going out in public entirely."

"I mostly work from home, so it would be a lot easier for me," I noted, "but there are a lot of emergencies that constantly come up. It's probably not feasible for me to just stay at home, either."

"At least we don't have Elliot's schedule," Hannah pointed out. "He travels so much."

"Well, if you didn't want your future husband to be gone all the time, then you shouldn't have married a pilot," I playfully remarked.

"He was just a pool security guard when we met," Hannah explained. "There was no travel involved there. He just had to be ambitious and get a more lucrative career."

"Wow, ambition," I exclaimed. "What a turn-off."

Hannah and I laughed over my sarcastic comment. Elliot was the pool security guard for the Exe Apartments at the beginning of their relationship, which to me, was a red flag. Kyle Kingsley was also a pool security guard at the Exe, and we all saw how that turned out. However, before he was working at a pool, Elliot flew planes for the military. After years of being in the Air Force, he decided to step back from that career when he decided that he rather live a quieter life. He was in his thirties, and was quite a bit older than Hannah, but their priorities were still pretty aligned.

Hannah also preferred a more laid-back lifestyle, so dating a pool boy didn't bother her. Guarding residents was a lot easier than protecting our country, but Elliot eventually changed jobs again. He still had a passion for planes, and therefore, decided to become a commercial airline pilot after his job at the pool wasn't fulfilling enough. It was a better career move for him, but it also meant that he was gone a lot. He loved his job, but I was pretty certain Hannah had mentioned that he was going to be working less hours once they were married.

"Reid is ambitious too," Hannah pointed out with a wink. "He made manager in less than three years of working at the restaurant."

I appreciated Hannah trying to hype up my potential wedding date, but I still wasn't excited about him being my plus-one.

"And, he has a passion for helping the homelessness problem in the city," she continued on.

"That's great," I replied nonchalantly.

"I can't wait to see you two hitting it off at my wedding and dancing together on the dance floor," Hannah confessed.

She continued to ramble on and on about how great Reid was and how eager she was to have him accompany me on her special day. I tried to stay calm and not let my true emotions show on my face, but when she brought up the idea of me potentially dating Reid after her wedding, I had to put a stop to the conversation.

"Hannah, can I tell you something?" I asked, interrupting her monologue about her former coworker.

"You can tell me anything," Hannah promised. "Is it something bad? Are you okay? Did you do something? Did I do something?"

I held her hand and took a deep breath.

"I truly appreciate you setting me up on a blind date," I confessed. "It was such a kind gesture, and Reid is such a great guy."

"I know, isn't he awesome?" Hannah exclaimed.

"However," I emphasized, "I don't find him nearly as great as you do. Truth be told, I actually find him incredibly boring."

Hannah looked at me speechless, but I was already on a roll so I continued on.

"While I was hanging out with Reid at Lucky's, I met this guy named Michael. Michael was fun, exciting, and everything that Reid was not. I ended up talking to the new guy the entire night, and I barely even spoke to Reid. I will still bring your former manager to your wedding as I want you to be comfortable with all your wedding guests, but I have absolutely zero interest in him." I finished my speech with a loud sigh.

There was a long pause until Hannah eventually spoke up.

"So, you'd rather bring Michael to my wedding instead?" Hannah innocently questioned.

"Oh, absolutely not," I claimed. "Well, I mean, it's possible that he and I would attend together."

Hannah looked at me confused.

"He and I have this bet that if we run into each other again, then I'll have to invite him, but I don't plan on running into him. I don't even want to see him again," I uttered.

"Well, why not?" Hannah inquired.

"Michael is...unpredictable," I said after trying to find the right word to describe him. "I can't read him, I don't know what he is thinking at any time, and he has this way of making me feel nervous around him."

"So, you like him?" Hannah continued with her line of questioning.

"No, I don't like him. But he's way more entertaining than Reid," I stated. "I didn't want to tell you or Avery about him because I wanted the focus to be on your wedding, and I didn't want you to think I was going to abandon the idea of inviting Reid. Like I said, I don't even want to see Michael again."

"It kind of sounds like you want to run into him again," Hannah reasoned. "And there's nothing wrong with that."

"Maybe a really tiny fraction of myself hopes that we see each other, but I don't want to run into the same situation as..." I paused, not wanting to bring up the traumatic event that our best friend had gone through.

"As Avery," Hannah finished for me.

I nodded my head, indicating that she had correctly finished my sentence.

"I understand your fear, but what Avery went through was a rare occurrence that shouldn't slow you down from dating. You used to be so confident around men, but ever since the incident a few years ago, I don't think I've seen you go on a single date," Hannah explained. "Avery's past isn't your future."

Understandably, watching your best friend have to rebuild her self-esteem and put her heart back together after being crushed by Kyle Kingsley was enough to put your own love life on hold. I knew that being assaulted and robbed were not normal dating experiences, but it had scared me to the point where I never let another guy into my life. I saw how men could be, and I didn't want to risk that happening to me.

"You're right about everything," I let Hannah know, "but that still doesn't make this any easier. I'll just attend your wedding with Reid, and then I can revisit the whole Michael situation another time."

"And risk losing the one guy who actually gets you excited about love again?" Hannah asked. "Absolutely not. I saw how your eyes lit up when you talked about him."

I turned my face away from her, trying to hide the illumination that I apparently gave off when mentioning Michael.

"Don't worry about disappointing me or Reid," Hannah started. "He will be fine not going to my wedding, and as your best friend, I want you to bring someone that actually makes you happy."

"Thanks, Hannah," I said with a sincere heart, placing my hands over hers. "You're a great best friend, and you are going to be a beautiful bride."

"Aw," Hannah responded, wallowing in the sweet moment. "I can't wait to meet Michael at my wedding."

"Well, there is only one problem with that," I noted. "I don't have his number or anything. We really left it up to chance. I have to actually run into him again in order to ask him to be my plus-one."

"How romantic!" Hannah cried out. "It's like you're living in your own little romantic movie."

"Yeah, hopefully this one has a happy ending," I revealed.

"It definitely will," Hannah confidently answered. "It wouldn't make for a good movie if it didn't."

She winked, knowing that I had just complained about how all romance films end in a predictable happy ending—not depicting real life—and now here I was, hoping for a fairy tale finale of my own.

"If it's meant to be, I'll run into him again," I said to Hannah, although I was mostly trying to convince myself that Michael and I's story didn't simply end at the grocery store.

"Well, since you met him at Lucky's," Hannah began, "why don't we go see if he's there?"

My eyebrows almost touched the top of my forehead, and my jaw dropped so low it almost hit the couch.

"Hannah, I can't just search the city for him. I'm pretty sure that's called stalking," I exclaimed.

"You aren't stalking him," Hannah defended. "You are simply putting yourself in a position that increases the odds that you will run into him."

"Sounds desperate," I uttered.

"Sounds romantic," Hannah shared.

It was true that Michael hadn't left my mind since the moment I met him. He seemed to have made a permanent residence in my brain. Every time I was around him, my heart would race, my skin would sweat a little bit, and my stomach would twist into knots. It had been a while since I had a crush on somebody, so I couldn't tell if the feelings I had when I was near him were my body telling me that I was enamored to be in his presence, or a warning sign to stay away from him. Fear and excitement gave off a similar reaction, and I assumed there was only one way to find out which one I was truly feeling.

"Your life is the plot of a romance movie," Hannah shared. "Don't make it a boring one."

"So your argument to get me to go to Lucky's is to entertain the viewers of my theoretical romance movie?" I inquired.

"I'm invested," Hannah shared.

It wasn't the greatest reasoning to get me to go out, but I'd surely never run into Michael just sitting at home. Besides, I had a movie I needed to carry on, and nobody wanted to see the main character sitting at home.

"I guess we are going to Lucky's then," I finally agreed.

"Yes!" Hannah shrieked. "I get to meet Michael!"

"It's not guaranteed," I explained to Hannah, who seemed to not realize that we were going to the bar blindly with no certainty whatsoever that he was actually going to be there.

"Oh, he will be," Hannah claimed.

"Yeah, and how can you be so sure?" I countered.

"Because he probably has the same idea. I bet he's already there waiting for you," Hannah stated.

I imagined walking into Lucky's and seeing Michael in another tropical shirt, seated at the bar with a hot chocolate in his hands, and an extra one waiting for me. I pictured his confident grin and soothing voice acting surprised as if it were a coincidence that we ran into each other, even though it was an obvious location to be at.

"What are you smiling at?" Hannah chimed in.

"Nothing," I said. "Let's go get dressed."

I quickly snapped out of the fantasy I had created in my head and brought myself back to reality. It was obvious that my heart was guarded after seeing what had happened to Avery. The violence she endured was indescribable, and I was nervous that I would end up in the same position—beaten, bruised, robbed, and tied to a chair. However, it was unfair to apply those hesitations to Michael as he hadn't shown me a single ounce of anger or cruelness. I barely knew him, but the few encounters I had with him involved hot chocolate and playful bets. It seemed the only crime that Michael was actually capable of committing was kidnapping my thoughts.

9

Long Time No See

I initially thought Friday nights at Lucky's were crowded, however, Saturdays were even worse. Five people had already stepped on my toes within five minutes of being in the establishment. I didn't wear my favorite pair of heels, so I wasn't that mad about the damage done to my shoes, but I did have a fresh pedicure that probably had shoe prints on it by now. People were shoving their way through crowds as if manners didn't exist, and the noise that echoed from numerous conversations all happening at once was almost loud enough to be heard over the DJ. Yet, I didn't mind not being able to hear the music that well, as I was pretty certain the bar was playing a song from Zane Wilder.

Unfortunately, the only spot at Lucky's that wasn't overcrowded by sweaty and obnoxious young adults was a tiny space in the corner by the restrooms. Therefore, my view consisted of people waiting in line to relieve themselves, and my nose was filled with the scents of musty fumes.

"I don't think he's here!" I shouted over the overwhelming noise.

I was screaming at the top of my lungs so that Hannah could hear me, but I was sure my words were still barely heard.

"How would you know?" she responded. "We've only been here for a few minutes."

"Trust me," I relayed. "If he was here, he would've made himself known by now."

On our way to the back corner of the bar, I made sure to take a closer look at the spots I remembered seeing Michael at the previous night. I didn't see anyone that came close to resembling him at the bar ordering a hot chocolate or playing a game of darts. I didn't pin him as the dancing type, but when we passed the dance floor, I looked for him there, too. There was no sign of him. Although it was impossible to have seen everyone at Lucky's, I was pretty confident in my ability to spot him in a crowd, and I had come up empty-handed. Even if I had missed him for some reason and he was hiding in a back corner like we were, he would have definitely come up to me by now because although I may not have noticed him, he always seemed to know where I was.

"Don't give up, Paige," Hannah announced, "I'm sure he will turn up sooner or later."

"I'm not giving up on anything," I insisted. "I just don't think he came out tonight."

"Well, either way, we are already out. We might as well make the most of it!" Hannah remarked.

She started dancing to the music and singing along to Zane's awful song. I loved seeing Hannah enjoying herself, and I truly wanted to join her in her fun, but the smell of dirty restrooms killed my vibe. Each time the bathroom door opened, I'd hear toilets flushing in the background. It was not the ideal atmosphere for getting into the dancing mood.

"Do you want to grab a drink instead?" Hannah proposed after I refrained from joining her solo dance party.

"No, I don't feel like standing in line for thirty minutes and subjecting my feet to be further trampled on just for a subpar drink," I replied.

"We could hit the dance floor?" Hannah mentioned as an alternative solution.

"I don't really feel like dancing," I remarked.

I could tell I was dampening Hannah's mood with every response. I didn't mean to rain on her parade, but I honestly didn't expect to feel the level of disappointment that I was experiencing. I didn't believe the odds of running into Michael that night were high, but I had gotten my hopes up and was starting to realize that I would not be seeing him tonight. My sour mood was also stemming from how upset I was with myself for how excited I got at the idea of potentially seeing a guy that I barely even knew. I hadn't shown interest in men or dating ever since Avery's incident, yet only after a few interactions with Michael, I was already thinking about him nonstop. Maybe it was because I was simply curious about him as he was hard to get a read on, or perhaps he resided in my mind because of his eagerness to always want to be around me. I kind of liked that a confident and poised man actually loved being in my presence. It gave off the sense that he would do whatever it took to be by my side, and I was attracted to that. He barely knew me, but it already felt like there was an unspoken loyalty between us. Unfortunately, the assumed bond that I had with Michael might have just been an illusion that I curated in my head as there was no actual proof that I had his trust and support. He didn't even show up tonight. I guess fate was trying to tell me to run for the hills instead of standing around Lucky's bathrooms, hoping that I might run into him.

"There's a pool table in the far corner of the bar," Hannah suggested as another potential option.

"I'm sure there's already people playing," I noted.

"I know," Hannah affirmed, "but watching a bunch of grown men argue over a game of billiards is probably more entertaining than watching the bathroom line."

"Good point," I said, "Lead the way."

I put a hand on Hannah's shoulder so that we wouldn't get separated in the swarm of people. She took a very polite approach in weaving around strangers, always kindly asking them to move. I would have definitely found a more forceful way to make it through the crowd, but it was probably best that Hannah's gentle soul was leading the way.

Hannah was right about the activities surrounding the game section of Lucky's Tavern being a lot more enjoyable than the views of people with full bladders, but I was extra excited about her suggestion because the pool table was an area that Michael could potentially be at. It was right next to the dartboard, a place where he might be if he was inside the building hanging out...or looking for me.

"Almost there," Hannah called out as she continued to maneuver through groups of people.

I continued holding on to her shoulder, eager to get to the pool table.

I had a firm grasp on my hopes of seeing Michael again, but it was hard as they were like helium balloons, trying to float and get carried away. I firmly anchored them down, ensuring they wouldn't soar out of reach and get so high that there was no way I could bring them back down. However, Hannah and I hadn't explored the section of the bar near the games, and that was enough to let one of my helium balloons of hope slip free, drifting upward before I could stop it. I was sure that after a few minutes of realizing that he wasn't there either, the floating balloon would pop, and all hope and excitement would die down. It wasn't fun—being in a constant game of wondering where Michael was—but I had to admit to myself that there was obviously something about him that was gravitating me toward him, or else I wouldn't have been this eager to see his face again.

"Oh, look who is here," Hannah shouted once we neared our destination.

"Michael?" I asked.

A rush of electricity ran through my body, and I frantically started searching for the one person I came to the bar for.

"No, silly," Hannah commented. "It's Reid!"

I quickly realized that Hannah had never seen Michael before, so of course it couldn't have been him. However, I was still upset that the man who approached us was Hannah's former boss, and not the guy who had me considering letting my walls down.

"Paige. Hannah," Reid exclaimed.

Even his greetings were boring and lacked enthusiasm.

"Reid! So great to see you!" Hannah shouted back in a more emphatic tone. "What are you doing here?"

"Well, your friend inspired me," Reid stated, pointing at me. "After watching her amazing skills, it motivated me to learn how to play darts."

"Oh, so you came to Lucky's to practice?" I questioned.

"Well, I haven't exactly picked up a dart yet, but I have been studying everyone's movement and taking notes on common tactics," Reid explained.

He held up a tiny notebook and turned his head to the side so that we could see the pencil tucked behind his ear. I thought it was extremely weird, but Hannah seemed to be impressed with his willingness to learn something new.

"You are going to have to show us your new skill sometime," Hannah relayed.

"Will there be a dartboard at your wedding?" Reid chuckled. "I can show off what I learned at the reception."

Reid continued to laugh at his own comment, but for Hannah and I, it was an uncomfortable encounter as we both knew that I had already decided that I didn't want him to be my plus-one. I was fully set on taking Michael, but neither of us had let Reid know that he wasn't going with me anymore.

"Actually, Reid..." I began, not wanting to break the bad news. However, I knew the longer I waited, the worse it would be. "I'm actually going to Hannah's wedding with someone else. I'm sorry."

The hurt look on Reid's face which expressed itself only a few seconds after I had finished my sentence was enough to make me want to take my statement back. He looked as though I had just stolen a puppy from him.

"Oh, okay..." Reid stuttered.

My heart broke as I watched his lip quiver and pools of water line the bottom of his eye lids.

"But no worries, Reid!" Hannah interjected. "You are definitely still invited."

"Really?" Reid stammered, the color slowly returning to his drained face and the corner of his mouth curving into a slight smile.

"Of course!" Hannah shared. "I want you there."

Reid lunged toward Hannah so fast that I thought he teleported to her. He wrapped her in a tight hug and began thanking her.

"I appreciate you so much," Reid disclosed. "I can't wait to celebrate with you."

"I'll text you the details," Hannah said once Reid finally let her go. "Unfortunately, I ran out of invitations."

"That's totally fine," Reid professed. "I'm just thrilled to attend."

If Reid wasn't so blinded by his excitement, he would have realized that he had just received a pity offer. He had no idea that the real reason she didn't have any more invitations was because everyone who was actually a planned guest had already received one.

"I need to get my suit dry-cleaned, and I have to schedule a haircut." Reid pulled the pencil from behind his ear and began writing in his notebook that he had used for his notes on playing darts.

"You still have a couple more weeks," I pointed out since he was acting as if she was getting married tomorrow.

"Do you think I'll have time to get my shoes shined?" he asked.

I looked at him quizzically as I had just clearly relayed that her wedding date was far enough away that he didn't need to panic.

"I need to put my darts on hold," Reid noted, putting the pencil back behind his ear. "I'll catch you guys later. I've got a lot of things I need to do before the wedding."

Reid abruptly pushed past Hannah and I, bolting toward the direction of the exit.

"He's so..." I paused, trying to find the right word describe the interaction that had just ensued.

"Motivated," Hannah said, incorrectly finishing my sentence.

I actually didn't know what word I was going to use, but that one was not on the list.

"Uh, sure," I muttered, confused as to how she found the recent events to be normal. "I can't believe you invited him to your wedding weeks before the official date."

"You saw his face," Hannah remarked. "I couldn't just watch him cry. He was so crushed to learn that he wasn't going with you."

"Do you even have space for him at the venue?" I asked.

"I'll make room," Hannah confirmed.

Hannah proved to me every day that she truly possessed the sweetest heart in the world. If I was in her shoes, I most likely would have let Reid feel bad for a few moments, and then move on from it. No way was I extending an invite less than a month before my wedding day.

"Well, I'm ready to leave if you are," I exclaimed.

"You don't want to watch a few games of pool?" Hannah asked, confused.

"The conversation with Reid was enough entertainment for the night," I shared.

I truly was tired and the conversation with Reid didn't help that, but the real reason I was ready to go was because during the whole interaction with Reid, my eyes were scanning every inch of the gaming area. Michael was nowhere to be found, and therefore, there was no reason to continue to be at Lucky's.

"You sure?" Hannah inquired. "How are you going to ask Michael to be your wedding date if you don't run into him?"

"I don't know," I answered.

I probably shouldn't have told Reid I wasn't going to the wedding with him until it was official that I was going with Michael, but it was too late now. There was barely any time left before Hannah's special day, and since I didn't get to see Michael and I had already denied Reid, I would most likely have to show up alone.

"We could come back next weekend?" Hannah offered.

"That's okay," I pointed out. "I think it just wasn't meant to be."

I raised my arm and rested my hand on Hannah's shoulder like earlier.

"Lead the way?" I asked Hannah.

Hannah smiled, although, her expression mostly showed that she felt sorry for me. I believed she could tell that I was disappointed that I didn't run into Michael, even though I didn't verbally express it.

She turned to face the exit, and as she had done previously, she politely weaved her way through the traffic of sweaty humans. A few more people had stepped on my toes on the way to the door, but I was so ready to leave the bar that I didn't have the energy to care.

The exit was only a couple of yards away, but it felt much further with how long it took to reach it. It would have been faster if we had bulldozed through everyone, but I was in no mood to cause a fight at Lucky's. I had endured enough public interaction for the time being. I was so confident going into the night that running into Michael would be a simple operation that the let down of not seeing him was affecting me more than I had anticipated. I just wanted to go to bed and start a new day.

"Why is it so hot outside?" Hannah asked, pushing through the exit doors.

A rush of heat suffocated us when we finally left the building.

"Because it's August," I shared. "And we live in a desert."

"I've lived here for years, yet I still never get used to the hot air," Hannah complained.

"You could move to Utah," I offered.

"I'd love to, but Elliot loves Vegas," Hannah explained. "He would never want to leave."

Our heels clanked against the parking lot pavement as we trudged through it, and Hannah continued to talk about how great it would be to explore a different state. I didn't want her to think I wasn't listening to her about the great attractions of Utah, but I didn't give her any eye contact as my sights were solely focused on counting all the bruises and cuts on my toes that I had collected from the night.

"Um, Paige?" Hannah shakily questioned in the middle of her rant.

"Yeah?" I answered, still walking alongside her and staring at my big toe.

"Someone's waiting for you at your car," she said.

I looked up and saw a figure of a man, leaning against my car with his arms crossed. He was facing our direction and watching us walk toward him. It was dark, so I couldn't make out his exact physical features, but it wasn't too hard to see the neon flamingos on his Hawaiian shirt. My previous mood of feeling extremely disappointed was quickly replaced with hope and excitement.

10

Patience is a Virtue

"One hour and thirteen minutes," Michael called out as he stared at his watch. "That's how long you waited at Lucky's for me."

"I wasn't waiting for you," I declared as Hannah and I approached him.

I expected to be a lot more afraid of a man who was standing at my car in the middle of a parking lot outside of a bar, but Michael was far from scary. Even in the darkness of the night, he still didn't seem the least bit intimidating. I could tell Hannah was initially frightened by his presence, but she too seemed to immediately ease all her nerves at the sight of him. I was glad to know that Michael's charming and stoic demeanor not only worked on me, but was also able to have an effect on Hannah. I was starting to worry that I was the only girl in the world who felt the need to lower my guard around him.

"I'm used to you stalking me by now, Michael, but this is taking it to a whole other level," I playfully remarked.

Michael chuckled and started stroking his jawline.

"Running into you at the grocery store was purely a coincidence," he bantered back.

"Oh, a coincidence," I sarcastically repeated. "Then what do you call waiting in the parking lot by my car?"

"The same thing you call going to Lucky's for the sole purpose of trying to find me," he answered.

"I wasn't looking for you," I lied. "My friend Hannah and I were just having a fun night out."

"Right, you randomly decided to enjoy a night out at the very bar we met at," Michael returned.

"That is exactly what happened," I explained.

"So, if it was pure chance that we decided to go to the same location tonight..." Michael began. "...then that must mean running into each other again would be..."

"Stalking," I finished for him.

"Destiny," Michael corrected.

"Wait," Hannah interjected. She was clearly not prepared to witness the interaction between Michael and I. Ninety percent of our conversations were either sarcastic comments or playful remarks. I found it fun, but Hannah appeared extremely confused. "I thought we did come to Lucky's to see if he would show up?"

I violently shook my head at Hannah in an attempt to get her to stop talking.

"What?" she questioned. "Aren't you supposed to ask him to be your wedding date? I thought you guys had a deal."

I smacked my forehead. The act of pretending that I wasn't purposely trying to find Michael was definitely over now, thanks to Hannah. Reading social situations was not her greatest strength. There was an element of mystery amongst Michael and I, and I wanted to keep it that way. I couldn't tell if he felt the same way about me as I did about him. I wondered if I also ran through his mind all day. He kept his cards close to his chest, and I wanted to mimic his behavior, but with Hannah by my side, no secret was safe.

"We did have a deal, didn't we, Paige?" Michael inquired, poking fun at the situation.

I felt my face get warm, and I didn't know what to say to save myself from the embarrassing situation, so I tried to mentally remove myself from the awkward moment by shifting my focus back to counting all the bruises on my feet. I looked down at my battered toes and tried to pretend I was somewhere else. I observed each toe one by one, moving from my big toe to my pinky, trying to decide which one got the worst beating. However, I didn't get to finish because in the middle of my evaluation, I felt a gentle grasp around the tip of my chin, which was used to carefully lift my face.

"You know, I was kind of hoping you'd show up tonight," Michael confessed. "I didn't want you to have to show up to the wedding alone."

There was still a subtle note of playfulness in his tone, but it was the first time that Michael had shown a slight hint of vulnerability. I was glad he picked that moment to reveal another layer to himself as it was hard to keep up the façade that I wasn't interested in him.

"Great!" Hannah shrieked, ruining the intimate moment. "Paige, now you have someone to bring!"

She hugged me out of excitement and then outstretched her hand toward Michael.

"I'm Hannah Livingston, but soon to be Hannah Stockton," she eagerly shared.

"Michael, but soon to be Paige's plus-one," he returned jokingly.

"I told you he was going to be here tonight," Hannah noted pridefully. "Wait, but how did you know where Paige was going to be? How did you even know this was her car?"

"Lucky guess," he replied smoothly.

Michael gave me a sly wink. The tiny shred of vulnerability that he had once portrayed was now gone, and he was back to being his completely mysterious self.

"Well, I'm excited to have you at my wedding, even though I don't know you that well," Hannah overshared.

"The pleasure is all mine," Michael exclaimed.

"Actually, you two don't even know each other that well, either," Hannah concluded. "Maybe you guys can go out to lunch or something?"

Hannah looked at me for an answer, but I didn't want to be pulled into the conversation. Michael and I had our own thing going on. We never planned when we would meet up—it would sort of just happen. She was altering our typical flow of things, and I didn't know how Michael would handle the sudden change.

"I'm free tomorrow for lunch," he shared.

Now, they were both staring at me, awaiting a response.

"Um, I can make tomorrow afternoon work," I nervously stammered.

I liked being around Michael because there wasn't any pressure. I could just be myself and let go of any expectations. However, formally making plans with him made it feel like a date, and the idea of going on an actual date was stressful to me.

"Noon?" Michael proposed.

"Sure," I muttered.

I could feel myself shutting down. I wanted to return to the free-flowing conversation and away from the rigid scheduling. It was all becoming too real, too fast. I liked it better when I could simply randomly run into him and have a brief witty banter session.

"This is the part where you give him your phone number," Hannah whispered loud enough for everyone to hear.

"Hm? My phone number? Oh, okay," I nervously replied.

I unzipped my purse and dug around in it for my phone. It was dark, so I blindly felt for it.

"It's right here," Hannah informed, reaching into my back pocket and retrieving my phone.

She immediately unlocked it and handed my device over to Michael.

He looked at me for approval before typing in his number, so I gently nodded my head.

"Oh, this is so exciting!" Hannah cried out.

While Michael was entering in his contact information, Hannah reached for her own phone that was ringing in her pocket.

"It's Elliot. I've got to take this," Hannah explained, staring at her screen.

She abruptly took several steps away from Michael and I in order to give herself some privacy to talk to her fiancé.

"I can see why you two are friends." Michael laughed while handing me my phone back. "She's very bubbly."

"Yeah, she's very energetic," I softly noted.

I could feel the typical dynamic between Michael and I return as soon as Hannah left. It eased my nerves knowing that I could feel comfortable around him again.

"So, things are getting pretty serious between us now," Michael jokingly offered.

"You're just my wedding date," I reminded him. "Don't get too excited."

"It's still a date," he countered, "so I'm definitely excited."

I rolled my eyes, but internally I appreciated his eagerness.

"Just behave yourself," I warned. "I don't want you embarrassing me."

"Don't I always?" he returned.

"Always what?" I questioned. "Behave yourself or embarrass me?"

"Both," he affirmed.

"Absolutely," I said with a smile. "But if you do anything dumb at the wedding, I swear I'll never speak to you again."

"Right, because you betting against ever seeing me again worked so well the last time," he sarcastically pointed out.

I stared at him unamused, annoyed that our previous bet resulted in a major boost to his ego.

"Paige, we have to go," Hannah breathlessly returned. "Elliot is upset that I'm not home right now."

"Why? It's a Saturday night," I explained.

"I promised him I would be home when he returned from his work trip, but now he's at the apartment and I'm not there," Hannah uttered.

Elliot had a tendency to be slightly controlling. At first, I thought he was concerned about Hannah's safety and well-being, but over time, it seemed as though he had ulterior motives. In my mind, he was extremely insecure.

"Okay, I'll take you back home then," I answered.

I reached for my keys and unlocked my car. As soon as the car was accessible, Hannah raced to the passenger seat.

Michael got the hint that it was time for us to go our separate ways, so he took a few steps away from my vehicle.

"So, I'll see you tomorrow?" Michael asked.

"Yes, at noon. There's a casual lunch spot around here. I'll text you the address. Don't be late," I instructed.

The idea of meeting formally was still a little unsettling, but the fact that the source of his excitement was from the idea of seeing me again made me feel good about myself.

Michael outstretched his arms and started slowly making his way toward me.

"What are you doing?" I asked as he got closer.

"I'm trying to give you a hug," Michael stated. "Unless, you rather me give you a kiss."

He gave me a sly smirk, but part of me refused to believe that he was a hundred percent joking.

In an effort to deny his offer of a hug and a kiss, I stuck my hand out. Hannah had basically exposed my true intentions tonight, and I was trying to preserve the idea that I wasn't completely into him yet. He wasn't the only one who could hide their true feelings.

Michael reached for my hand, but instead of completing the handshake, he wrapped his other hand around my waist and pulled me toward him. I was quickly swept off my feet before finally landing in his arms.

"You know, we don't always have to act like there isn't something more between us," he asserted while hugging me.

"I don't know what you're talking about," I replied, opting to continue to ignore the obvious connection that was there. Sometimes, it was just easier to pretend that we were normal friends instead of facing the real feelings that resided.

I pulled away from the hug, as I was sure Hannah was in the car worrying about what Elliot was going to say.

"I'll see you tomorrow," I said.

As soon as Michael stepped out of my way, I darted toward my car. When I reached the driver's side door, I flung it open, hopped into the seat, and started my vehicle.

I needed to head home in order to take Hannah back, but I was also relieved to create some distance between Michael and I. I wasn't sure how much longer I would have been able to keep my composure. It was a lot easier put on a tough act before the hug. Now that I had experienced what it was like to be touched by him, I knew I was in trouble.

11

Brotherly Love

Whatever could possibly go wrong on a Sunday morning went wrong. The old me used to conquer dates as if they were a normal daily activity such as brushing my teeth, but now I couldn't even remember my own name. I didn't entirely know whether lunch with Michael counted as a date or not. Of course, I was going to give off the impression that it was simply two friends sharing a meal, but that didn't change how nervous I was. Whether we labeled it a date or not, it still felt like one, and therefore it resulted in me running around my apartment trying to find my car keys. If I didn't locate them within the next ten minutes, I wouldn't be able to make it to the restaurant on time, and the hard time I had given Michael about being tardy would have been a complete waste. Instead, I would have to endure his entitled lecture about timeliness. Hopefully my keys would simply reappear in my hand, but I was in such a rush to get Hannah home to her antsy fiancé last night that I couldn't remember where I last had them.

The entire morning had been a disaster. Losing my car keys was just the cherry on top of an already unfortunate series of events. I had burned the tip of my ear when I was straightening my hair, I ripped the seams of my favorite pair of jeans, and I couldn't tell if my makeup was classy or clown-like. My best friends were both at their significant others' apartments, so nobody was home to calm me down and tell me that I was overreacting. I still hadn't gotten the chance to tell Avery about Michael, however, I wouldn't have been surprised if Hannah had told her already. She had a tendency to overshare.

I double-checked every inch of the apartment for any sign of my car keys. They were usually in my purse, but I had already dumped out all of the contents and didn't have any luck finding them there. I didn't remember sitting on the couch when I got home last night, but I still made the effort to remove each cushion, hoping they would magically show up in the deep abyss of the living room furniture.

"Remodeling?" Graham questioned as he entered my apartment without knocking.

He was used to coming over and having free access as his girlfriend obviously lived there, but he may have gotten too comfortable with his ability to pop in and out willingly. One of the main reasons he decided to live in the same complex as me was so that he could keep an eye on me, and he definitely took full advantage of that.

"Have you seen my car keys?" I immediately asked.

"Um, no?" Graham answered, confused as to why I would think to ask him that.

"I'm late for...something, and I need to find them," I uttered, not wanting to divulge my dating life to my older brother.

"Well, where was the last place you had them?" he asked.

"Obviously if I knew the answer to that I wouldn't be tearing this couch apart," I snapped back.

Graham had evidently returned from working out as he was still in his sweaty gym clothes. He made himself at home by navigating his way toward my fridge and retrieving the orange juice as if it were his own place. Thankfully, he opted to pour himself a glass. I was nervous that he felt comfortable enough to drink it straight from the carton.

"While you're searching for your keys," Graham started, "see if you can find your sanity. I'm sure it's lost in here somewhere, too."

"It's not funny," I huffed. "I need to find my keys now, or else I'm going to be late."

"Right," Graham started. "You are going to be late to the very top-secret place you won't tell me about."

I rolled my eyes at him as he continued to stare at his helpless sister while he mooched off my orange juice.

"Where's Avery?" I asked him. "She will actually offer some assistance."

"She's at my apartment, but she's very busy editing some photos she took last night for our social media page," Graham explained. "Did you know that Zane Wilder was there?"

"Yeah, I heard," I responded, unamused.

I wasn't the slightest bit impressed that an entitled celebrity dined at his restaurant, but Zane's presence at Iron Nine would probably spark a lot of excitement. I decided to continue looking for my keys on my own as

I didn't want to interrupt Avery's workflow. She was really excited about Zane being there, and I was certain she got some good photos of him.

"How about I help you find your car keys?" Graham began slurping down the rest of his glass of orange juice. "But you have to tell me where you plan on going."

"No deal," I refused, moving my search from the couch to the coat closet.

"Hm, you must really like him," Graham noted.

I paused my pursuit and stared at my brother, wondering how he found out about Michael. Maybe Hannah had told Avery, and then Avery must have shared it with Graham.

"Why are you looking at me all crazy?" he questioned. "You think I don't know you by now. I've only known you my entire life. I can tell when you are nervous about a date."

Graham was leaning against the kitchen counter but stood up in order to rinse his glass. He turned on the sink and started cleaning his dish. At least he was a courteous guest.

"It's not a date," I countered. "I'm just meeting someone for lunch."

"Is it a guy?" Graham probed.

"Yeah," I replied.

"Is anyone else joining you two?" Graham inquired.

"No, it's just us," I answered casually.

"Then it's a date," Graham concluded.

The coat closet was a lost cause, so I started shuffling through the drawers in the kitchen.

"Hannah said I needed a date to her wedding, so I invited someone," I explained. "We are going to lunch to get to know each other better."

"You asked someone to go to a wedding with you, and you don't even know him?" Graham asked.

"It's complicated," I uttered. "You wouldn't understand."

"I might not understand completely, but I can tell you really like him," Graham shared. "When I first started dating Avery, I also got nervous and couldn't properly dress myself."

"What are you talking about?" I asked, still digging through random drawers.

"Your shirt is on inside out," Graham pointed out.

I looked down at myself, noticing that the wrong sides of the seams of my blouse were exposed.

"Crap," I muttered, "I can't find my keys, and I can't dress myself, either."

I turned away from Graham and quickly adjusted my top, ensuring that it was correctly on that time.

"Let me give you some brotherly advice about boys," Graham stated. "Come, sit down."

Graham gestured toward the nearest chair, while he took a seat at the kitchen table.

"Graham, I don't have time for this. I need to find my keys," I rebutted.

"You're already going to be late, Paige," Graham said. "You might as well hear what I have to say."

I stood firm, still not wanting to waste my precious time listening to my brother's obnoxious advice.

"I'll help you look for your keys if you sit down and hear me out," Graham proposed.

"Ugh, fine," I murmured.

I didn't want to know what he had to say, but I had given up on looking for my keys, so I decided to take a seat. I searched the entire apartment over and over, and I still couldn't find them.

"Now, when you start dating someone," Graham started as soon as I sat down, "you need to be careful."

"Graham, I'm twenty-five, not sixteen," I reminded him.

"I know, but you will always be my little sister," he affirmed, "and I don't want to see you get hurt."

"You don't want to see what happened to Avery happen to me," I clarified, knowing the point he was trying to make.

My brother looked at me with hurt in his eyes, most likely reminiscing on what had happened to his girlfriend.

"I've also known you my whole life," I continued on. "I know what you are trying to say."

"Please, just be careful," Graham cautioned.

"I will. I promise," I assured him. "Trust me, the only thing that this guy has in common with Kyle Kingsley is his hair color."

"Wow, you're going out with a blonde?" Graham asked, clearly surprised. "Blondes were never your type."

"They still aren't," I confirmed, "but this guy is...different. Besides, it's just a casual date. Nothing serious. Well...if I make it there. It's already noon, and I haven't even left yet. I should have already been there by now."

Graham shuffled around in his chair, reaching into the side pocket of his gym shorts. A clanking sound echoed throughout the kitchen when he pulled out my car keys and slid them across the table.

"You forgot them in the fridge," Graham revealed. "Right next to the orange juice."

"You couldn't have given these to me, like, five minutes ago?" I shouted.

"I could have," he admitted, "but what would be the fun in that?"

"You're ridiculous," I uttered, swiping my keys off the table.

I quickly got up from the kitchen table, car keys finally in hand, and raced to my room to grab my purse. The restaurant was less than ten minutes away, but it was already past noon. I reached for my phone and sent Michael a quick message, notifying him of my late arrival. I didn't want to know the satisfaction he was going to feel when he read my text, realizing that I couldn't show up on time.

"Have fun on your date," Graham called out as I raced through the kitchen to head to the front door.

"It's not a date," I sharply reminded him.

"Will I get to meet him before Hannah's wedding?" Graham asked.

"I don't know," I answered, reaching for the door knob. "I can't predict the future."

"Does he know you have a protective older brother?" he inquired.

"Graham, I'd love to answer all of your questions, but I have to go," I said.

"Okay, I'll wait right here for you so when you come back you can tell me all about it," he claimed.

"Please, don't," I returned. "Don't you have a restaurant or something to be at?"

"I'm off today," he proudly shared.

Time was ticking by and I was becoming even more late, but at least I was already halfway out the door.

"You don't have anything better to do with your free time than obsess over my dating life?" I said to him.

"It's not a date," he replied with a wink.

"Whatever, just don't eat all my food," I declared.

"Have a good time," Graham returned right before I shut the door.

I was glad to finally have been able to leave my apartment, but it was already past noon, and I hadn't even gotten into my car yet thanks to my brain that chose to have a mental lapse last night. I must have grabbed a late-night snack and decided that my keys would make great friends with the orange juice.

I already knew Michael was going to have some snarky comment to say about my tardiness. I could picture his smug face after indulging in the satisfaction of watching me walk into the restaurant after our decided time. I reminded him to not be late, but I guess I was the one who needed the lecture. However, that didn't stop the excitement of knowing I was on my way to see Michael from flowing through my veins. I was about to be face-to-face with the guy whose hair color I didn't like, who thought that tropical attire was appropriate for a night out, and who always wanted to make a silly bet...yet, I couldn't have been more excited to see him.

12

Imprisoned

There was a beautiful essence of spontaneity that I greatly appreciated. The fact that there wasn't an exact arrangement or any preplanned details was fascinating to me. Sometimes, spur-of-the-moment happenings created the best memories. An impulsive adventure, such as randomly going to Lucky's to find a potential wedding date, created a sense of mystery—constantly wondering which impromptu event would happen next. Something about letting the universe decide the next course of action made life fun. I believed that the spontaneous run-ins that I had with Michael added an element of excitement to our friendship. When we would meet coincidentally or without any preset plans, everything seemed to fall into place. Our encounters were even more special when we just let fate choose our next move.

On the other hand, when we had conversations about seeing each other again and actually made real plans, the level of ease that we had seemed to dissipate. In the past, there was no specific time that I had to be anywhere in order to see him, and now, I couldn't even show up on time. I was twenty minutes late to our prearranged lunch, which made me feel incredibly horrible about myself—especially since I had warned him not to keep me waiting. I believed Michael could tell that I was incredibly sorry about my tardiness as he didn't give me a hard time about it when I showed up. In fact, he didn't even say much to me at all. Our typical free-flowing conversations and flirty banter were kept to a minimum during that afternoon. All Michael and I knew was spontaneity, excitement, and chance meetings, so we didn't know how to handle a proper date. Even if it was just a casual lunch between two friends, our brains couldn't seem to fathom the idea that we had actually planned to meet up, and we were somehow supposed to converse in a normal setting.

"So, what are you going to order?" I asked Michael, trying to keep the awkward silence to a minimum.

"Hm, I was thinking about the club sandwich. How about you?" he responded formally.

"Um, probably just a Caesar salad," I replied casually.

I didn't recognize Michael or myself with how shy we happened to become over a simple meal. I seemed to have lost my confident persona along with my car keys back at my apartment, but was only capable of finding one of them before heading out the door.

"I heard the grilled cheese was also good," Michael added.

"I've never had it before, but I'm sure it's delicious," I answered.

"Maybe I'll get that instead," he contemplated.

"Can't go wrong with cheese and bread," I assured.

I tried to cut through the tension with a lighthearted comment, but the awkwardness remained.

I had already decided on a salad a while ago, but Michael still seemed to be contemplating his options. While he continued to scan his menu, I pulled out my phone to read the job posting that I had published that morning. I didn't think many people would notice it on a Sunday afternoon, but I already had three applicants schedule an interview with me on Monday. The posting hadn't even been out for a full day yet, and I was already seeing a lot of activity on it. I was taking Avery's advice seriously by trying to find an assistant to help me with simple tasks that took up a lot of my time and kept me from focusing my attention on larger business matters. However, I believed the real reason I felt an urge that Sunday morning to publish the open position to a few job boards was my growing friendship with Michael. I still wanted help tackling the mundane parts of my job, but instead of using the extra time that would be freed up to study the market, look at expansion strategies, and hire more nannies, I foresaw myself spending more time with him. I loved the growth that my business had that resulted from me throwing myself into my career for the past two years, mostly because I had given up on the idea of dating after seeing what happened to Avery. However, Michael showed me that there was more to life than just working, and that I didn't have to always carry this fear of falling for someone.

"Do you smile at your phone like that when I text you, too?" Michael questioned.

I hadn't realized that he had finished looking at the menu, so having my phone out was completely rude and disrespectful, but I was also excited to hear the playful sarcasm beaming from his voice again. I figured the awkwardness of our date was starting to wear off, and his true self was being brought out again.

"Sorry, I was already bored of hanging out with you," I jokingly returned.

My comment was lighthearted, but there was some honesty intertwined in it. I wanted him to know that I sensed that things were off between us.

"Oh, wow. Late, on your phone, and calling me boring...you are the worst first date I have ever been on," he bantered.

"It's not a date," I said with a wink.

"You are the worst plus-one I have ever had," he playfully corrected.

The waitress briefly interrupted our conversation in order to take our drink orders, but I was adamant on keeping our conversation light and fun, so as soon as she left, I kept our normal banter going.

"Was it weird knowing that you didn't have to follow me in order to see me this time?" I asked.

"Super weird," he jokingly shared, although I could hear the truth behind it.

"I think I like you better when you stalk me," I flirtatiously confessed.

"Should I follow you to your car after this?" he asked.

"Yeah, and then you can watch me drive home so you can see where I live," I answered.

"Maybe I've already done that," he slyly mentioned.

"I wouldn't be shocked if you had. You are all about the element of surprise," I noted. "I don't think planned dates are your thing."

"This isn't a date." he winked.

I laughed at his comment, and I assumed it was safe to say that we both had noticed the awkward tension at the start of the lunch. It took a moment for the newness of us actually being together on a planned occasion to wear off, but it was also kind of refreshing to see him not as confident as he usually portrayed. His shyness humanized him a bit, and his innocence was just as attractive as his cockiness.

The waitress returned to disrupt our conversation again by placing an ice water in front of each of us. I was hungry and eager to order, but I also wanted a few moments to talk to Michael without any interruptions.

"Ready to order?" she cheerfully piped up.

"Yes, she is going to have..." Michael quickly interjected, lifting up the menu and pointing to a specific spot on it. "She likes to be surprised."

The waitress wrote down the item on her notebook without saying the food item out loud. Our rigid lunch date was turning into a fun game—something that Michael always seemed to incorporate when we were around each other. I could easily see how others may find his unpredictable behavior off-putting, but I loved every second of it.

"Well, in that case," I began, raising my menu and shielding it from Michael. "He will have..."

I frantically skimmed the menu, looking for the most outlandish thing I could find on it. The menu wasn't huge, and with some more time I probably could have guessed what Michael had picked out for me. However, the waitress was patiently standing next to me, waiting for me to select something for him.

"He can have an order of this," I announced, pointing to the grilled cheese, "but can we remove an ingredient?"

"Um, sure?" the waitress asked, confused.

I pointed to the word *bread* on the menu, in which the waitress returned an even more quizzical look.

"Are you sure?" she asked.

"Oh, I'm positive," I answered proudly, handing her my menu.

She quickly wrote down the order and collected the menus.

"Your food will be out shortly," she relayed.

"I'm sure it will," I cheerfully said, knowing that his lunch wouldn't take a lot of prep time. Grilled cheese without bread couldn't require too much attention.

As soon as she left Michael and I alone again, my phone buzzed, indicating a notification. I didn't fully pick it up, but I snuck a quick glance to see what it was. A giant smile emerged across my face as another candidate had applied for my recent job posting.

"You must really like whoever is texting you," Michael commented.

"Jealous?" I smirked.

"I think so," he shared.

"Sorry, it's just a notification on my job posting," I revealed, not wanting him to think someone else had my attention. "My friends think I work too much, so I'm trying to hire an assistant. I was just alerted of another application being submitted."

"What do you do for work?" he sincerely asked.

"I run my own business," I explained. "I match caregivers to families."

"Oh, I'm actually in the market for one of those," he remarked.

"Really?" I inquired. "Do you have kids or something?"

I made the assumption that he was childless, but now I was greatly anticipating his answer.

"No, but I'll hire you to watch me," he joked. "That way, you won't have to do it for free."

I groaned at his comment. There was only one person in this friendship who was a stalker, and it definitely wasn't me.

"What about you?" I asked curiously. "What do you do?"

"I own a car detailing business," he replied.

"So, you wash cars for a living?" I questioned.

"Something like that," he said.

I was trying to downplay Michael's career, as I didn't want to seem impressed by him, but the fact that we both owned our own businesses was amazing to me. I knew how hard it was to run a company, and the fact that Michael did too was very attractive to me.

Michael began reaching into his pocket until he eventually pulled out his wallet. "Judging by the state of your vehicle, you could benefit from a little cleaning."

He pulled out a small, white piece of paper and handed it to me—it was his business card.

"King Cars," I read aloud. "You aren't serious."

"It's catchy," he defended. "You should come by the shop and help me out one day. The address is on the card."

"Oh, I know nothing about cars," I stammered. "I wouldn't know what to do."

"I just wash cars for a living," Michael said, mocking me. "How hard can it be? Consider it a way of making us even."

"Even?" I questioned.

"It's the least you can do since I saved you from going to the wedding alone," he explained.

"You did not save me. I would have been perfectly fine going by myself," I defended.

"Whatever you say," he replied.

I stared at his business card and had an internal battle on whether or not I should help him out. It was another opportunity to see him again, but we both knew how things went between us when we actually planned our meetups.

"Fine, I'll help you," I eventually agreed. "But only because you are giving up a day of your time to go to this wedding with me, not because you 'saved me'."

"So, I'll see you tomorrow then?" he smiled back at me.

"I'll show up when I feel like it," I returned, keeping the spontaneity between us.

He took a sip of this drink, but I could still see him smirking behind his glass. I believed he liked the fact that I could keep up with him and his silly games.

"Wear something that you don't mind getting a little grease on," he instructed. "We are going to get down and dirty."

"Can I just borrow one of your hideous shirts?" I inquired.

"What? You don't like tie-dye, either?" he asked, looking down at his top.

"Have you ever heard of a plain white T-shirt?" I questioned.

"No, I haven't. Tell me more about it," he sarcastically responded.

He leaned forward as if I was about drop a bucket of knowledge on him about clothing styles, but instead I simply laughed at him. My laughter must've been contagious because he happily joined in on it. We probably looked like two weirdos, causing a scene and hysterically laughing over seemingly nothing. He and I couldn't even keep a straight face, and when we tried to stop, we just burst into another fit of laughter.

I couldn't put a true definition to the feeling that I had in that moment with Michael, but it was as if nothing else in the world mattered. Any concerns or stressors seemed to just melt away, and nothing but pure bliss existed. The walls that were guarding my heart were no longer standing strong. Each encounter with Michael was a blow to the defense, and I didn't know how much longer I could be around him without completely succumbing to the feelings that were growing for him. Maybe my efforts to protect myself were actually hurting me. I wasn't guarding my heart anymore...I was imprisoning it.

"Order for table five," the waitress announced as she returned with our platters. "Grilled cheese without the bread for the gentleman."

I almost fell out of my chair when I saw her set a plate of melted cheese in front of Michael.

"And for the lady, a hamburger with French fries," she explained.

"Wait, what?" I questioned, staring at Michael. "...I actually like burgers."

"Me too," he agreed, stealing a fry off my plate.

I blankly stared at the delectable food in front of me, as the real joke was on me. I was going to be eating a juicy burger while guilt was going to be eating me. I had to watch him only have a few slices of cheese for lunch.

"Bon appétit," Michael replied with smirk as he cut into the gooey mess.

"I bet you never had a meal like that before," I uttered as I began cutting my burger in half so that I could share it with him. "Best first date ever?"

"By far," he affirmed.

That time, neither of us denied the fact that this was more than just a casual lunch between friends, and I knew it was finally time to end my heart's prison sentence and let it go free.

13

When Can You Start?

"I don't work weekends, before 10 a.m., after 2 p.m., or between the hours of noon and 1 o'clock," the candidate explained during the virtual interview. "Oh, and I definitely do not wear suits to work."

"Well, this is more of a casual work environment," I explained. "Most of the work can be done from home, but on the occasional times when you need to run an errand for me or if we need to have an in-person meeting, I do not expect you to wear business attire. However, can you please elaborate on your availability? What hours can you work?"

"Run an errand?" the candidate repeated. "What does that mean?"

I pulled up the job posting that I had published on a few websites, including my own. I scrolled to the end of the document and found the description portion of it.

"This role involves managing a variety of tasks, including answering phone calls, handling incoming mail, maintaining and organizing the calendar, and responding to emails in a timely manner," I read directly from the job posting. "The ideal candidate will have a reliable mode of transportation, as this role consists of running errands that may include, but are not limited to, picking up packages, traveling to clients' houses, and occasional business meetings."

After reading directly from the document, I looked up and noticed that the girl I was interviewing appeared completely uninterested in the position. I wasn't sure what her expectations were when she applied for the role, but I thought my job posting was pretty clear.

"Maybe my mom will let me borrow her car sometimes," she eventually replied.

I had a list of questions that I went through for every candidate. She was my fifth interview of the day, and the fact that she had lasted longer than fifteen minutes made her the leading candidate, which wasn't saying much.

The first two didn't even show up. The third person received an offer from another job in the middle of our interview, so she didn't even finish. And the fourth woman was almost eighty years old and fell asleep during one of her answers. Although my current interviewee had been the best out of the previous ones, I still wasn't inclined to hire her at all. I didn't feel our work ethics entirely aligned. She took time out of her day to participate in an interview so I wanted to give her the time she deserved, but since I had no desire to offer her the position, I skipped to the last few questions.

"So, what is your hourly rate, and when is the earliest you can start?" I asked, trying to quickly wrap up the interview.

She picked up her phone and began going through it with great intent.

"I have a few trips planned in August," she explained, squinting at her phone. "I wouldn't want to spend the last few weeks of the summer working."

"That's okay. I have a wedding to attend over Labor Day weekend, anyway," I shared. "Should I mark down that you're available to start the second week of September?"

"On second thought," she continued, "I wouldn't want to start a new job during my birthday month. I'm turning nineteen. It's the last year I'll be a teenager, and then after that I'll be old and in my twenties. I need the whole month to plan for my special day."

"Okay, so, October?" I asked, even though the question was merely a way to finally get an answer and move on. There was no chance that I was going to hire her.

"Maybe November," she countered. "I can't work on Thanksgiving, though."

"This position would not require you to work the day of Thanksgiving," I noted.

"The day? I need the whole week off, at least. Maybe even two," she remarked.

"How about I just put down that you can start in January of the following year, and we can go from there," I offered.

I debated closing my laptop and pretending that my internet wasn't working, but I continued to suffer through the interview.

"Well, can I still get paid until then?" she questioned. "I need money for my birthday party."

"I can't pay you until you start working," I explained, confused as to whether the candidate knew how the job market worked. "The starting hourly wage for this position is twenty-five dollars an hour. Are you comfortable with that?"

"Twenty-five?" she exclaimed. "I would have to work a whole day just to cover the price of my nails."

She wasn't the brightest candidate, but at least she was somewhat good at math.

"What rate are you comfortable with?" I asked.

"At least, like, a hundred an hour," she responded.

"I'll make a note of your start date and hourly wage, and we will be in touch. Thank you so much for your time," I quickly said.

The entire interview lasted less than twenty minutes, but it felt like it had gone on for at least two hours.

"Oh, wait. There's one more thing I forgot to ask," she abruptly interjected. "My dad is a police officer, and he said that I should have my employer participate in a background check. Are you open to that?"

"If I decide to offer you the position, I'd be more than happy to undergo a background check," I stated, giving her a fake smile.

"Amazing! Oh my, I can't believe I am going to get my first job!" she yelled in a celebratory manner.

"We will talk soon. Thank you for your time," I said before quickly ending the virtual interview so that she couldn't ask me another question.

I still had one more interview for the day, but since I had ended the last one early, I had about ten minutes to regroup myself before another person asked me to pay them a ridiculous amount, explained their inability to start in a reasonable amount of time, and asked me to provide them a report of my criminal history.

Anywhere but sitting at my desk sounded like a better place to be, but the kitchen was especially calling my name. I was pretty sure I had a half-eaten sandwich in the fridge ready to be devoured. It wasn't going to fix all the trauma I had gone through in the interviews, but it would at least provide me a temporary happiness.

I pushed myself away from my desk and stood up from my chair. An imprint of my butt still remained in the cushion since I had been conducting interviews the entire morning. I didn't think I had gotten up from my chair in over four hours. However, the power of a ready-to-eat sandwich was all the motivation I needed to give myself a break from a stressful day of work.

"Wow, I don't recognize you without a laptop in your hand," Avery joked when I walked out into the kitchen.

Instead of responding, I simply let out a giant sigh.

"Woah, rough day?" Hannah chimed in.

They were both scouring the kitchen, presumably also trying to find their next meal.

"I actually took Avery's advice for once and have been interviewing candidates to help handle some of my workload," I shared.

"Oh, that's awesome! I saw your job posting yesterday," Hannah relayed. "How have they been going?"

"If you are deciding between two people, choose the one that likes cats more," Avery sarcastically added.

I headed over toward the fridge and began moving a few items to the side in order to find my sandwich.

"Well, unless I want to hire a woman who is too old to endure the full length of an interview without falling asleep, or a girl who doesn't fully understand the definition of a job, then I am out of luck," I explained.

"I'm sure the right candidate is out there," Hannah optimistically noted.

"Did you finish all your interviews for the day?" Avery asked.

"I have one more," I informed them, "but my expectations are low."

I continued to browse the fridge, but I couldn't find my lunch.

"You know what solves every stressful day?" Hannah proposed. "Bowling!"

"Yeah, I don't know about that," I said as I continued to rummage around some old dairy products.

"Too late, you are invited," Avery inserted. "We are going bowling with Graham and Elliot tonight."

"Great, fifth-wheeling a bowling date. That is exactly how I want to end my day," I said. "Have either of you seen my sandwich by the way?"

"You could invite Michael?" Hannah offered.

"No way," I denied. "Too soon. I just saw him yesterday. If I invite him to go bowling, then it's going to look desperate."

I was already planning to go to his car shop toward the end of the week. I couldn't also invite him to a bowling night.

"Michael?" Avery asked. "Who's Michael? I was thinking she could invite Reid so she can get to know him more before your wedding."

"She's not going with Reid anymore. Michael is her date now," Hannah explained.

"Have either of you seen my sandwich?" I asked again.

"While you were at Iron Nine, Paige and I went to Lucky's Tavern to find Michael. Apparently they had a bet where if they saw each other again, then he had to go to my wedding with her," Hannah revealed. "We couldn't locate him, but he was literally waiting for Paige at her car."

"Wait, what?" Avery shouted. "I need all the details."

"Okay, but first," I grumbled, giving up on my search and walking over to them, "where is my sandwich?"

Neither of them had to answer my question as my lunch was clearly gone. The only thing left was the wrapper that it was encased in, which was currently crumpled up in Avery's hand.

"Oops," she began, "I thought it was Graham's. I can make you another one, though."

"Sure, but I have to go finish my last interview of the day first," I explained.

"But what about Michael?" Avery asked. "I need to hear the full story."

"I'll tell you at bowling," I answered as I started heading toward my room.

"Fine, but don't forget!" she called out as I was steps away from my bedroom.

"Don't forget to make me another sandwich," I jokingly replied.

I shut the door behind me to block out the noise coming from the kitchen, as I was sure Hannah was going to tell Avery her version of the story before we even left for bowling. Hannah was a chatterbox, and Avery was impatient.

I adjusted myself back into my desk chair, mentally preparing myself for the last candidate of the day. I just hoped the final person would at least make it through the full thirty minutes of the allotted time.

There were still two minutes until the scheduled interview, but I got a notification that the candidate had already entered the virtual meeting room. I didn't know whether that was a good or bad sign that they were early, but I figured the sooner we started, the sooner we could end, so I hopped into the interview.

When I first joined the virtual meeting room, only my face was displayed. The graininess of the screen made my makeup skills look worse than they actually were, but honestly, my appearance was one of the last things on my mind. I just wanted to get the day over with.

After a few seconds of only staring at myself, the candidate eventually turned on their camera and popped up on my screen.

"Reid?" I shouted once I saw his familiar face.

"Hi, Paige," he beamed with a glowing smile. "How are you today?"

I quickly pulled up the resume that was submitted, confused as to how I didn't see this coming.

"Your resume says your name is Isaac Young Jr.," I read aloud.

"That is correct," he confirmed. "Reid is my middle name. I often go by it in order to not get confused with my father, as I was named after him."

"Right," I hesitantly responded.

"Hannah said you were looking for an assistant. She sent me the job posting yesterday, so I figured I'd apply," he confessed.

"You do know this job isn't glamorous, right?" I explained, uncertain as to how he could be so eager about a position that solely consisted of handling mundane tasks.

"I read the job description and thought it was right up my alley," Reid alerted. "I love organization and order. I'd be happy to assist you on any of your needs."

I thought back to Lucky's when I witnessed Reid taking notes on how to play darts. I thought his tactic was odd and unusual, but his eagerness to learn was definitely an asset to the role that I had posted.

"Plus," Reid started, "I already know one of your employees."

I didn't know how his relation to Hannah was of any relevance to the job, but maybe he was using her as a reference.

The thought of going from being his potential wedding date to being his potential boss was a crazy turn of events. I was hesitant to continue on in the interview process, but his boring personality traits were actually perfect for the mundane tasks that were required. In fact, he might even label the daily assignments as fun.

"This is a part-time role that can turn into a full-time position. The starting pay is twenty-five dollars an hour. Is that within your expectations?" I asked.

"That is perfectly fine with me," Reid exclaimed.

"Well, the hours can also be pretty unpredictable at times," I shared, trying to get him to think realistically about the job. "Although I am not expecting you to work forty hours a week, sometimes weekend hours are needed."

"I don't have anything else to do on the weekends," Reid affirmed.

His casual energy was annoying in a social setting, but for being my assistant, it was perfect.

"If considered for the role, when could you start?" I inquired, so far impressed by the potential of having Reid as my assistant.

"Whenever you need me to," he answered.

I wasn't necessarily thrilled at hiring someone who was initially introduced into my life as my blind date, but I didn't see a reason as to why I shouldn't hire him. He had a great attention to detail, he liked boring assignments, and I already knew he liked to learn. Not to mention, he showed up on time and actually seemed interested in the position. Admittedly, I had a lot on my plate, and it was time to finally receive some help.

"One last question," I began, fully convinced that I had finally found my new assistant. "Do you want to go bowling tonight?"

14

Spare Me

There was a pattern to the flow of noises that was constantly fighting for my attention. First, quick yet purposeful footsteps pattered against the floor in a methodical manner. Next, a quiet, vibrating boom would hit my ears, resembling the sound of thunder. The following noise consisted of a ferocious rumble, as a hard object raced across the hardwood. The finale to the sequence of events was a loud crash, and a bunch of patrons either cheering or groaning at the results. The bowling alley was a succession of patterned sounds that continuously tried to pull my attention in numerous different directions. However, as loud as the noises were, they couldn't compete with the sound of Avery's voice describing her courageous encounter with pop star Zane Wilder.

"You actually had a conversation with one of the most famous artists in the entire world? Multiple award nominations. Sold-out tours. Heartthrob celebrity," Hannah continued on.

"Well, not necessarily a full conversation...but close!" Avery explained.

"Wait, tell us the story again," Reid instructed. "From the very beginning."

I was supposed to be attending a double-date night, with Reid and I there as just friends, but it had turned into a gossip session. I took a few turns bowling, but I quickly lost interest in the activity. Talking with Hannah, Avery, and Reid was a lot more entertaining than trying to knock over a bunch of pins. Our lane started with six bowlers, but after the excitement of the sport died down, Graham and Elliot ended up being the only ones actually playing the game.

"Okay, so I was taking pictures of the ambiance of the restaurant for our website the entire night," Avery began. "I snuck in a few photos of Zane, but as the night went on I figured that it would be awesome if instead of taking pictures, I actually got to be in one."

"I can't believe you secretly photographed him," Hannah uttered in shock. "You're like the paparazzi."

"I would've had the same thought process," I chimed in.

"Can we see the photos you took?" Reid asked.

"I'll show you all later," Avery replied. "Anyways, it took almost the entire evening, but right before he was about to leave, I took the opportunity to race over to his table and ask for a picture with him. I pushed past his bodyguards and everything."

"How many were there?" Reid questioned.

"Were they huge?" Hannah asked.

"Were they drunk?" I followed up, confused as to how a girl as tiny as Avery managed to find her way into the presence of Zane Wilder, who was heavily guarded by security personnel.

"They were literal giants who were presumably sober, but I cannot confirm nor deny. But here comes the best part," Avery continued on. "When I asked Zane for a photo, he nodded his head!"

Avery pulled out her phone and started showing us the selfie that she took with him.

"And then, I thanked him for the photo...and he smiled at me!" Avery shrieked.

Her chest was heaving up and down from the excitement of recapping her exhilarating night, which had consisted of meeting a famous pop star.

"Oh my gosh," Hannah exclaimed, staring at the picture. "You talked to Zane Wilder. You guys are, like, friends now."

"Well, maybe not exactly friends," Avery corrected, "but that's why I've been hiding away in Graham's apartment for a bit. I had to get the photos edited so that I could update our website. I included some of Zane, but not the one we took together. That one, I will keep to myself."

"Paige and I definitely miss you when you spend the night at Graham's, but it was for a good reason," Hannah concluded.

"Yeah, but I feel like I missed a lot. You both went to Lucky's without me, and Paige has a new love interest. What else have I missed?" Avery inquired.

"I got a new job," Reid piped up. "I'm working for Paige now."

All eyes turned toward me after Reid's sudden revelation. I didn't blame their obvious shock as I also wasn't expecting to employ our mutual friend, but he ended up surpassing all of my expectations. It helped that there wasn't a single candidate who gave him any sort of competition. The decision was pretty easy.

"He's going to help me with some of the administrative tasks of the business so that I can focus on other things," I confessed.

"I'm proud of you for finally allowing yourself to get the help that you deserve," Avery complimented.

"Congratulations, Reid!" Hannah shouted. "Are you also a wedding planner? I could use some help, too."

Hannah followed her comment with an awkward chuckle. It was evident that her upcoming special day was causing her an extreme amount of stress.

"Do you still have a lot to do?" I asked. "Is there anything Avery and I can do to help?"

"I can be of assistance too," Reid agreed.

"Thanks, guys," Hannah somberly replied. "I think I've got it taken care of. It's just been hard because of how much Elliot travels. I wanted this to be something that we do together, but I've been doing most of the planning myself."

"Have you told him that?" I questioned.

"Yeah, but his job is helping pay for our wedding, so he can't quit," Hannah explained. "But he said he would reduce his hours after we get married."

Hannah's words told one story, but her face told another. The tone in her voice sounded preppy and hopeful, but her heavy eyes and frowned lips showed that she wasn't as confident as she sounded. I hoped Elliot noticed Hannah's frustrations as much as we did, and that they were able to come up with a compromise to their issue. Maybe he truly was going to alter his schedule after the wedding, and therefore, Hannah only had to endure his constant absence for less than a month longer. However, I really wished he was there for her during the planning stage. If he could make time to go bowling, then he could make time to help plan a wedding.

"I'm sure it will be a beautiful ceremony," Avery commented. "You are going to feel so relieved once it's all over and you can focus on you and Elliot."

"Yeah, I'm still excited for it," Hannah affirmed. "I just can't wait for the day to be here."

"Me too," I said. "It will be a fun day."

"Oh yeah, I'm sure you are extra excited for it." Hannah winked.

"He's just my wedding date," I defended, knowing that she was hinting at the fact that Michael was going to be there.

At that point, he was just my plus-one, though, I was beginning to warm up to the idea that the wedding was only going to be the beginning of our story.

"Please tell me about this mystery man," Avery pleaded. "I need to know more about this guy. I haven't seen Paige's cheeks blush this red since college."

I felt my face, unaware that my fair skin had turned a completely different shade. Although I couldn't see the pink tones filling my cheeks, I could definitely feel the warmth. It was an obvious giveaway that Michael meant more to me than I led on. I was curious if the bodily reaction also happened when I was talking to him because if that was the case, the confident persona that I tried to give off when around him may have failed before it had even started.

"Does anyone else want to play?" Graham inserted himself into the conversation carrying a giant bowling ball.

My brother disrupted my conversations more times than I could count, but I actually appreciated his timing that time.

"We're busy, Graham cracker," Avery replied, utilizing the cheesy nickname she had given him.

"Well, we've got the Graham cracker right here," he said, sliding into the bench next to her, "and now I've got my chocolate." Graham pulled Avery closer to him and their faces ended up inches apart. "Should we finish off this s'more with a marshmallow?"

Graham whispered his next sentence into Avery's ear. I couldn't tell what he was saying, but I didn't want to know, either. It was probably an obnoxious flirt attempt as whatever he said made Avery giggle, and then they ended up kissing.

"Gross!" I chanted, still not used to seeing my brother and best friend make out.

I always gave both of them a hard time when they showed any sort of affection. Truthfully, they were a good match for each other, but sometimes I reminisced on the times when Avery and I were younger and she found my brother as repulsive as I did. According to her, it wasn't until our senior year of high school when she actually started finding my brother attractive—but since he went to a different college than us, that crush died out. However, when Graham came to Las Vegas to surprise me for my birthday after we first moved out here, Avery's dormant feelings for him were awakened, and she ended up falling for him all over again. It was certainly hard to fathom someone being attracted to my brother, but he was the perfect guy to help piece her heart back together after Kyle Kingsley had put it through a blender. Graham was my annoying older brother, but he was also the most caring person in the world.

"Hannah, do you want to take a turn?" Elliot asked, as it appeared nobody else wanted to play.

"No, thanks," Hannah politely declined. "I'm having fun with the girls...and Reid."

Reid smiled, happy to be included. He seemed to be an unofficial member to Hannah, Avery and I's trio.

"Well, I paid for you to bowl," Elliot explained. "You should have told me that you didn't want to play so I could have saved my money."

"I didn't know I was going to end up hanging out with my friends instead," Hannah defended. "And I did take a few turns."

"I just figured you would be smarter about this. We are paying for a wedding. We don't have time to waste money on bowling if you're not going to play," Elliot lectured.

I could tell Hannah was embarrassed by her fiancé's behavior by the way her eyes frantically bounced around, looking at everyone in the vicinity.

"I'll play for her," Reid offered, standing up from the bench.

"I'm trying to talk to my future wife. Please stay out of the conversation," Elliot scolded.

Reid slowly sat back down, choosing not to go to war with Elliot.

"I don't really feel like bowling right now," Hannah shared. "I'm sorry I wasted your money."

"Or, you could not be sorry and not waste my money," Elliot began, "and actually take a turn."

"She doesn't feel like playing," I chimed in.

"You and Graham seem like you are enjoying yourself," Avery uttered. "You don't need Hannah to take her turn."

Elliot started having a mini tantrum. His face turned red, his body was fidgety, and I swore I saw some smoke escape his ears.

"I'm so tired of people inserting themselves into my relationship," Elliot huffed.

"Hey man, calm down," Graham announced. "Let's just let the women talk."

"And me!" Reid chirped to ensure he was included.

"No, I'm seriously over it. Everyone always has an opinion. I just want my future wife to have a good time bowling, and you all are trying to paint me to be this horrible guy," Elliot griped.

Hannah stood up from her spot on the bench and joined his side.

"I'll take a turn," she said, taking the bowling ball out of his hands. "I know you mean well."

She started caressing Elliot's arm, and it seemed to calm him down.

"I just want to focus on us and our relationship," Elliot spoke.

"Me too," Hannah agreed with a smile.

They both walked off toward our reserved lane, seemingly in a good place. His outburst sent alarm bells in my head, but Hannah seemed to understand him on a level that I didn't.

"Reid, why don't you and I order our group some pizzas?" Graham asked. "I heard this place is known for their good bowling and good food."

I believed Graham was hungry, as we all were, but I assumed he mostly wanted to start a new topic of conversation in order to move on from the awkward encounter that had just occurred.

"Sure, I'll come with you," Reid agreed, standing back up and walking over toward Graham.

"Extra pepperoni!" Avery added.

Graham gave her a quick peck and a sly wink before him and Reid headed toward the front of the alley to order our group a few pizzas.

Avery and I were the only ones left as the rest were either getting food or taking their forced bowling turns.

"What was that all about?" I asked. "I've never seen Elliot have a melt-down like that."

"Wedding jitters?" Avery proposed.

"I hope so," I replied hesitantly, as Elliot's recent behavior didn't sit right with me.

"So back to you and Michael," Avery brought up with a smirk. "Is he hot? Is he tall? Is he muscular?"

She started listing off all the qualities of my usual type, but since it was only Avery and I left to talk, I didn't mind spilling all the details to her.

"He's...blonde," I answered.

"No!" Avery gasped.

I had sworn off guys with that hair color since I started noticing boys. Something about lighter hair had never really been that attractive to me, even though my hair was a perfect mix of blonde and brown and could be labeled as either one.

"But he is tall, and he definitely works out," I added. "There's something about him that's mysterious and intriguing, yet also feels familiar—like I've met him before, or that he was perfectly made for me. I don't know how to explain it."

"Sounds like love," Avery playfully pointed out.

"I don't know him enough to say that I love him," I explained.

"Because you have only met a few times?" Avery asked.

"It's true that I've only hung out with him a couple of times," I answered. "I'm actually planning on seeing him at his work sometime this week. But it's not really about the number of times we have met. I feel like even if I hung out with him twenty more times, I would still feel the same way. It's not exactly that I don't know him...it's that I can't understand him. I can't read him at all."

I thought back to all the conversations I'd had with Michael. Sure, I knew basic information about him, such as his name, his job, and a few of his hobbies, but I knew there was so much more to him to uncover. He would give me tiny bits of insight into his life, and I just hoped that the trail of crumbs would soon lead me to the jackpot of truly knowing his full self. I really liked Michael, but I also knew that the person I was falling for was only the version of himself that he actually let me see. There were obviously hidden parts about him that he hadn't brought to the light yet. The mystery to him was attractive, but I was also extremely ready to solve the case.

"Well, when can I meet him?" Avery asked. "Do you have a picture of him?"

"I don't have a photo of him," I relayed, "and the first time you see him will most likely be at Hannah's wedding. Him and I aren't necessarily the best at planning when we meet up."

"Aren't you seeing him in a few days?" Avery asked.

"Yeah...kinda," I answered. "I'm going to show up to his work this week unannounced and hope he's there."

"You're not going to tell him you're coming?" Avery questioned, confused.

"It works better to surprise him," I said, not knowing how to explain that Michael and I thrived off the element of coincidence, fate, and spontaneity.

"Well, I can't wait to meet him," she uttered. "He sounds like a good guy."

It felt good to gossip with Avery about boys again. I hadn't had any newsworthy dating stories since before I gave up on the idea of love after watching what Avery had gone through. It felt normal to gush about a guy to her and give her all the details. Both she and Hannah were very supportive in my journey of navigating the dating world again, and I realized that although Avery was the one who went through a horrific event, I was the one who was still holding on to that time in our life. Hannah went on and got herself a fiancé, and Avery had moved on with my brother. Everyone had put the past behind them, yet I was still holding on to it for dear life. Michael was helping me put myself out there, but he was also helping me move on from the past. Hurt, anger, and frustration were history; love, happiness, and hope were my new future.

15

Wash, Rinse, Repeat

Today was the day I really realized I had no life, or rather, a life that solely revolved around my career.

It was Reid's first day on the job, and I found training him harder than I had originally thought—but not in the way I had expected. He was great. In fact, he was phenomenal. Reid showed up to the apartment early. He had an eager attitude, and he even brought me a latte to start the morning. I had originally set aside the entire week to teach him everything he needed to know, but he caught on so quickly that he had learned his role by lunchtime. After only a few hours, Reid had already created a color-coded calendar, a to-do list spanning the entire month, and suggestions on how I could work more efficiently. I was so impressed with his organizational skills that I was certain that if I had given him a few more hours with my email account, he probably would've had my whole inbox categorized in folders and in order of importance. I let him go home early because of how much he had gotten done in just the few short moments that he had been at the apartment. Honestly, the hardest part of Reid's employment was that he took on so many of the tedious tasks that I had been doing since the start of my business that this was the first free Tuesday afternoon that I'd had in a while...and I had no idea what to do with it.

The next few days were supposed to consume all of my time training Reid in his new position, but that had already been completed before the sun even reached its peak. With all the extra time I had on my hands, I could've researched the industry a bit, worked on expansion plans, or anything else that I had put to the side because other things were pulling my attention. However, the point of hiring an assistant was to free myself up in order to have a life again and explore a world that didn't consist of stressing over my business. I had to pace around my room for a bit, chomp on a few snacks, and flip through a bunch of television channels before finally admitting to myself what I really wanted to do with the rest of the day, but eventually I caved in to the temptation and found myself sitting in the parking lot outside of King Cars.

It was in the unofficial handbook of Michael and I's relationship to not organize the next time we hung out. It was supposed to only be a surprise to him, but I ended up surprising myself as well as I didn't expect to be outside his workplace roughly forty-eight hours following our lunch date. I was planning on waiting at least a few more days before arriving unannounced, but fate, the universe, destiny, or whatever word anyone wanted to use to describe the unexplainable force that constantly pulled Michael and I together, was working overtime that day and must've really wanted him and I in each other's presence again.

I enjoyed sitting in the parking lot of Michael's business and admiring the empire he had started. I barely knew him, but a sense of pride overcame me when I took in my surroundings. Being there made it really sink in that he had a successful business. I was in awe that the guy who had eaten a slice of cheese in front of me and challenged me to a game of darts was also an owner of a car detailing company. He clearly had a lot going on to keep him busy as they weren't short on customers. My car was easily masked by the many vehicles surrounding me. Michael obviously knew what I drove since he had waited for me outside my car before, but even he would have had a hard time finding me in the sea of automobiles. I was nervous that Michael would be too busy to talk to me and that I had chosen the absolute worst day to show up, but I couldn't remember a time when he had appeared less than excited to be around me. The thought of his face lighting up when he saw me was enough to give me the courage to finally get out of my car and head inside his workplace.

I exited my car with a lot of emotion and enthusiasm, but by the time I reached the front door, my stomach became a butterfly exhibit. I didn't know why I was so nervous to see someone that I'd already had multiple encounters with, but my confidence always seemed to change from a personality trait to a costume when I was around him—and I was pretty sure he could see right through me. Thankfully, I was given a few more moments to collect myself, because when I walked inside, there were numerous employees populating the space, but none were the one I was looking for.

I debated taking a seat in the waiting area, hoping Michael would some-how sense that I was there and come find me, but I quickly realized that the idea was a terrible one. I didn't know how long I'd be waiting before he actually realized I was there, or how long it would take another employee to notice that I had shown up to the shop without waiting for a vehicle to be serviced. Instead, I decided to walk over to the only available employee behind a giant computer screen and hope that my nerves would subside by the time that I got to see Michael.

"Good afternoon," I proclaimed with a smile.

"Welcome to King Cars," a young gentleman expressed. "Do you have an appointment with us today?"

"No, I'm here to see Michael," I informed him.

The man behind the computer looked at me, confused. His red polo and khaki pants made him appear as though he worked for an insurance company rather than a car detailing business, so I wasn't sure why he was the one looking at me in a weird way. I should've been the one skeptical about him. I wasn't sure I trusted a man in khakis to thoroughly clean my car if I was truly there as a paying customer. He must've just been the one to solely check people into their appointments. I was certain he had a laundry stick on him in case grease from a car accidentally splashed onto his pristine clothes.

"I don't believe we have an auto detailer here named Michael," the employee hesitantly began. "Are you sure that's his name?"

"I mean, I wouldn't be surprised if it wasn't. He apparently owns this place, but that could be fake too," I jokingly said aloud.

I had never considered the possibility of Michael giving me a false identity and fake place of employment, but at that point in our relationship, nothing really surprised me anymore.

"Oh, that Michael," the employee returned.

There was a wave of recognition once I let him know that I was looking for the owner of the establishment, and any unease about Michael potentially lying to me about who he truly was suddenly seemed to dissipate.

"He's extremely busy today, but I can get you an appointment with him." The employee began methodically clicking away at the keyboard in front of him. "His next availability is in three weeks."

"Three weeks?" I repeated.

"Do afternoons or mornings work better for you?" he continued on. "Our business hours are from 7 a.m. to 6 p.m."

I was confused as to how Michael seemed to have plenty of time to have lunch with me the other day and follow me to Lucky's Tavern, but I couldn't make a formal appointment with him until about a month later. It was truly a testament that our relationship thrived in chance encounters as there was no way I was going to schedule a formal meeting with him in three weeks.

"Can you just tell him that Paige is here to see him?" I pleaded. "He knows who I am."

"Is he expecting you?" the employee asked.

"No, he never is," I answered truthfully.

In my head everything made sense, but out loud I sounded like a crazy person begging to see the busy owner who had no idea I was coming, or potentially even existed.

"Well, he works on an appointment-based scheduling system. I can take your information down and call you if there's a cancellation?" the man offered.

"No he doesn't. He works off spontaneity and stalking," I corrected.

"Excuse me?" the employee inquired.

"Never mind," I uttered. "Can you just get him for me, please? It's an emergency."

"What kind of emergency?" he pried.

"One that only concerns your boss," I fired back with a hint of attitude.

"Ma'am, if you would just schedule an appointment..." he began.

"I don't do appointments, and I'm not waiting for someone to magically cancel theirs. I asked for Michael. Do not make me ask again," I firmly instructed.

I assumed my sudden change from a calming patron to a feisty customer sparked his change of heart in finally deciding to go locate his boss. I wasn't happy that I had to unleash the firecracker side of my personality in order to get what I wanted. Usually, I reserved it for times when I wanted to bug Graham, but at least the employee decided to abort his station at the front desk and disappear through a set of doors in order to fulfill my request.

I expected to be waiting quite a bit before my demand was met, as I was sure Michael actually was busy and the employee was probably too hesitant to interrupt his boss, but he returned in a short amount of time profusely apologizing, not to me, but to the owner of the shop who was closely following behind him.

"I was told someone was begging for the owner," Michael said to me, ignoring his apologetic employee. "I knew it could only be one person."

"Oh, please. I wasn't begging," I responded, sending a quick glare at the messenger who had clearly misunderstood the situation.

"Are you here for business or pleasure?" Michael smirked at me.

"I'm here to help you," I clarified, trying not to get too sucked into his confident persona which I was jealous he was able to maintain in front of me.

"Ah, so both," Michael concluded with a wink. "Follow me."

Michael began heading back through the doors that he had just walked through, and I quickly followed in his footsteps.

"I'm sorry," his employee whispered as I walked past him.

I simply returned his apology with a smile as I wasn't sure if it was aimed at me or his boss.

Michael ended up leading me to an area of the building that appeared to be a spacious garage. It was a huge concrete space filled with several cars that were being worked on. I was in awe of the employees who were hard at work, turning old run-down vehicles into shiny new prized possessions. However, my trance was abruptly broken when a towel smacked me in the face. After making impact with my nose, it slid down my body and I caught it before it hit the ground.

"You're on towel duty," Michael instructed. "The final step of the detailing process is an exterior car wash. All you have to do is dry the car. Can you handle that?"

"Did you just throw a towel at me?" I ignored his question and returned one of my own.

"Bathrooms are to your left," Michael said, pointing to the restrooms. "Don't take too many breaks."

"Too many breaks? How long do you plan on me being here?" I uttered.

Michael looked at his watch before answering. "We close at six."

"That's in like four hours!" I relayed.

"Great, you can do math," Michael alerted. "I'll come check on you halfway through."

Michael began to take off, leaving me to work on the line of soaking wet cars in need of being dried.

"Wait, wait," I said, running after him, towel in hand. "I wasn't planning on working like an actual shift. I just came to help out a little."

He stopped his strut and turned to face me. His six-foot-three frame towered over me, and the dim lighting in the garage made his scowl look even more intense.

"Paige, this is a place of business," Michael shared. "And in my business, we work hard. Can you manage four hours of hard work?"

"Um, yes sir?" I answered.

"Good, I'll see you in a bit," he noted before walking off.

Michael at work was a completely different person than the guy I was used to seeing. In public, he seemed care-free and all about having a good time. His smile never faded, and the only thing competing for attention with his outgoing personality was his obnoxious choice in attire. However, when he was in business mode, he was stern and forceful, yet purposeful. His movements were sharp and precise, and he appeared to have control over everything that was going on around him. It was refreshing, attractive, and it reminded me of myself. I, too, knew how to have a good time, but when it came to running my business, I didn't play about that. Michael was a boss, a leader, and a force to be reckoned with—Michael was the male version of me.

His leadership style resonated with me, and it made me want to do the best job I could for him, even if it was just drying cars. I knew that if the roles were reversed, I would've expected everyone working under me to give it their all, so I wanted to give him that same respect. There were a few other employees assigned to towel duty, and although I wasn't given specific directions on how to dry a car, I knew there was probably a preferred technique. I spent a few minutes studying those doing the same job as me, and once I felt comfortable enough, I began mimicking their movements. Some of them smiled at me or nodded their heads in approval, so I felt I was doing the job correctly.

I actually got lost in the art of wiping down vehicles and watching how the other workers were able to remove droplets without leaving streaks or water marks. I came into the day not knowing a thing about cleaning cars, but sometime during my shift at King Cars, I shifted from a novice to a pro. Michael stuck to his word and came by a few times to check in on me and the status of his employees, but besides that, I was left on my own for four hours towel-drying cars.

The camaraderie in the garage was also encouraging as guys would be seen helping each other out or picking up the responsibilities of another. I usually worked on each vehicle by myself, but when I was drying the last car of the day, everyone joined in to help me finish it off. I wouldn't necessarily say that I gained new brothers that day, but the mutual respect of working on a task together for that long was enough for me to at least consider the other employees as friends.

"Thanks for helping me, Adam and James," I uttered to the last few men who had helped me complete my final task of the shift. All the detailers had their names sewed into their uniforms, so I learned them pretty quickly.

"Want us to stay behind and help you clean your station?" Adam kindly offered.

"No, thanks," I politely declined. "It's already past closing time. Go home to your families. I can take care of gathering up the used rags."

"Just place them in the bin in the far corner," James instructed, pointing to a box filled with used towels. "We'll wash them first thing in the morning. Are you coming back tomorrow?"

"Oh no," I informed them. "I was just volunteering for the day."

"Volunteering?" Adam questioned. "As in you just worked for free?"

"Wow, the things you do for love," James commented.

"Woah, I'm not in love," I defended. "I was simply helping out a friend."

"Yeah, sure," Adam sarcastically noted.

"When I help my friends out," James began, "I bring them food or help them start their car—not spend my entire day working at their shop."

"I guess we are super close friends then," I explained, trying to fight the blush that was attempting to make an appearance on my cheeks. "I'm sure he has people come by and help him all the time, right?"

"If you are asking if Michael is dating anyone," Adam started, "the answer is no."

I thought guys were supposed to be oblivious to everything that didn't revolve around sports or cars, but these two employees were very capable of reading between the lines.

"And if you're asking if you should get involved with him," James added on, "the answer is also, no."

Adam and James burst out laughing simultaneously.

"Well, why not?" I shakily asked, not sure if I actually wanted them to answer. I knew there was more to Michael than what met the eye, but I wasn't sure what was hiding behind the personality that he portrayed. "What's wrong with him?"

"What's not wrong with him?" James replied, which made them both revamp their laughter.

"There's a reason he is single," Adam explained.

"What's the reason?" I asked.

Adam and James exchanged apprehensive looks, and the lighthearted laughter and boisterous chuckles were now just distant memories.

"He's a good guy," Adam shared. "We don't mean to scare you."

"Yeah, he's great," James agreed. "He just..."

"Surrounds himself with the wrong people," Adam finished.

I didn't really understand what they were trying to warn me about. We all have had friends in the past that may not have made the best decisions, but I didn't think that was enough to prevent me from getting to know him. I didn't know who Michael hung out with in his free time, but he seemed to surround himself with amazing employees.

"But maybe you're the positive influence he needs," Adam uttered. "He could use a calming presence in his life."

"Yes, he needs a girl like you—sweet, kindhearted, and can put away the dirty towels so that we can go home," James joked.

"Don't worry, I'll collect the towels," I said, staring at all the dirty rags on the ground. "You guys get out of here."

"Thanks, Paige," James remarked.

"Maybe we'll see you again sometime?" Adam asked.

"I'm sure I'll be back," I relayed with a smile.

I appreciated them helping me throughout my shift, but I was more grateful for the insight that they had given me on Michael. I knew that he possessed a sort of mystery to him, and I figured that I had finally solved the case. It seemed that he had probably been associated with the wrong crowd and didn't want me to define him based on his friends' actions. Whether he wanted to tell me who he had been around or what they had done was irrelevant to me. I based my feelings for Michael on who he was and not who his friends were growing up.

I watched Adam and James head home for the day, leaving me alone in a garage full of soiled rags that needed to be placed in a designated bin. The day was long and grueling, but I had no regrets as I got to learn more about Michael than I had in the past few days. He was truly an interesting guy, but I was finally figuring him out.

"What are you doing?" a thunderous voice echoed throughout the empty space.

"I was just cleaning up, boss," I returned with a hint of sarcasm since Michael was far from being in charge of me.

"We only put the towels up once all the vehicles have been wiped down for the day," he informed me.

"I am done," I remarked, gesturing toward all the clean cars.

"You missed one," Michael said.

I looked around the garage, and although it was an enormous space, each vehicle that I saw was clean and, most importantly, dry. I turned to look up at Michael and ask him what car I had missed, but he left me alone to figure it out for myself. I assumed he had meant that the cars were not dried to his standard, so instead of trying to find the one car that wasn't clean enough, I began wiping down all the vehicles I had already done. It would take me a while to go through all of them again, but maybe that was Michael's way of wanting to spend more time with me even though he wasn't in the garage.

I usually liked the games that he played, but one that consisted of manual labor wasn't necessarily my idea of fun. I groaned a bit and muttered a few things under my breath as I went through each car again, but I still had a mindset of wanting to do a good job for him. There were probably about twenty cars that I still had to redo, but my answer as to which one still needed drying became very apparent when after a few minutes of wiping down vehicles, one of the garage doors opened up and Michael drove in a new vehicle that was clearly soaking wet. He parked the white truck directly in front of me and eagerly hopped out of it.

"Got time for one more?" he cheerfully asked, dropping his hardened boss role for the day. Despite still being at the shop, he had returned to his normal self since it was outside of business hours.

"I could not think of anything else I'd rather be doing right now," I sarcastically remarked.

"Great," Michael replied. "Make sure you don't miss a spot. I don't want any water marks on my truck."

"Your truck?" I repeated.

"Yeah, I like to drive around in a clean vehicle, too," he answered.

I was slightly annoyed that I was going to be spending the overtime wiping down Michael's own truck, but I wasn't as mad when I saw him pick up a towel and start drying, too. That time, I was clearly aware of his tactic to spend more time with me.

Since he was back in his playful mood, I decided to take revenge from earlier on in the day when he had thrown a towel at my face. I had already gathered a pile of used towels that I planned on placing in the bin, but since they were conveniently sitting next to me, instead of throwing only one at him, I chucked the whole pile his way. None of the rags had directly hit him in the face, but I thought ten towels hitting him and soaking his shirt was definitely funnier than the single one he had thrown at me.

I was expecting an outlandish and over-the-top reaction to the numerous dirty rags that had just soiled and dampened his shirt, however, he barely reacted. Once the rags had pelted, him he simply shrugged off the towel attack, looked down and noticed the wet uniform clinging to his body, and then slowly removed his shirt. I almost soaked my own top with how much drool was dripping out of my mouth when I saw his exposed skin. I was privileged enough to be able to see the body that Michael possessed. His chiseled abs and defined muscles squeezed as his arms continued wiping down his truck. I thought his biceps were going to bust through his skin with how toned they were. He looked even more fit under the dim lighting of the garage, and for a second I was confused as to whether I was staring at a grown man's body, or a work of art—or perhaps both.

"I know it's hard for you to dry a car without towels since you just threw them all at me," Michael pointed out, "but some help would be nice."

Michael was daring me to walk over to him and resume drying, but I had no idea how I was supposed to be that close to him while his naked skin was tempting me. I didn't think he was aware of the allure that his body gave off, but it was extremely hard to look away from. I kept staring at the area where his bare skin met the top of his belt buckle and trying to imagine what the rest of him looked like.

"You seem to have the exterior covered. Is there anything you want me to do inside the vehicle?" I asked, trying to find some way that I could distance myself from the temptation beaming in front of me.

"Actually, yeah. If you could help me get rid of some of the junk in the backseat," Michael exclaimed, "that would be extremely helpful."

"What do you have back there?" I asked, curious as to how much trash could accumulate in the back row of his truck.

Michael set his towel down and opened his truck's door. I walked over to the opposite side of the vehicle and did the same.

"There's just a few items back here," Michael said.

He was modest in his description of the interior. I could barely see the floor as almost every inch of it was covered with some sort of miscellaneous item.

"It's like a garbage can back here," I uttered, observing all the junk.

"More like a mall," he countered, pulling out some old clothes that were stuck under bags of random car parts.

"I don't know where you shop," I began, "but this is definitely not a mall."

"Speaking of shopping," Michael added, "I was thinking you could help me pick out something to wear for Hannah's wedding since you are so concerned about my attire."

"You do need help with your style," I shared with a slight chuckle.

"I could pick you up tomorrow," Michael acknowledged. "I'll have a clean car."

"Um, I'll just meet you there," I returned while removing a broken fishing pole out of the backseat. I couldn't imagine what other sorts of treasures were hiding inside.

It was hard to reach the junk in the middle seat, so I took the leap of faith and hopped inside the truck to give myself a better chance of getting the items that were out of reach.

"You don't want me to give you a ride?" Michael asked, joining me in the backseat.

"You're still technically a stranger, and my parents told me never to get into a car with someone I didn't know," I said, but quickly realized I was currently in the back of a truck with him.

"Hm, yes, it's probably best to listen to your parents," Michael said sarcastically.

I continued to throw out items from the backseat and a small pile of trash formed outside the vehicle. I tried to keep my mind busy as my eyes were constantly attempting to fixate on the bare chest that was sitting right next to me.

"So, how can I not be a stranger anymore?" Michael asked. "What do you want to know?"

"Um, I don't know," I returned as my brain was not functioning at its best. My chest collapsed and my breaths were short as I was already nervous around him when he was completely covered. Now, without a shirt on, I couldn't even think straight. "What's your favorite part about owning your own business?"

"I like defying the odds," he proclaimed. "Growing up, nobody thought I could hold a job, and now, I run a company."

"I like that answer," I proudly returned.

I respected his response and understood where he was coming from. One of the motivations that I had for continuing on in my business was the idea that I was doing something that most people would never even attempt in their lifetime.

"So, am I still a stranger now?" he jokingly asked.

"Yes," I playfully returned. "Friendships are a two-way street. I'm learning about you, but you also have to get to know me."

"I want to learn about you," Michael declared.

"Well, what do you want to know?" I questioned.

"I want to know what you taste like," he confessed.

"Excuse me?" I gasped.

That time, I decided to ignore my attempts at trying to shield my vision from his exposed skin, and actually face him. His naked upper body stared back at me, and I almost melted into his hand that suddenly started caressing my cheek.

"I want to know how you taste," he said again.

I couldn't formulate a reply even if I tried. Every response that popped into my head was either something corny that I heard from a movie, or a jumbled mess of words. I tried to play it cool and pretend like his recent statement didn't affect me, but I could feel myself cracking under the pressure. Since words weren't formulating and my face was giving too much of my thoughts aways, I simply crashed my mouth against his. It was a release to all the tension that had been building up between us. The fake confidence and the façade that I wasn't interested in him instantly melted away with every kiss, groan, and moan. I was completely enamored with Michael and every inch of his being.

As the mirrors began to fog up and our own clothes added to the displaced items already inside his truck, it was clear that our craving for each other was mutual. And, after hours of drying off damp vehicles, I realized I was more soaked than I'd expected—but not in the way I thought I would be.

16

Are We There Yet?

I let Reid work from home today since there was no point in making him drive all the way to my apartment for minimal tasks that he had already been thoroughly trained on. He probably could have accomplished everything on his plate from a tree house if I was being honest. After working a shift at Michael's business and gaining an employee's perspective, I realized how important it was to find, train, and retain good talent, so the first thing I did when I woke up was inform Reid of the higher hourly rate that I was going to base his new pay on, and I offered him a full-time position that he gladly accepted. He was the reason why my calendar went from a chaotic jumble of scheduled events to a clear, clean, and concise organized list, and he was also the cause of another free afternoon that afforded me the time to hang out with Michael again. I was grateful that he wanted to use my expertise on fashion before picking out an outfit for Hannah's wedding, but I was also excited about another opportunity to see him.

We didn't have a set time to meet, but it was already well past noon. Michael was either patiently waiting for me at the mall, or tracking the GPS that he had most likely placed on my car since he somehow always seemed to know where I was. I had sat down at my computer that morning telling myself that I would only answer a few emails, but I got sucked into my work and didn't realize the time until it was already well past lunchtime. I probably would have kept working and forgotten to check the clock even longer if it wasn't for the arguing coming from the common area of the apartment. I liked that our unit's layout was an open concept, with the kitchen and living room merging together, but it also made conversations echo. I could clearly hear Elliot's raised voice.

"What do you want from me, Hannah?" I heard him shout. "I have been working extra shifts to pay for the wedding, so I can't be around as much.

Do you want the wedding paid for, or do you want me around? You can't have both."

I was very protective of Hannah. She had strong opinions, but she often had a difficult time standing up for herself. Therefore, I didn't let her fiancé utter another sentence before I abruptly left my desk and entered the living room, putting myself in the middle of their argument.

"Is everything okay out here?" I asked.

Hannah was innocently sitting on the couch, petting Tubs, Leo, and Toby. The three calm cats were soaking up all the love and affection, while my rambunctious cat, Benny, was playing with his toys nearby. It was a sweet scene minus the angered fiancé who was ferociously standing over them.

"We're fine," Elliot answered on behalf of both of them.

"I'm sorry, did we interrupt your work?" Hannah apologized.

"No, I'm actually done for the day," I explained. "I'm about to head to the mall to meet Michael so I can help him find something to wear to your wedding."

I looked at Elliot, who was still fuming. I wished he could've read my mind so that he could hear all the threats I had in my head against him for yelling at my best friend.

"Do you want a ride?" Hannah offered. "Elliot and I are meeting with our wedding planner at our venue. It's only about ten minutes from the mall. We are leaving here shortly."

"Sure!" I enthusiastically responded, trying to sound grateful for the ride even though I was only agreeing in order to make sure my best friend was okay. "Let me grab my purse, and then I'll be ready whenever you guys are."

To me, hitching a ride from them didn't seem like the most efficient option as I had my own car and could've easily driven myself. I didn't know how long it was going to take Hannah and Elliot to meet with their planner, and I definitely couldn't predict how long it would take Michael and I to find an outfit for him, so coordinating the pickup time would have been difficult. In my head, driving myself to the mall would have made the most sense, but after hearing Elliot yell at Hannah and witnessing his current attitude about having to do some wedding duties, I believed her offer was more than just a mode of transportation—it was a safety measure. Elliot was infuriated, and Hannah probably did not want to be alone with him while he was in that state.

I gave Hannah an emphatic smile, silently alerting her that I was there for her, but she either was rejecting my sympathy or pretending like she didn't need it as she didn't return a smile back. Maybe I had misinterpreted the whole situation and had confused Elliot's raised voice with extreme anger when really it could've just been stress from work. Perhaps I missed an entire side to the argument and had mistakenly placed all the blame on him. Either way, I didn't like the scowl that was plastered all over his face, and I wasn't fond of how he was talking to Hannah. Whether she was actually in danger or not, I was still glad that I was going to accompany her in the car. If she truly was afraid of her fiancé, at least she could feel safe during the car ride.

I quickly scurried into my room to fetch my purse. Hannah had mentioned that they were leaving shortly, but I didn't know that the timeframe meant within the next thirty seconds. As soon as I returned to the living room with my belongings, they were both standing by the front door, waiting for me.

"Ready to go?" Hannah politely asked.

"Yes," I kindly replied, speed-walking over to them. "Thanks for offering to drive me."

"It's no problem at all," Hannah noted. "It's on the way, and I'm sure you're nervous to see Michael."

I didn't know if Hannah actually believed that, or if that was her excuse to have me come along with them, because I actually wasn't that nervous to see Michael that time. It was a planned date, in a public setting, with a guy who gave me goosebumps from simply smiling at me—a recipe for an anxiety attack—however, for the first time, I actually felt a sense of calmness about seeing him. I believed it wasn't Michael himself who was causing all of my nerves prior to meeting up with him, but the idea of the unknown. He was a stranger to me, and I could tell he wasn't revealing his true self. I didn't know him, and I couldn't predict his behaviors. However, after working a shift at King Cars, I got to learn more about him than I had ever imagined. I got to see what he was passionate about, I was made aware of his insecurities regarding who he surrounded himself with, and I got to discover that his tongue tasted like a sweet mix of sugar and confidence. After yesterday, I felt like I truly knew Michael emotionally, mentally…and physically.

"Is there anything specific I should know about your wedding before I find Michael something to wear?" I asked as the three of us walked down the hallway of the apartment toward the parking deck. I was hoping my small talk would allow Elliot some time to calm down. "He really gravitates toward bright colors and funky patterns, but I don't want him to clash with your wedding theme. In all honesty, he would show up in a flamingo bathing suit if you let him."

My joke produced a chuckle out of Hannah, but Elliot simply grunted at my remarks.

"Can we talk about something other than the wedding?" he inquired. "That's all you girls talk about. I'm already about to be tortured with wedding talk enough today, so can we keep the conversations about it to a minimum, please?"

"Babe, we are just excited for our big day," Hannah argued as she reached for Elliot's hand. He held onto hers, but more so out of spite.

"Then you two should have been the ones to meet with the wedding planner," he explained. "I don't know why I'm even going to this."

"Weddings are not just for the bride," I interjected. "It's your day as much as it is hers."

"Well, Hannah doesn't have a job, so it's easier for her to attend these useless appointments," he shared.

"Um, she does have a job. In fact, you're talking to her boss," I fired back.

Hannah let go of Elliot's hand and turned her attention toward calming me down. She was always the peacekeeper, however, her future husband's insult was a jab at me, as well as her.

"Watching kids is not a job," Elliot reasoned. "I fly complicated aircraft carriers, and you wipe kids' noses."

"Babe, that wasn't very nice," Hannah proclaimed.

"Han, you know I have been having a stressful time at work lately. All the extra hours I have added to my schedule have been overwhelming. I just wanted to spend my off day hanging out with just you," he explained.

"Because you love me?" Hannah flirtatiously prompted.

"That's why I am marrying you," he responded, kissing her rosy cheeks.

If Hannah hadn't been walking in between Elliot and I, I probably would have unleashed a side of me that I would have been ashamed of later. I didn't appreciate how he treated her however he wanted, and then just kissed and apologized for it later. It wasn't fair to Hannah. For my best friend's sake, I kept my mouth shut while Elliot led us through the corridors and to the garage where his car was parked.

Walking into the parking garage made me realize that I should have given Elliot Michael's business card because he could have really used his services. His car's exterior was caked with dirt, and as I got closer to his vehicle, I could tell the interior wasn't much better. I opened the door to his backseat, and although it wasn't as cluttered as Michael's truck, it was definitely stained and gave off an interesting odor. I climbed into the seat behind the driver and braced myself for the ten-minute drive ahead of us. I immediately cracked the window once Elliot started the car and hoped that the smell wouldn't rub off on me. I'd hate for my scent to be the reason why Michael decided to forgo being my date to the wedding, although I highly doubted that a few musty fumes would turn him off.

The drive to the mall was quiet...but awkward. For some reason, Elliot didn't like to utilize the radio, so we were simply sitting there, riding in silence. It was better than hearing Elliot's complaints, but too much silence gave my nervous system an opportunity to kick in and rile up my anxious thoughts. I had made it the whole day without stressing over seeing Michael, and I wasn't going to use the drive over there obsessing about what could go wrong. Therefore, I decided to disrupt the quiet.

"Thanks again for giving me a ride," I piped up, leaning forward from the backseat. "I'm glad the venue isn't too far away."

"Shh," Hannah hushed. "No more wedding talk for the day, remember?"

"Um, okay," I uttered sinking back into my seat.

I despised Elliot's childish behavior and inability to control his anger, but I could see why he hadn't changed. He was apparently rewarded for his poor attitude as Hannah was now on his side and in agreement that the wedding shouldn't be discussed any further, even though Hannah was extremely excited for it.

"So, Reid actually turned out to be a really good employee," I relayed, choosing a different topic to talk about. "Thanks for urging him to apply."

"Oh, has he been?" Hannah exclaimed, turning her head to face me. "I've been meaning to ask you about him and how he's doing. I'm glad to hear it's all working out!"

"Wait, Han, you were the one who told Reid to apply?" Elliot questioned.

"Yeah, Paige was looking for an assistant, and Reid is a really good organizer," Hannah revealed.

"Extremely good at organizing," I added on.

"Oh, I see what this is," Elliot continued on. "You wanted to have a male coworker so you could flirt with him. Didn't you already work with him before?"

"We used to work at a restaurant together, but that's not why I told him about the open position," she defended. "I wouldn't do that."

"Sure, Han, sure," Elliot mocked, tightening his grip around the steering wheel. "You totally wouldn't do that."

"I'm serious, babe. I just thought he would be good for the job," Hannah stated.

"Are you some kind of wizard? Some kind of fortune teller? Can you see the future?" Elliot prodded.

"No..." Hannah hesitantly answered.

"Exactly, so you didn't know if he would be a good fit or not, but you suggested him anyway," Elliot griped. "I can't believe you. Asking for male attention right before our wedding is not a good look."

Hannah faced the window in order to try and hide her cries, but I could see the tears streaming down her face in the reflection of the window.

"I know this isn't my place, but Elliot you have got to stop," I threatened.

"You're right. It's not your place," he insisted.

"Alright, I've held my tongue long enough," I began.

"Paige, please don't," Hannah begged through agonizing sobs.

I took one good look at my best friend's pained expression, and the last thing I wanted was to do anything that would hurt her more than she already had been.

"Elliot clearly does not want to meet with the wedding planner today," I muttered toward Hannah. "Why don't you come to the mall with Michael and I? We could use another person with some actual fashion sense."

"She's coming with me," Elliot declared, eavesdropping on our conversation. "That's my future wife, and we have a wedding to get ready for."

"Oh, so now you want to talk about the wedding," I said to him.

Thankfully, I was secured in the backseat by my seat belt because if I hadn't been buckled up, I would've banged my head into the back of Elliot's seat when he slammed on the brakes.

"Get out," he demanded. "Get out of my car."

I was about to muffle Hannah's ears and give Elliot an earful of words that my parents would not be proud of, but when I looked out the window and noticed my surroundings, it appeared that we had arrived at the mall.

Granted, it wasn't directly in front of the door and I would have to do a little walking, but at least we had made it there.

"Hannah, are you sure you don't want to go shopping with me?" I asked her a final time.

"I'll be fine," Hannah said with puffy eyes.

"Han, do you love me?" Elliot asked her.

She nodded her head.

"And do you know that I just want the best for you?" he questioned.

"Yes," Hannah sniffled.

Elliot reached across to the passenger seat and pulled her toward him, hugging her weeping body and kissing the top of her head.

"Marriage is hard, but we can do this together," he whispered to her.

I rolled my eyes as the pattern of unruly behavior followed by affection was getting old.

"Text me when you get to the venue," I uttered toward Hannah as I exited Elliot's car. "And when you make it back home. And throughout the entire day."

As soon as I shut the car door, Elliot drove off in a hurry.

Kyle Kingsley was the initial reason why I didn't trust men anymore, but Elliot was the reason why I continued with that mindset. My expectations of finding a good guy were already at rock bottom, and I just hoped that Michael wouldn't turn out to be another Kyle or Elliot. I was about to spend the afternoon with a guy that was either going to restore my faith in the idea of dating, or crush the sliver of hope I had left that love was real.

17

Shop 'til You Drop

I couldn't get out of the car soon enough. I didn't think anyone could have paid me any amount of money to sit in a car with Hannah and Elliot while they were fighting. I wanted to be there for Hannah, and I would have loved it if she had exited the car as fast as I had, but I didn't want to get in between her and her fiancé. She was evidently old enough to make her own decisions, and she chose to stick by Elliot's side. Some may have called her loyalty admirable, but I certainly couldn't have endured that type of treatment from a partner. However, Elliot and Hannah's relationship was theirs to mend. I had my own love life to figure out, and my first task was navigating through a mall and trying to find a six-foot-three, blonde, sculpted man who knew his way around the inside of a car...and a woman.

I loved our "coincidental meetings", but I wasn't sure if they were sustainable. I was in a location swarmed by hundreds of people, and none of them were the person I was looking for. I wasn't even sure if Michael was at the mall. It was pretty late in the afternoon, so I couldn't have blamed him if he had gone home by now or back to work. Considering how busy his shop was, I knew he didn't have all the time in the world to hang out. We probably should have rethought our spontaneous plans when it came to meeting in a crowded place. It would have been better if Michael had given me a certain spot to find him, or at least a specific time, but I guess it was all part of the fun and games.

There was a mall directory near the elevators, so I used that as my clue to finding him. It felt like I was on a scavenger hunt, although I wasn't certain if there was even a prize at the end still waiting for me. I figured if I really couldn't locate him, I'd simply just call him, but I didn't want to give up that easily. I wanted to find the pot of gold at the end of the rainbow mall adventure.

I scanned the map and quickly read the list of stores inside. If I knew Michael as well as I thought I did, there could really only be one store that he was hiding out at. The store I was looking for was on the same floor that I was currently on, but unfortunately, it was on the opposite side of the mall. The energy running through me from the excitement of seeing him and the game we were presumably playing fueled my long stroll to the other side of the building where I found myself walking inside a space that solely sold Hawaiian shirts. It was pretty obvious that the first stop of the twisted version of a scavenger hunt was going to take place in that store. However, trying to find my next clue was more difficult than I had anticipated. I thought there was going to be an obvious sign or clear next clue, but I was left confused as I meandered around the colorful shirts without a single idea of what I was supposed to be looking for. If his plan was for me to purchase one of the atrocious polos, then the game was going to be over quicker than it had started.

"Are you searching for something in particular?" one of the store attendants stopped and asked me. He looked obnoxious in his attire that he clearly had picked out from the racks.

"Um, this may sound silly, but has anyone given you like a clue or a hint?" I returned.

"I don't think so..." the employee hesitantly replied.

"Did anyone tell you to look out for a girl aimlessly walking into your store?" I questioned.

"No..." he cautiously answered, evidently confused by my line of questioning.

"Sorry, I'm on a wild goose chase trying to find someone, and I assumed the first stop was this store. He really likes your clothes for some reason. No offense," I said.

I realized my comment was basically a jab at the store, but my mind was concerned with finding Michael and not on complimenting the pineapples printed on the employee's shirt.

"You're playing hide-and-seek in the mall?" he asked.

"Something like that," I answered. "Well, at least I think so. Honestly, I could be making up this entire game in my head, but I won't know for sure unless I try."

"Well, maybe he is hiding in a store that has to do with something that you like instead of what he's in to," he suggested. "Do you like jewelry? All men like to get their women a new necklace."

"He's just my friend," I informed him, though I wasn't exactly clear on what we were at that point, "but I do like sparkling diamonds."

"He could be there," the employee alerted.

"I doubt he knows his way around gems," I said with a chuckle, "but I guess it doesn't hurt to try. Thank you for your time."

I left the store almost as quickly as I had bolted out of Elliot's car, and I found another mall directory. I scanned the list of jewelry stores, but I wasn't in possession of a lot of confidence as I was simply following the suggestion of a random mall employee who dressed worse than Michael. I highly doubted he would position himself among shining jewelry as I had never noticed him wearing any, but I let out a tiny gasp when I read the name of one of the stores.

"Hot Chocolate Jewelry," I read aloud. "That has to be my next stop."

I raced back toward the complete other side of the mall, as of course, the answers to the clues couldn't be in stores right next to each other—they had to be at the furthest possible point away. It took me a good ten minutes to journey back to the part of the building where I had just come from, but eventually I made it to the jewelry store that specialized in brown gemstones. It gave the store its name of Hot Chocolate, which happened to be the drink that we had first ordered at Lucky's Tavern.

"Hi! Are you interested in trying our latest ring collection?" the jeweler politely offered when I entered the premises.

"No, thank you," I kindly declined. "I'm only here to look."

"Well, let me know if I can be of assistance," she called out.

I returned a sweet smile and then frantically began to search through all the merchandise. There had to be another clue hidden among all the crystals. Michael wasn't making the scavenger hunt easy. I doubted if I was playing the game right or if there even was a game at hand. However, I still wasn't ready to give up. I was in the middle of a competitive game, which meant there was an aspect of winning to it—and I wanted to win.

I pretended to be interested in the necklaces and bracelets on display as I intently studied the items for any sort of clue. When I couldn't find anything that resembled an inkling of where Michael's next location was, I shuffled over to the earrings section. After a few minutes of staring at all the brown gems, I came up empty. The ring section was the last area that I hadn't observed yet, but I wasn't excited to search for my next clue right in front of the jeweler. I didn't want to be informed about the current sales or latest promotions.

"Is there anything of interest to you?" the store attendant calmly uttered. "I can offer you a few suggestions."

"Um..." I remarked. I was stalling as I was really trying to find something out of the ordinary. However, even after combing through the entire store, I was unable to locate a clue.

"I couldn't find anything, but thank you," I gently muttered.

I slowly walked away from the store, defeated because I hadn't noticed anything. I knew the jewelry store was a bad idea.

"You know, usually the obvious choice is right in front of your face," the jeweler pointed out before I was out of earshot.

"Um, thanks," I replied, as I gingerly walked back over to the map of the mall.

I was disappointed in myself as I took pride in my gaming skills, and I couldn't complete one simple scavenger hunt.

I scanned the map again, trying to find a store that I had previously overlooked, and of course, I missed the one store that he was surely waiting for me at—Michaels. It was an infamous craft store that happened to be attached to the mall. It was so clear that he was hiding out in a store with the same name as him. I wasn't sure how I missed it the first few times, but I darted—almost ran—right to it. I probably looked like a freak who was obsessed with arts and crafts by the way I made a beeline for the store. I was so proud of myself for finally cracking the code, and nothing could get in my way. Nothing could stop me from getting to my destination, except for the sight of Michael eating a pretzel at the food court. I stopped dead in my tracks when I saw him. He had led me on a wild scavenger hunt to ultimately end up finding him enjoying a snack. I detoured from my original route, and marched right over to him, aborting my mission for the craft store.

"Seriously? The food court?" I exclaimed as I walked over toward the table he was sitting at. "I ventured all the way around this mall for you to be at the food court eating a pretzel?"

I was huffing as all the walking combined with the amount of breath it took to lecture him was leaving me winded. I occupied the empty seat across from him, grateful to finally be off my feet.

"Um, I'm sorry?" Michael said, handing over his salty snack. "Did you want some?"

"No, I don't want your pretzel," I explained. "I followed all the clues but you just led me on a wild goose chase!"

"What clues?" Michael inquired.

"The store that sold Hawaiian shirts. The jewelry store called, Hot Chocolate," I listed out. "Michaels!"

"The craft store?" he replied.

"Yes, the craft store!" I loudly proclaimed. "I followed all of your little hints and played along with the scavenger hunt, but you were at none of the locations! The food court was not a part of the game."

I could feel my face turning red, and at any second my eyeballs were going to fall out of my head, but I spent almost an hour looking for him, and I was in no mood for any more silly games.

"I didn't lead you through a scavenger hunt," Michael shared while he pulled out his phone. "I texted you where I was."

Michael's screen displayed a message he had sent me, clearly indicating that he was going to grab a pretzel at the food court. I must've been too wrapped up in the game I thought I was playing that I forgot to check my phone. I reached for my own to ensure that he had actually sent me a text, but it didn't take long for me to confirm that he was telling the truth.

"Oh...oops," I uttered, severely embarrassed. "You like to always have some type of gamble or game up your sleeve, and I thought this was just another one of those."

"It's okay, you don't have to explain yourself," Michael said with a cheesy smile. "It's not every day that you can make a girl squirm twice in less than twenty-four hours."

He licked the salt off his finger, but ended up prolonging the action by sucking his fingers and winking at me in the process.

"Michael!" I screeched, kicking him under the table. "We are in public."

"Wow, and you're screaming my name again. Must be my lucky day," He flirtatiously remarked.

I checked my surroundings to see if anyone was eavesdropping on our conversation or noticing myself melting in my chair.

"Anyways," I began, changing the subject or else we'd probably end up in his backseat again. "Are you ready to gain some fashion sense today?"

"Yeah, just let me finish my pretzel first," Michael confirmed.

He still had about half of his treat left, but I didn't mind enjoying the moment with him.

"No prints, no stripes, and no crazy patterns," I directed. "Oh, and please do not choose a tie that is neon colored. We are in and out of each store. If we don't love something that means we hate it, and we put it down and find something else. Efficiency is key."

"Anything else, boss?" Michael teased.

"Yeah, actually...um...do you think you could give me a ride home after this?" I asked.

"I thought we were strangers," Michael remarked after taking a bite of his pretzel. "Your parents told you not to get in the car with someone you didn't know, remember?"

"I think we are past the point of strangers now," I noted.

"Past the point as in now we are acquaintances...comrades...pals..." Michael listed.

"Yeah, past all those," I affirmed.

"Buddies...friends...dating..." Michael continued.

I almost choked on the air after hearing the last word that he had mentioned.

"We are definitely not dating," I refuted. "We are far from that."

"Okay," Michael casually stated as he crumpled up the wrapper that the pretzel he had finished was encased in. "Whatever you say."

I wasn't ready to be a girlfriend yet. There was still a lot to learn about Michael, and there was still a lot to learn about myself. He and I were surely headed in that direction, but I figured it was too soon to put a label on it—or maybe that was another defense I had built around my heart to distance myself from putting my feelings in any type of position to be hurt. Maybe dating Michael was as fun as getting to know him...maybe we were basically dating now.

Michael stood up and left me alone at the table while he went to throw his trash away. Well, I guess I wasn't completely by myself as he had also left his phone. I trusted Michael, and I didn't consider myself nosy, but when a phone buzzes and lights up right in front of me, it's hard not to look at it—especially when a name pops up that I recognize. Adam's name blared across the screen, and I was curious as to what his employee was asking him about in the middle of the day. I figured it was something about the shop, but Michael's phone was positioned where it was facing me, so I didn't even have to try that hard to read the message. I took one more little peek and read the text glaring at me:

Did she find all the clues yet, or is she still running around the mall?

I smirked to myself after reading the text...I knew it was a scavenger hunt.

18

Five-Finger Discount

"This is the last one we are trying," I explained to Michael after numerous unsuccessful trips to various stores. "No matter what, we are getting your outfit from here."

"What if all they have is camouflage?" he jokingly returned.

"Then you will show up to the wedding looking like you are in the military," I answered.

I hadn't been to a mall in a while, but from what I remembered, they were supposed to be a retail paradise. I envisioned having so many options to choose from that I'd end up buying at least five dresses. Now, I understood why online shopping was the emerging preferred method of buying clothes as everything Michael and I saw was either out of budget, or out of style. I believed we tried almost ten different places before I decided to give up and have him take me home, but since there was one more store that we hadn't tried on the way to Michael's car, we decided to make it our last stop.

It wasn't a promising option, as most of the suits on display appeared as though they were tailored for a junior high prom, but I wasn't sure if he could order an outfit in time if we shopped for them online, and I definitely didn't feel like going to another mall. After this, I was going to plop in my bed and nap away the stresses gathered from being surrounded by ugly fabrics.

"I think you should wear this," Michael suggested, holding up a long white dress.

He seemed proud of himself for finding a somewhat decent item.

"I'm a bridesmaid, so I already have my dress. Besides, I can't wear white to a wedding," I replied. "That's like rule number one."

"So, then, no to this one as well?" Michael inquired, holding up another white outfit. However, it was a mostly sheer, lingerie set.

"Absolutely no to that," I chuckled, observing the very revealing outfit.

Michael always found a way to incorporate fun into everything. As much as he was nice to look at, his uplifting presence was the most enjoyable part about being around him. Clearly, I wasn't the only one who noticed his attractiveness or his charismatic demeanor. There was a pair of girls shopping in the same store as we were, and one of them seemed interested in Michael. I tried not to make my glares noticeable, but every time I looked at her, she was staring at him with stars in her eyes.

"Oh, come on," Michael continued on, "I'm sure Hannah would love if you showed up in this."

"That's not even enough fabric to cover my thumb," I uttered.

Michael took a minute to observe the tiny cloth that was in front of him, and ultimately decided to put it back on the rack. However, the way he smirked when he picked up the revealing outfit made him look ten times more attractive, and the girl nearby noticed that as well. That time though, I stepped in front of her gaze and gave her a threatening stare back, daring her to continue to drool over him.

"What if I buy it for you so you can wear it on a different occasion?" Michael flirtatiously began.

"Well, I'm not going to say no to that," I teased, dismissing the strange woman and focusing my attention back on Michael and our mission of finding him a wedding outfit.

"I'll hold on to it for now then," Michael shared as he winked at me, picking the outfit back off the rack.

"There's no way I can pull that off," I said, eyeing the lingerie that was clearly meant for a model.

"She probably couldn't fit in it either," a girl snickered as she walked past us, and I recognized her as the one who was gawking at Michael.

She was accompanied by someone who I assumed was her friend by the way she giggled at the rude comment.

"Excuse me?" I said.

"Ignore her," Michael whispered, walking over to me to provide some comfort. "She's just bored with her life and wants to create drama."

"Ignore her?" I repeated. "Did you hear what she just said?"

"She's not worth it," Michael muttered, diverting my attention toward another article of clothing.

He picked up another dress off the rack and held it up in the air.

"Do you like polka-dots?" he playfully suggested.

"Not even on cows," I replied.

I appreciated Michael's positivity and attempt to uplift my spirits, but my mood was immediately crushed again when the two girls circled back toward us. I guess they decided to utilize a divide-and-conquer approach as one of them stood in front of me, while the other decided to try and capture the attention of my wedding date.

"Can I help you?" I snapped at the girl who approached me.

"You look like you could use some assistance," she said in a condescending tone. "I'm only trying to be helpful."

"Well, you can be helpful by leaving us alone," I relayed, stepping around her and interrupting the girl who appeared to be trying to flirt with Michael. The friend was clearly intended to distract me while the other one made her move.

"Oh, I'm sorry," the flirtatious girl uttered without remorse. "Is he your boyfriend or something?"

I was fuming, but her question made me pause my rampage for just a second. Michael wasn't my boyfriend, but he wasn't just my friend, either. It wasn't the time or the place to explain my relationship with him, and it definitely wasn't her business.

"Um, yeah, actually that's my girl," Michael answered for me. "And if you will excuse us, we actually have somewhere to be."

Michael walked past the desperate females and joined me at my side.

"Let's get out of here," Michael warned, setting down the sheer lingerie set and placing his hand behind my back in order to gesture me toward the exit. "We can find my outfit at another store."

"No!" I rejected, probably sounding like a spoiled child. "I have seen enough disrespect for the day. I refuse to tolerate any more."

Michael evidently wasn't in the car with me when I got dropped off at the mall, but I had already endured a car ride of watching my best friend get berated by her fiancé. It killed me to sit back and do nothing, but I wanted to let Hannah handle the situation how she felt best. Therefore, I held my tongue and soaked in the discomfort of listening to Elliot treat her horribly. Part of my feelings may have also been dug up from the deep-seated anger that I had planted within myself regarding witnessing Avery's poor treatment from Kyle. The past few years had been sprinkled with watching two people I cared about get treated completely awful by horrible men. Although the two girls in the store were utterly disrespectful toward me, it was just the cherry on top to all of my bitterness that I had been holding on to.

"Paige, it's not worth it," Michael scolded firmly. "Trust me."

"We can't let them get away with this!" I argued. "They deserve to reap the consequences of their actions."

I felt a little ashamed and embarrassed of the side of me that was coming out in front of the guy who had brought up the idea of dating only a few hours prior, but I had finally hit my limit. It was the last time I was going to stay silent—and probably the last time I'd see Michael again. I doubted he would want to see me after witnessing the karma that I was about to embody for those rude girls. Revenge was best served in the heat of the moment. There was no time like the present.

"Just walk away..." Michael calmly instructed.

"Oh, I'm definitely going to walk somewhere," I answered.

I started my stride right for the snickering girls, but I didn't make it far before I was swiftly lifted off my feet and thrown over the shoulder of someone who smelled like car grease.

"Michael, what are you doing?" I shouted as he hoisted me off the ground and carried me toward the exit.

"I've seen the ugly side of anger," Michael explained. "It can change your life for the worse if you let it."

I bobbled on his shoulder as he paraded me across the floor. I wasn't certain what Michael was warning me about, but it wasn't like I was going to do anything illegal. A few choice words with some spoiled brats didn't sound like something that would alter the course of my entire life.

"I was only going to—" I began, but my sentence was cut short when my words were replaced by the sounds of the store alarms when he carried me through the exit.

A few employees immediately ran over to us, and coincidentally there were a few mall cops in the area that darted toward the sound of the alarm and joined the party. Michael gently let me down and tried to take control of the situation.

"Is there something wrong?" he questioned. "We didn't buy anything. We only looked around for a minute."

"Can we check your purse and pockets?" one of the mall cops asked.

"Sure, but I told you we didn't get anything," he firmly responded.

Michael seemed timid and hesitant when it came to standing up to the mean girls, but he was not at all afraid of law enforcement. Maybe he didn't take mall cops seriously, but either way, he didn't seem too fond of the police.

Michael stretched out his arms and let one of the cops pat him down while I handed my purse over to one of the store employees so that he could check it. Being thrown over a burly man's shoulder caught the attention of a few fellow shoppers, but an even bigger crowd began to form around all the new commotion.

"See, we didn't get anything," Michael affirmed after his pat-down was finished. "It must've been a false alarm. Can we go now?"

"Not exactly," the employee with my purse remarked as he pulled out an extra large lingerie set that was clearly from the store since the tag was still on it.

"That's not mine," I profusely insisted. "I swear I did not put that there."

"Then who did? Who else would have done it?" one of the cops interjected. "Put her in handcuffs."

I was forcibly spun around, and my wrists were pinned together behind my back by one of the mall cops. I felt a cold, metal restraint tightly grip my wrists in place. I was being arrested in front of a crowd that had now doubled in size, and in front of the man I was developing feelings for. The situation was wrong, it was unfair, and more importantly, it was happening to the wrong person. I looked up and saw the bratty women snickering as I was being arrested. One of them even waved at me as I was being dragged away. Karma must've gotten misdirected and hit me instead.

"Stop! Where are you taking her?" Michael shouted as he tried to get in the way of the men who were pulling me through the mall in cuffs.

"We are going to detain her while we straighten everything out," the cop explained. "Please get out of our way. You can see her once we process everything."

I had a giant man on either side of me, and they pushed past Michael as if he weighed nothing. I struggled against the cuffs, but it only made me look more pathetic. I was already being displayed to shoppers as a low-life, petty criminal. I was getting pulled further and further from the scene of the crime until the sound of the same alarm echoed through the mall again.

Our parade around the building was stopped as everyone turned toward the blaring noise. Out of the corner of my eye, I could Michael see standing outside the store with a handful of clothes in his arms that all still had the tag on them.

"Another shoplifter," one of the mall cops exclaimed.

"Busy day on the job," the other concurred. "I'll handle it. You just take her to the basement."

I was left to be accompanied by only one officer. Some of the crowd had lost interest in my situation and decided to divert their attention toward Michael, however, it was still embarrassing to walk around in handcuffs. The route to the basement was long and consisted of many stairs and back doors, but I preferred the quiet staircases as at least it meant there weren't any bystanders staring at me. Eventually the journey had come to its end when I was locked in some sort of cage. It appeared to be the mall's version of a jail cell, but it resembled a steel-caged storage closet. My surroundings were not ideal, and I griped the whole way to the cell, but soon enough, I was joined in the makeshift prison by my new cellmate.

"Is there room for one more?" Michael said, trying to make light of the situation while he was being thrown into the cage with me.

"We are in big trouble, aren't we?" I nervously asked.

"Don't worry," Michael said, flashing me a slight grin. "We'll figure something out. It's not the first time I've been in a situation like this."

"Really? You've been in jail before?" I inquired as I glanced around the tight space, observing the cracks in the concrete floor and the loose bricks in the wall.

"A few times here and there," he shared. "Nothing serious, though. Just...dumb stuff. I was with the wrong people at the wrong time."

I remembered back to when Adam and James had explained that Michael's major downfall was the people he had surrounded himself with. It sounded like there was more to the story than I was being informed of, but I wanted to respect his privacy, so I didn't push for any more details.

"I swear I did not steal that lingerie set," I explained. "Those girls planted it in my purse."

"I know," he said in a soft tone. "This is probably just the first time the cops have had any activity since the mall opened, so they are taking their jobs too seriously. We'll get out of here sooner or later."

A lump formed in my throat, and I felt bad that I had become another person that Michael had surrounded himself with that ultimately resulted in him ending up in another unfortunate circumstance.

"I'm sorry, Michael. I really didn't mean for any of this to happen," I said.

"Is this revenge for putting you through the crazy scavenger hunt?" Michael asked with a sly wink.

"I like to keep you on your toes," I returned playfully.

I had a feeling that we were in a lot more trouble than Michael was leading me to believe, but at least, for now, we weren't alone in it—we were together, and that's all that mattered to us.

19

Family Over Everything

I never considered myself to be claustrophobic, especially since I spent most of my days confined to the four walls of my bedroom. I worked there, slept there, and even ate there sometimes. I could vividly remember a few days when I never even left my desk. My apartment wasn't that big of a space, either. Although it was a three-bedroom unit, I didn't spend too much time in Avery or Hannah's rooms. Therefore, it felt like the apartment really only consisted of the living room, kitchen, and my own bedroom. It was normal for me to see the same paint chips, only interact with my roommates and cats, and stay in a small area for a long period of time. I figured all of that practice would have made me a prime candidate for thriving in a prison, but even in the makeshift jail cell in the basement of a mall, I knew it was only a matter of time before I would lose all my sanity.

I was pacing around the small cage, replaying the recent events and trying to decipher the conversation that the mall cops were having in the other room. Their voices were loud enough to hear, but I couldn't exactly tell what they were saying. If I had to guess, they were probably giving Michael and I's height and weight to the closest prison so that they could have our uniforms ready by the time we got transported there. It was already hard enough to survive in a fenced-in janitor's closet, so I knew my time in a real correctional facility would be far from easy.

"What's your death row meal?" Michael chirped while sitting on the floor and picking at the crackling concrete floor.

"Excuse me?" I exclaimed, caught off guard by his morbid question.

"What do you want your taste buds to experience for the final time?" he clarified.

"Um, I don't know? Probably a steak from my brother's restaurant," I answered. "Why are you asking me this?"

"Well, they are probably going to lock us up and throw away the key for stealing a few articles of clothing," he followed up with a slight smirk.

I took a seat next to him, giving my pacing episode a break.

"What would you want to eat?" I calmly asked.

"A peanut butter and jelly sandwich," Michael confidently replied.

"You are not serious," I responded. "That's what every kid has for lunch. You don't need to be on death row to request that."

"It's simple, yet nostalgic," he proudly said. "After a long summer day of playing in the creek behind our house, my mom would always prepare the most delicious peanut butter and jelly sandwich any kid has ever tasted."

I watched Michael's eyes light up at the distant memory of eating one of his favorite meals from when he was younger. I could tell that such a simple activity was one of the highlights of his childhood, and I briefly wondered if that was a good or bad thing.

"Grape or strawberry jelly?" I asked, hoping to keep such a nostalgic memory going for him.

"Definitely grape," he exclaimed.

"You already lost me by choosing a peanut butter and jelly sandwich as your last meal, but preferring purple jelly over red might be the worst thing you have ever said to me," I jokingly remarked.

Michael scooted away from me and grabbed at his chest in pure horror.

"I will not take the disrespect toward the flavor of grape," he uttered with sarcasm.

"We can't all have mature taste buds," I teased, moving toward him and refilling the space he'd created when he scooted away from me. Even a few inches of separation from him felt like miles away when I was under such duress.

"Well, tell me about your taste buds," he inquired. "How do you like your brother's steak cooked?"

"Medium, for sure," I relayed.

"Hm, bloody steak," Michael said, studying me with a face of disgust. "I knew you were a vampire."

I leaned my head against Michael's shoulder as we both sat against the wall of our cell.

"Maybe I can try your mom's sandwich with grape jelly, and you can try my brother's steak cooked medium," I proposed as I nestled up against him.

"I'd love that, but my parents passed away a while ago," he somberly disclosed.

"Oh, I am so sorry," I said, instantly regretting bringing up his deceased mom.

I wrapped my arms around him in an effort to comfort him, and he put his heavy arm around my shoulder. Michael and I always bantered with each other, but we had never embraced each other in such a tender way. It was my intention to comfort him during the sad conversation, but he was comforting me in that moment just as much.

"I still struggle with the fact that they are gone sometimes," he continued on, "but I am getting better as time goes on."

"What were they like?" I asked.

"My mom was the happiest person in the world. I don't think I have any memories of her where she wasn't smiling. She was always singing, and she appreciated all the little things in life," he explained. I could feel his heart thumping against his chest, and I thought I shouldn't have made him reminisce about his mom and dad, but I could also hear a glimmer in his voice as if he hadn't talked about them in a while and was glad for the opportunity to keep the memory of them alive. "My dad was tough, but he meant well."

The eagerness in Michael's voice when talking about his mother was not present when he mentioned his dad, so I figured it was best to not ask any more questions about the passing of his parents, especially his dad.

"What about you?" he asked. "What is your family like?"

"Well," I began, understanding how Michael felt when talking about his family. It was nice to take a moment and really appreciate your loved ones. "My brother is a chef, and he makes the most delicious food anyone has ever tasted, but I'll probably never tell him that to his face. My mom is overprotective. I'm in my mid-twenties and she is still super concerned about what I am doing with my life. She lives in Michigan, so she calls me every weekend to check in on me, but she calls my brother every day to make sure he is watching me closely and keeping me out of trouble. My dad is similar in personality to my brother. They are both more on the reserved side, but my mom and I are more outspoken."

"Do you think she would like me?" Michael genuinely asked.

"My mom?" I clarified.

"Yeah," he confirmed. "Do you think she would approve of me?"

I lifted my head off Michael's shoulder and sat straight up so that I could try and read the expression on his face. He seemed sincerely concerned that there would be something about him that would make my mom view him as a flawed man.

"She would love you," I smiled, offering him the reassurance that he needed.

Michael smiled back at me, seemingly relieved that my mother would potentially like him.

I never really thought about him meeting my parents, as our relationship had always been in a limbo state. We weren't necessarily just friends, but we never discussed an official title. However, it was apparent that Michael was thinking about me in a way that was more than just someone he had a flirty friendship with since he brought up the idea of dating earlier today at the food court, and now he was mentioning meeting my mom. He always portrayed a tough exterior, and sometimes Michael was hard to read, but I was picking up on the hints he was dropping, and I was excited that I was finally getting the confirmation I needed—our feelings for each other were mutual.

"Thank you, by the way," I said, staring into his beautiful eyes. "You didn't have to steal those clothes just to get arrested with me."

"If you go down, I am going down with you," he reassured. "Besides, I know those girls planted the lingerie set in your purse."

My blood started to boil at the mention of the evil women. Jealousy was an ugly look on them.

"One of them was clearly into you," I grunted.

"Should I have handled it differently?" Michael asked. "I tried to be polite while still letting her know that we are together."

The limbo state of our relationship continued as there still wasn't any clarity as to what we were, however, hearing Michael say that we were together sounded really nice, and I was seriously warming up to the idea of eventually viewing him as my actual boyfriend.

"You handled it perfectly," I affirmed before doing something that I had been dying to do all day.

I grabbed either side of Michael's face and pulled him toward me until his lips met mine. It was a quick kiss, but the intent behind it had a more profound impact than the short duration may have signaled. Michael and I didn't operate under societal norms. We didn't plan our meetups, and we definitely didn't use labels. We communicated more through action than actual words. Therefore, my kiss wasn't just telling Michael that I liked him—it was telling him that I was with him. We were each other's person, and we didn't need words to confirm that.

"Alright, time for your phone call," one of the mall cops bellowed as he walked into the janitor's closet where Michael and I were being caged. "You each get to call one person to come and pick you up."

"Wait, you mean we are getting out of here?" I asked, standing up and walking over the fence that separated me from the mall cop.

Michael got up from the ground and stood next to me to get a better listen of the good news.

"Per our mall policy, the monetary amount of the items you stole was not enough for us to process you any further," the cop explained. "However, you will be banned from the establishment for a month, and you must have someone come and sign you out."

"You won't have to worry about us coming back," Michael shared.

The mall cop wasn't amused by his comment, but he calmly unlocked the gate and gestured for Michael to exit the cell.

"I'll take you one at a time for your call," he instructed.

I could tell Michael was hesitant to leave me alone, as he didn't want to leave my side. In order to move him along, the cop gently tugged on his arm to lead him out of the cell. Once he was fully out, the cop locked the cage back up and took Michael into a nearby room. I didn't like being enclosed alone, but I could still hear the base of Michael's voice as he made his call, so I knew he was close.

The few minutes of separation made me feel uneasy, but his call was quick and efficient, and it didn't take long for the officer to lead Michael back to the cage and exchange him for me.

"Your turn, miss," he said, holding the door open with one hand and the keys in the other.

I slowly inched my way toward the exit and blindly followed the cop into the next room where the second officer handed me my cell phone.

"Make it quick," the one with my phone directed as he gave it to me.

Thankfully, I had a great support system in Las Vegas of people who would drop anything to bail me out of a mall prison. Honestly, there were numerous people who I could depend on to rescue me. However, there was one person who had been there for me since birth, and after a couple of rings, my brother Graham answered the phone.

"What's up, Paige?" he said. "I'm at work. Do you need something?"

It took me a while to try to find the right words to say without freaking him out, but I also wanted him to quickly understand the situation so he could come get me. I didn't have time to explain how I was wrongfully framed. I just needed my brother.

"You know the mall by the bakery you like?" I hesitantly started my story.

"Yeah, why?" he questioned.

"I've been arrested for shoplifting, and I need you to come pick me up," I briefly rattled off.

"What?" Graham shouted through the phone. "Arrested?"

"I'll explain everything later," I promised. "Can you please just get here as soon as you can."

There were a few seconds of silence before he spoke again.

"I'll be there in ten minutes," he exclaimed before hanging up the phone.

Graham sounded understandably upset, but at least he was on his way.

I shakily handed my phone back to one officer while the other led me back to the entrapment.

"Back so soon?" Michael jokingly let out as I was being locked back in the cell with him.

"I told you my brother was in charge of keeping me out of trouble," I explained. "He's going to be angry, but I also know he's going to get here fast."

"Yeah, I called my brother, too," Michael shared. "He is also overprotective."

"Got to love our brothers," I stated. "They get on our nerves, but they also bail us out of a mall jail."

Michael and I took a seat back in our original spot near the back corner of the cell. We knew we wouldn't be waiting long, but it was more comfortable to be seated next to each other than standing awkwardly in the musty janitor's closet. It was also nice to resume the position of leaning against each other. Instead of focusing on the sticky situation we found ourselves in, we simply chose to enjoy each other's company.

"I'm surprised you called your brother," I eventually piped up. "I figured you would've called Adam."

"My employee?" Michael asked. "Why did you think that?"

"Well, after working a shift at your car shop, I can tell he is really responsible," I shared. "And he really cares about you."

"Yeah, he is a good guy," he agreed.

"You should promote him," I suggested. "He knows how to dry a car better than anyone I've ever met."

"Hm, telling me how to do my job?" Michael playfully added. "I'll make sure I bring that up to Human Resources."

I reveled in Michael's constant ability to get me to smile through every situation.

"I should get promoted, too." I laughed. "I completed my shift without any customer complaints. It was actually a fun time."

"So, does that mean you will be back?" he encouraged.

"I think I could squeeze it into my schedule." I smiled.

I was incredibly grateful that Avery had encouraged me to find an assistant, because although Michael and I were simply having a lighthearted conversation, I actually could make time to come by the shop again since Reid was such a wizard with organization.

I was also thankful that I had made a bold move in kissing Michael earlier, and showing him how I truly felt, because the roles were quickly reversed, and I was now on the receiving end of the affection. He had taken the liberty to reciprocate the action, and we found our lips pressed together once again.

"Paige," he calmly said, peering into my soul, "I'm not strong enough to lose you."

"And I'm not weak enough to let you," I returned.

Michael kissed me again, and for the first time, I actually felt the vulnerability radiating from him. I heard the walls around his heart crumble. I saw the chains around his soul shatter. The guards protecting his ability to love had been removed from their post, and the door to his feelings was now open. Michael was finally letting me in.

"One of your brother's is here to pick you up," the mall cop announced as he walked into the tiny room.

Michael and I reluctantly stopped kissing and stood up. We didn't necessarily enjoy being contained in a mall basement, but we had grown closer to each other from the experience.

I was expecting to see Graham closely follow the officer, as I knew my brother was on a mission to race here as fast as he could to save his only sister, but when I saw the man behind the cop, my heart sank into my stomach. My body had a visceral reaction to the sight of the man that had just walked into the room to pick up his brother. I didn't know if I wanted to cry, puke, or both. I slowly walked backward until my back hit the wall and I couldn't get any farther away from him. My body was shaking from fear, but mostly anger. I slid down the wall and sank to the floor as I watched the officer unlock the cage to let Michael out.

"Hey, Paige," Michael's brother said with a smirk. "Long time, no see."

"Get away from me," I shakily uttered as I curled up into a ball in the corner of the cell.

Michael looked confused as his brother and I exchanged words.

"Do you two know each other?" he asked as he left the cell.

"Yeah, that's Avery's best friend," his brother answered. "You remember Avery, don't you, Mike?"

Michael appeared as if he saw a ghost. The color drained from his face, and he offered me the most apologetic look.

"Well, I'm sure we'll see you around," his brother said with a wink.

Michael was clearly too stunned to react. He didn't utter another word to me. His brother and the mall cop had to help guide him out of the room as he was too shocked to move. They left me alone in the cage while I waited for my own brother to arrive. I was scared, I was sad, and I was sick to my stomach...I had fallen for Kyle Kingsley's brother.

20

Better Left Unsaid

I was sprawled out in the middle of the living room floor while Hannah's and my cats climbed all over me. We were all fighting for the same spot on the carpet where the sun's rays were squeezing through the crack in the curtains and providing a nice blanket of warmth. I guess I could've gotten up and pushed the curtains back so that more sunshine could be let in, but I was enjoying my spot on the ground. I had marked my territory first, so I let the cats fight for whatever space was left. The older cats were smart and found the crevices between my legs to nest in. Toby and Leo rested by my ankles, while Hannah's pet, Tubs, opted for the area around my upper thighs. However, the rambunctious kitten that Avery had gotten me for my birthday a few years ago chose the route of trying to create space by moving me or another cat out of their spot. I thought Benny would have calmed down by now since he wasn't a baby anymore, but I didn't think he would ever outgrow his wild side. He was a natural-born ball of energy. I was used to fighting for space with the cats anyway, as it was overwhelming to have four felines in a three-bedroom apartment. I was the main culprit, as three of the four belonged to me. Toby and Leo had been in my life ever since I rescued them from the dumpster behind my high school. If they had been capable of being functional members of society and knew how to operate a vehicle, I probably would have called them to pick me up from the mall yesterday instead of Graham. My brother didn't yell at me or lecture me on what happens when you steal. He had simply dropped me off at the apartment and returned to work—which was honestly worse. I would have much rather had him get his anger over with than hold on to the disappointment that I had caused him. I was sure there would be a time when we would have to discuss what had happened, but I was hoping that the conversation could hold off for just a while longer.

It was nearing the end of summer, which meant the pool was closing soon, Hannah's wedding was just around the corner, and business was a lot slower. Families were usually taking their final vacations at this time of year before school started, so parents didn't need any babysitting since they typically took their kids along and wanted to spend time with them. Work was already slow since Reid continued to tackle tasks that I used to spend hours on, so now instead of stressing over incoming emails, answering frequently asked questions, and tweaking the company website, I spent my Thursday lying on the floor covered in cat hair. However, the extra time on my hands really showed me what I was missing out on. I didn't think there was much going on during the workweek as everyone had their own jobs, but there were so many memories that I had created and things I got to do because I chose to step away from my desk. Something as simple as staring at the ceiling while cuddling my pets and listening to my best friend's gossip on the couch was a memory I could have missed out on if I had decided to spend the day locked in my room. If I weren't hanging out in the living room, I would've spent most of the day scrolling on my laptop, finding anything and everything that I could do to help improve my business and take advantage of the slower time, while the other part of the day would be spent behind closed doors crying my eyes out from the fact that I had just seen the most evil person in the world.

Michael was related to the cruelest man to walk the planet. Kyle not only broke my best friend's heart, but he also instilled a permanent fear in her, and in me, too. Nobody ever imagined that he would break into our apartment and attempt a robbery while bruising an innocent girl's face and innocence. I knew he had completed the crime with the help of his brothers, as although Avery refrained from giving the police Kyle's identity, she did reveal that he was accompanied by two other men—and she later confessed to me privately that those accomplices were his brothers. I never really asked too many more questions about the incident because I didn't want my best friend to have to relive the trauma, and she was obviously reluctant to share any further details regarding the event. I just tried to be there for her and help her heal while listening whenever she did decide to divulge a new detail about the crime.

I thought I was being a good friend by supporting her in any way that I could, but dating the brother of the man who had laid hands on her was the ultimate betrayal. It would negate any support that I had offered her in the past. Last night, I just stayed in bed, trying to come up with an explanation as to how the Kingsley brothers had ended up back in the picture, but there were no perfect words. I knew I had to tell her, but I also knew that it would bring up a lot of buried scars. I contemplated waiting until after Hannah's wedding, which was an attempt to save the drama until after her special day, but I was afraid that Kyle would find a way to run into Avery and tell her about Michael and I before I had a chance to—and I couldn't risk that.

My thoughts were so focused on how I was going to protect Avery from the bomb that I was about to drop on her, that I didn't pay attention to my own injured heart that had let itself become vulnerable but had now retracted behind the newly built walls around it. I was heartbroken for Avery, knowing that her worst enemy was back lurking in the shadows, but I was also hurting for myself. Out of fear, I kept my love life to a minimum. I took a chance on the one guy who was able to help me pull myself out of the dark hole I had dug. Ultimately, I ended up in a worse place than I had started. I had numerous arguments with Avery in the past regarding her poor choice in men, and now, I was no better than her. I'd fallen for a Kingsley, too. She and I were one and the same.

"Paige, what do you think?" Avery chimed in from the couch that she and Hannah were outstretched on.

"Huh?" I blurted, wrapped up in my own thoughts. "What do I think about what?"

"Were you not listening to any part of the conversation?" Avery asked.

"Avery's parents are thinking about moving back to Michigan," Hannah said, filling me in on the discussion that I had completely zoned out of.

"Good, I think they should go back," I affirmed.

"But how else am I supposed to keep a close eye on them?" Avery shouted. "They left me once, and now they are trying to leave me again."

"I'm sure my parents wouldn't mind looking out for them," I advised. "They clearly have no problem making sure they always know my exact whereabouts."

"See," Hannah relayed. "You should support their decision. Paige's parents will help. Besides, I think we all know that this city isn't the best environment for them."

"I guess," Avery hesitantly muttered. "I'm about to go meet them for lunch, and I'm still unsure how I feel about them moving."

"Well, they aren't leaving today," Hannah relayed. "Just feel out the conversation and see how it goes."

I felt bad for missing out on a conversation that I knew was near and dear to Avery's heart. Her parents had abandoned her during high school to travel the world when her dad won the lottery. They came back into her life a few years ago when her father's gambling habit had squandered all their winnings when they took a trip to Las Vegas to visit Avery. Now, they were stuck in the city trying to rebuild their lives. My mom had given Avery's mother a job to help get her back on her feet, and she seemed to be doing a lot better than when she first started. It sounded like her parents had finally saved up enough money and were in a good enough place to move their lives back to their hometown. I was sure Avery knew how much her family had wanted to go back to their roots, but even though their relationship was rocky, I knew she liked having them close by. Their desire to move probably felt like another attempt to abandon their only daughter, but I felt that the situation was completely different than the first time they had left her. Her parents had traveled the world out of greed, and I believed them wanting to go back to Michigan was out of love. In order to be better parents, they needed to be better people. Avery's dad still had relapses with his gambling addiction, and being in a city surrounded by casinos was not ideal for him. Although it would be painful at first to watch her parents move across the country, I figured it was in everyone's best interest that they escape Sin City.

"I'll just hear what they have to say and try to understand their reasoning for leaving," Avery shared. "Besides, I want to make sure I'm in a good head space with them before your big day, Hannah. I do not want any unwanted stressors."

"The wedding is only a few weeks away. Are you excited, Hannah?" I asked, trying to add to the conversation even though my mind was elsewhere.

"Yes, I can't wait!" she screeched.

"I'm excited to meet Michael," Avery interjected.

"Um, about that," I shakily replied.

"Oh, don't tell me you got cold feet already," Avery remarked.

"You don't have to be scared to bring him around," Hannah confirmed. "He is a great guy. Trust me."

"Well, I'm not so sure..." I offered. "We went to the mall yesterday, and I found out some things that rubbed me the wrong way..."

"Oh no," Hannah started. "He hates cats, doesn't he?"

"No, it's not that," I remarked.

"Does he think pineapples belong on pizza?" Avery guessed. "Because that is a complete red flag. I can tell the quality of a guy based on his food preferences."

"I mean he likes grape jelly over strawberry jelly," I informed them.

"Oh, Paige!" Avery shouted. "You can't break up with him over that."

"Well that's not—" I started.

"Just keep getting to know him," Hannah interrupted. "I'm sure he can learn to love strawberry jelly."

Avery and Hannah laughed over what they thought was the real reason why I didn't want to bring Michael as my wedding date. Their laughs echoed throughout the living room, startling the cats that were lying on top of me. I wasn't sure how Avery was going to handle the news about Kyle being back in Vegas and Michael being his brother, but it was a secret that I could not hold on to any longer.

"Michael is great. You both will have a great time at my wedding. I'm sure everything will be perf—," Hannah began, pausing mid-sentence. She was scrolling through her phone when she stopped talking, so it was evident that she had just seen something that had disrupted her entire train of thought. "My photographer just canceled on me!"

"No way!" Avery screeched. "Less than a month before your wedding!"

"This can't be happening," Hannah cried out, getting up from the couch. Her body obviously didn't know how to react as she simply stood there frozen. "I need to meet with my wedding planner immediately."

Hannah stumbled across the living room, heading toward the key holder so that she could retrieve her car keys. The way her hands were shaking hysterically made it obvious that she was in no position to drive.

Avery quickly popped up from the couch and raced over to Hannah, taking the keys from her hand.

"Let me drive you," Avery insisted. "I'm heading to lunch with my parents, anyway. I can drop you off on the way."

Hannah either couldn't respond because of how hysterical she was, or didn't respond because she didn't have enough time to as Avery was already gesturing her out the door.

"Call me if you need anything," Avery shouted in my direction. "We will be back tonight."

"Sounds good," I somberly answered, disappointed that I was still holding on to a grave secret.

"By the way," Avery slipped in before shutting the front door. "Give Michael another chance. Life is too short to deny yourself the love you deserve. I'm sure there's nothing about him that is worth letting him go for."

"If only you knew," I whispered after she had already left the apartment. "If only you knew."

21

I Knew You Were Trouble

My life had turned upside down in a matter of moments. After finding out that my mysterious, yet charming, wedding date was actually spawned from the same parents as Kyle Kingsley, the man who had obliterated my best friend's sense of self, I couldn't make sense of anything anymore. It appeared as though our mutual connection was as shocking to Michael as it was to me, but I wouldn't have been surprised if his whole purpose of getting to know me was to allow his brother back into Avery's life. It was probably the plan from the beginning. His stalking tendencies and always knowing where I was were most likely due to the conniving gene that he shared with his brother. Our coincidental meetups and spontaneous run-ins were not so cute anymore—they were creepy. I was playing with fire by sleeping with the enemy. Life was no longer as I knew it.

It was becoming more apparent that the giant secret that I held was going to have to stay hidden until after Hannah's wedding. Clearly, the future bride was not in a stable emotional state after her photographer had abruptly canceled on her, and I didn't want to drag Avery's happiness down with the awful news. I couldn't have the bride and one of the maids of honor being an emotional wreck on the big day. Today was my chance to deliver the shocking revelation. It was now or never, and considering Avery was currently driving a hysterical girl to her wedding planner and then heading to meet up with her absentee parents, my window of opportunity had closed. I would have to keep the information close to my chest for a few more weeks and hope that the wedding would occur before the secret had a chance to eat me alive.

I decided to go to a place that may have somewhat doubled as my sanctuary when I was tired of being confined to the apartment walls, and when the weather was nice enough to go outside. It would take a lot of calming and peacefulness to halt my racing mind, an amount that may be too much to ask of the place, but I was hopeful that the Exe Apartments' pool would help. It was a weekday afternoon, so it was one of the rare times when a summer party wasn't happening. I was hopeful that only a few residents were going to take advantage of the nice weather and tranquil environment, but thankfully, after removing four cats off of me and maneuvering through the apartment hallways, I was pleasantly surprised to see that the pool deck was completely empty.

I guess I shouldn't have been too shocked as I assumed most people were working—I surely would have been glued to my computer at that time. However, it was a nice change to not have to fight for a pool chair and to be able to grab one in the perfect spot. It was positioned so that I could see the full view of the pool, and it was half-shaded and half in the sun, keeping my chair at the perfect temperature. The chair was already fully reclined, so I took the liberty of positioning myself on it, lying my stomach against it, and letting the sun warm up half of me. The cats would have loved it.

I ditched my phone and put it on silent, lying it face-down on top of my bag. Avery and Hannah were too busy to need me, and I didn't want the ringing of my phone to disturb my peace. Michael had been blowing up my phone ever since I'd left the mall, and I obviously hadn't responded and clearly had no intention of ever talking to him again. It was still unclear what his true intentions were, but either way, he was no longer a part of my life. In fact, I found it completely disrespectful that he would think to reach out to me. He was there when Kyle decided to rob our apartment, and therefore, he was just as guilty whether it was his idea or not. He hurt my best friend, and I wasn't going to give him the chance to hurt me, too. I wasn't sure what type of girl he thought I was, but I wasn't about to keep him in my life just because he was cute and charming. He obviously had a thing for stalking, robbing, and beating up girls.

The pool was supposed to calm my thoughts, but it only fired up my anger even more. Kyle Kingsley used to work at the pool deck, and the memory of him still lingered around. I was getting more upset as I continued to replay his face in my mind. I felt my body heat up with frustration, but the half of my body that was baking in the sun suddenly became the same temperature as the rest of me. The sun must've gone behind a few clouds, or there was something blocking my rays. I repositioned myself, sitting upright so that I was no longer on my stomach in order to investigate the mysterious disappearance of my heat source.

"Wow, you still live here?" a voice that mimicked nails on a chalkboard uttered. "It's been years since I've been here, but some things never change."

"Bold of you to show your face here," I responded, peering at Kyle's towering body.

He took a seat in the pool chair next to me so that we were facing each other.

"How's it going, Paige?" he snickered across from me.

"What do you want, Kyle?" I hissed.

"Aw, you still have the same bitter attitude," he teased.

I casually reached behind me for my purse, trying not to alert Kyle of my action. When I finally felt my phone, I slowly turned my head and tried to dial for the police. However, before I could make any progress, I felt a strong grip around my arm. I looked down and saw white knuckles squeezing tightly around me. They were attached to an arm that was decorated with an evil-looking serpent tattoo.

"I wouldn't do that if I were you," he threatened.

"Why not?" I grimaced through my teeth.

"I think you are going to want to hear what I have to say first," he assured.

Nothing that Kyle could've said would have piqued my interest enough to abandon my plan of calling the cops, but I reluctantly left my phone by my purse as his grip was starting to cut off my circulation.

He eventually let go of my arm, and the smile that crept across his cruel lips showed me that he was satisfied with my decision to comply with his wishes.

"Why are you here?" I mumbled.

"Well, I had to retreat back to Sacramento with my brothers after the little incident with Avery," Kyle began, "and now I'm back."

"It wasn't a little incident," I corrected.

"You're right. It wasn't little because she is a giant liar," he shared.

"Your attempt to rob Avery was not her fault," I defended.

"Ah, see Paige, that is where you are wrong," Kyle sneered.

Kyle leaned in closer as if he was about to tell me a secret, but I moved further away from him as we were already sitting too close for my comfort. He smirked again, seemingly pleased that his presence was rejected by me.

"Do you really think Avery would have ended up in that position if she hadn't lied to me about her father's fortune?" he asked.

I refused to answer as I didn't want to waste another breath on the conversation.

"Unlike Avery, I am not a liar, and I promised her I would come back—I promised her that she would see me again," Kyle revealed. He leaned back to a normal upright position. "So two years later, that is why I am here—to fulfill my promise."

"She's in a happy, healthy relationship, and she has never once thought about you," I lashed out, trying to snap him out of his fantasy that Avery would actually want to see him again.

"Then, explain this," Kyle exclaimed, pulling his phone out of his pocket and showing me a text from Avery that showed her apologizing for misleading him.

"That message was dated almost two years ago," I explained, trying to defend her.

I was disappointed in Avery for reaching out to Kyle, but I understood that she was in a vulnerable position during that time period, as that message was sent roughly a few days after she had left the hospital.

"It shows she is still thinking of me," Kyle explained. "I mean you can't blame her, right? You also fell for a Kingsley."

He winked in my direction, and I tried everything in my power to not give him the reaction he was looking for, but I was sure he could sense my frustrations.

"It would be such a coincidence if I happened to run into Avery now, wouldn't it?" he snickered.

"Stay away from her," I hissed.

"Stay away from my brother," he returned.

Kyle's evil gaze intensified, and it felt like he was staring straight into my soul. It was as if he was trying to threaten me with his eyes in case his words weren't enough to convince me. However, I didn't need an evil stare to force me to stay away from Michael—I was already trying to run as far away from the Kingsley brothers as possible.

"I'm not talking to him anymore," I exclaimed.

"Good, then you won't have a problem going to his shop and officially cutting things off," he remarked.

"There's no need to do that," I objected. "I'm already ignoring his texts and calls."

Though it was the truth, it hurt saying those words out loud. My heart was still recovering from Michael's infiltration.

"He keeps blowing up my phone," I shared, "but I haven't responded to him. I can prove it to you if you let me show you my messages."

I reached for my phone, pretending as if I was about to pull up my text message history. I was hoping my love for theatrics and drama would help my acting skills portray the fact that I was adamant about showing Kyle that I hadn't responded to his brother. However, my main objective was to make a second attempt at calling the police.

"Nice try," Kyle hissed as he returned with another tight grip that latched around my arm before I could dial any numbers.

I whimpered from the force of his fingers slowly imprinting into my skin.

"My brother is a little odd—you know that, Paige," Kyle stated, squeezing even harder. "He doesn't see silence as rejection."

"Obviously, neither do you. It must run in the family," I managed to croak through the pain. "And that doesn't sound like my problem,"

"Well, now it is your problem. You are going to march into his shop and tell him that you are done with him for good," he declared. "I can't have someone who is fond of dialing the police for every minor inconvenience around my family."

I was starting to lose feeling in my arm, so I simply nodded my head to let him know that I understood. Kyle had no right to cut me off from Michael because of my reasonable attempt to alert the authorities that an actual criminal was in front of me, but there was no arguing with him. He had a plan in his mind, and he wanted it executed.

"You leave my brother alone, and I'll leave Avery alone," he reinforced, finally letting go of my arm.

As soon as I was free from his grip, I frantically grabbed my belongings in order to leave the pool deck. My arm was aching, and I didn't want to stay and figure out what other pain he could cause me.

I debated running for my apartment and locking myself in my room until the police arrived, but I would do anything to protect my best friend from her evil ex, and it sounded like the best way to shield her from Kyle was to fulfill his request.

"I'll go see your brother tomorrow," I reluctantly replied.

"No, you are going now," Kyle demanded.

"I can't go now," I refuted. "I need...time."

I didn't know exactly what I meant—time to process Kyle's return, time to understand that I had fallen for a Kingsley, time to grieve the loss of

Michael. Either way, marching down to King Cars and officially ending whatever I had going on with Michael seemed too sudden. I just wanted a moment to breathe. However, after denying Kyle's demand, I looked into his eyes and saw nothing but a dark hole. He was serious, and it was obvious that there would be consequences if I didn't agree.

"Fine," I eventually said, "I'll go right now."

I angrily stood up from my pool chair out of fear of what would happen if I didn't comply, and made my way toward the exit.

"You're going to wish you would've stayed in Sacramento," I whispered to him, before walking past him.

I had a mission I had to complete in order to keep Avery out of harm. Despite the outlandish request, I was eager to do something that would deter Kyle from ever crossing paths with Avery again—and to finally escape his death stare and unsettling presence. My arm was still throbbing from where he had gripped it, and I wasn't keen on finding out what else he could do.

"You're going to wish you never messed with my brother!" Kyle shouted back at me as I continued to walk away from him.

"I already do," I said only to myself.

22

Confrontation

I numbly drove to Michael's workplace without second-guessing my actions. Any thought that tried to pop into my mind, I immediately blocked out. All I knew was that I needed to officially end things with him, and that's all I was capable of thinking about. When I felt my focus drifting away from what Kyle had demanded of me and more on my connection with his brother, the temptation to turn around lurked in the back of my head. I couldn't let the tiny shred of my heart that still longed for Michael's presence to take control because my car would have been headed in the direction of Avery instead of Michael's office. I needed to remember the trauma that Kyle had caused Avery, and how I was being a great friend by protecting her from coming into contact with him again. Her bruised face and shattered spirit replayed in my mind as I tried to keep my mission at the forefront. However, as hard as I tried to concentrate on the goal at hand and hate the man who was related to my best friend's abuser, a part of me still wanted to run into his arms and have him face the problem with me. I so badly wanted Michael to rescue me from the terrible nightmare I found myself in. Yet, when I pulled into the parking lot of the car shop and realized King Cars was just an abbreviated version of his last name, I knew that there wasn't going to be a knight in shining armor ready to save me—Michael Kingsley was the enemy, and I had to end things with him once and for all. No more random meetups, and no more rogue scavenger hunts. The man I met was not the man who I was currently marching out of my car to go see. Kingsleys could not be trusted.

I knew it wasn't going to be as easy as storming through the building doors and catching Michael standing in the lobby, but it didn't stop me from still hoping that our spontaneous streak would continue, and that I would happen to run into him. That dream was mostly crushed when I walked inside and didn't see any sign of the owner. However, the employee behind the desk was the same one from when I had first visited the shop. He smiled at me, presumably out of recognition, but his kind expression quickly faded when I stormed past him and headed for the door that led to where the garage was.

"Ma'am, you can't go back there!" he yelled at me as I breezed by him.

His voice was sharp and demanding, but his bite didn't match his bark. He was screaming at me to stop my progress, but he didn't move from behind the desk. There was no attempt on his part to halt my aggressive march, so I continued to push through the door that was clearly marked for employees only. I worked a day at the shop anyway, so I technically wasn't entering an area that was off-limits to me.

I raced through the hallway that ultimately led me to my destination, fueled by anger and fear. The garage was packed with employees working on cars, but my eyes were focused on the Kingsley brother who stood across the room. His bulging muscles and authoritative demeanor weren't as attractive when I knew that he had used them to break into my apartment and harm my best friend—but I guess even the most beautiful things can be used as weapons if given to the wrong person. The abnormally large biceps and veins that laced his arms had caressed my face, but they had also beaten Avery's.

"Woah, look who it is!" Adam shouted when I neared his work station.

"She's back for another shift," James joined in.

I meant to force a slight smile in their direction, as my anger was nowhere near directed at the two men who had helped me when I worked at the shop. In fact, I kind of missed their lively spirits and was actually happy to see them again. However, I believed my intended grin came out in the form of an intense glare because when I looked in their direction, the joy on their faces quickly drained. They appeared as if they were staring at a ghost, or a mystical creature that only existed in books. Even they couldn't fathom the amount of anger that was plastered all over my face, but honestly, I didn't recognize myself, either. I hadn't been this enraged since the first time a Kingsley had entered into my life.

Adam and James seemed as curious as everyone else who I angrily walked past to see what could have possibly led me to be in such an enraged state. Surely all the employees had their fair share of angry customers, especially since they worked on cars for a living, but I didn't think anyone was prepared to see an apparently innocent girl stomping through the garage. All eyes were on me except for the one pair who I really cared about. Michael's back was facing me when I approached him, but either my loud footsteps or the smoke fuming from my body alerted him of my presence before I could say anything.

"Paige," Michael said when he turned around. His voice was a mix of surprise and hope. "What are you doing here?"

"Oh, I'm sorry," I angrily replied. "Should I have broken into your shop in the middle of the night and then beaten you? Would that have made for a better entrance?"

"Paige, please," he begged. "I know you're upset with me, but there's a lot you don't know about that night. Let me tell you the full story."

Michael tried to gesture me toward a quieter place to discuss what he and his brothers did to Avery. My voice was echoing throughout the garage, but I honestly didn't care if our whole conversation was broadcast to the entire world. He needed to finally face the consequences of his crimes.

"I don't want to hear how you pummeled my friend's face," I exclaimed.

"It wasn't me. I swear," he whispered, trying to lower the tone of the conversation. "Kyle planned the entire thing, but Eli was the one who hit her."

"And you did nothing wrong. You're totally innocent," I sarcastically remarked.

"I'm not saying that," he said, "but I truly didn't know that my brothers were going to hurt Avery that night."

"So believable," I groaned. "You always have an excuse."

"I'm telling the truth," Michael explained.

He gently placed his hands on either side of my shoulders and tried to pull me closer to him, but I brusquely brushed off his touch.

"Get away from me," I sharply stated.

"Paige, I am so sorry," he pleaded. "I am so so sorry."

Graham and my dad were on the more emotional side than most guys, but still, it had been a while since I had seen either of them cry. My dad's eyes briefly watered when he sent me off to college, and my brother shed a mini tear when he visited Avery in the hospital after her attack, but watching Michael clearly sobbing in front of me was the first time I had seen a man cry in a while. I felt my anger immediately subside, and it was replaced with remorse. I tried to put into practice what I had done on the drive over there and remember all the awful things his family had done, but it was harder when someone I cared about was crumbling right in front of me.

"I don't...want to see you...ever...again," I shakily croaked, trying to fight back my own tears. I needed to quickly officially end our relationship before I forgave him and ran into his arms.

Michael slowly nodded his head, understanding my anger and sniffling back a few sobs in the process.

"So, no more wedding date?" he managed to say.

"No more wedding date," I answered, crushed.

It was the most painful breakup I had ever gone through, and I wasn't sure if we were ever officially together. However, my heart didn't need the title of him being my boyfriend to still feel every ache and pain of letting him go.

I briefly removed myself from the heartbreaking moment and took a second to see if everyone was still staring at us. Clearly, Michael was extremely respected by all of his employees as the once full garage was now an empty space. They had all given their boss the privacy to mourn.

I took a few steps toward Michael and gave his arm a gentle rub in an attempt to comfort him. It was hard to watch his heart shatter in front of me, and although it was a long shot, I was hoping he would understand that the innocent touch was actually my way of showing him that I didn't want us to end like that, either. Kyle robbed my best friend out of love, and he robbed Michael and I out of it, too.

"Maybe we will see each other again?" Michael stuttered through a few tears.

"I don't think there will be a next time," I let out. "Goodbye, Mike Kingsley."

I walked away from him, allowing him to cry alone in his own shop.

It honestly felt awkward to call him Mike, as I had always known him as Michael. However, Michael was sweet and kind. Michael was the one who couldn't stand in front of me for longer than two seconds without making me laugh. Mike, on the other hand, was a gravely evil man who would rather watch a girl suffer than stop his own brothers from carrying out such a violent act. I would always miss Michael, but I would never forgive Mike.

23

Two Truths and a Lie

"The fries are a bit oily, and they could have crisped the edges more, but overall the flavors are there and the sodium level is appropriate," Graham described as he ate another fry. "Actually...on second thought," he shared as he licked his finger. "They may be too salty."

"Graham, we are at a random diner, not a five-star restaurant," I pointed out.

"Well, maybe our next sibling lunch date could be at one," he relayed.

"Sure...if you are paying," I returned, stealing one of his fries—they definitely had too much salt.

Graham and I had always been close growing up. Our family used to do a lot of bonding activities when we were younger and often had planned dinners together. I used to think my dad's demand of prohibiting phones at the table was an unnecessary rule, but looking back, some of my fondest memories from my childhood came from the laughs around a pot roast. With our parents still residing in Michigan and Graham and I living in Las Vegas, our family participated in fewer activities together. We aimed to at least plan a trip once a year, but trying to work with four different schedules proved to be a hassle. To maintain the bond we fortified growing up, Graham and I prioritized finding time to hang out just by ourselves. We frequented our sibling dates less and less as running a restaurant and starting a business hindered any free time we had, but I still looked forward to the time when I got to spend some quality time with my brother.

"I think I like your food better than mine," I revealed as I continued to pick the fries off his plate.

"Yeah, most people would agree with you," he remarked. "I'd choose chicken strips and fries over a house salad any day."

"I know. I wasn't really hungry, so I figured I'd just order a salad," I answered.

"That surprises me," Graham started. "You always order an entrée that comes with fries—even if you had just eaten five minutes ago."

I glared at my brother, curious to see if his comment was a dig at my eating habits. It was obvious he didn't mean anything negative by it, though. He was only pointing out a normal habit of mine that I hadn't followed that time. Thankfully, he didn't realize that my lack of appetite and my refusal to order my normal meal was because my mind was still preoccupied with Michael. Lately, my nights didn't consist of much sleep as the effort of trying to ignore my broken heart kept me up.

It had been several days since I had confronted him, and the guilt of holding on to the secret was nagging at me. There were numerous times when I wanted to pull Avery and Hannah to the side and divulge the fact that the Kingsley brothers were lurking around Las Vegas again, but something always came up that prevented me from telling them. However, the main reason I kept my lips closed was that Hannah's wedding was right around the corner. In a few days she would become Mrs. Stockton, and the stress of wedding planning would soon come to an end. Elliot and Hannah's relationship had been strained with all the stressors that came with coordinating such a big event, and I didn't want to add to it, but it was almost time for them to reap their benefits.

Avery and Hannah continued to hound me about bringing Michael as my plus-one, but as the big day neared, they stopped trying to push me to have him attend. They still insisted on me finding someone to go with, but when I told them I would find Reid during the reception, their apprehensions were eased. Lately, Reid had been the solution to all my problems—lightening my workload, acting as my wedding date—I wondered if he also knew how to get rid of Kingsley brothers.

"So, do you want to talk about what happened at the mall now?" Graham asked with a wilting French fry between his fingers. "Or are you still salty?"

He chewed the greasy potatoes with his mouth open as he laughed at his own joke.

"It's not funny," I stated while groaning at him.

"I know it's been a while since the incident occurred, but we still haven't talked about it," he said.

"Yeah, because you have been busy cooking food and kissing my best friend," I remarked with a hint of passive-aggression in my tone. I truly did think that Graham and Avery were a good match for each other. It just sucked that it resulted in me spending less time with my two favorite people as they were usually occupied by each other.

"I do enjoy both those things," Graham uttered with a wink, "but I also enjoy hanging out with my little sister and making sure she stays out of trouble. There must be something going on in your life that I don't know about for you to resort to stealing. Is it because of that new boy you're talking to?"

"No," I sharply replied. "He isn't in the picture anymore..."

"Oh, sorry for bringing him up then," Graham noted.

I picked up my fork and began to play with my salad—trying to distract my mind from the conversation at hand.

"It's just not like you to do something like that," he pointed out.

"I didn't take anything," I strongly assured. "Some girl planted the items in my purse."

"Now, why would someone do that?" Graham gasped.

"Because everyone is a liar and nobody can be trusted," I lashed out.

I realized the anger that I had felt toward Michael was coming out in the form of me yelling at my brother.

"Is everything okay, Paige?" Graham asked sincerely. "You don't seem like your normal self."

I could tell he was worried about me. I wanted to assure him that I could handle whatever I was dealing with on my own, but I wasn't sure how good of a job I was doing.

"I'm fine," I answered. "I think I'm just sad that things didn't work out with the guy I was dating."

"Well, I can assure you that your person is out there," Graham said. "You just gotta keep looking."

"How do you know if you found, 'the one'?" I blurted out.

Graham forcefully blinked and leaned back in his chair, clearly caught off guard by my question.

"Well...um...that's a tough one to answer," he returned.

"Do you pick your soulmate, or does fate make the decision for you?" I continued to interrogate.

I was either dumb for choosing the completely wrong guy to fall for, or I was dealt a bad hand of cards and my destiny was to end up in the position I was in. Either way, I wished I could go back in time knowing then what I knew now—I would have never given a guy in a Hawaiian shirt a chance.

"I believe Avery and I were put in each other's lives for a reason," Graham eventually responded. "Although what she went through was extremely sick, it brought us closer together. I guess what I am trying to say is that sometimes difficult times lead to beautiful results."

"Yeah, well, probably not in this instance," I blurted out.

"Why do you say that? What happened with the guy you were interested in?" Graham asked.

I could keep a secret from Avery and Hannah, but it was a lot harder to refrain from telling Graham the truth. He could always tell when I was lying anyway, so I found no point in trying to make up a story. Besides, I couldn't hold on to the information by myself any longer, and I needed someone on my side—and perhaps for some protection, too.

"The guy I went on a date with...Michael..." I began.

"Yeah?" Graham commented.

"His full name is Michael Kingsley..." I said in a low tone. "Kyle's brother."

The sound of glass plates clanking against the metal table when Graham slammed his fist down echoed throughout the restaurant. A few heads turned in our direction, but Graham was too enraged to notice, and I was too choked up to care.

"Did he hurt you at all?" Graham gritted through his teeth.

"Not physically," I shared.

"Does Avery know?" he inquired.

"No, I'm not telling her or Hannah until after the wedding," I informed him.

Graham's face quickly went from pale to red as he began to fully process the news that I had just told him.

"I'm ordering extra security around the apartment and Iron Nine," he started. "I'm going to call the cops, and we are going to have him arrested immediately. His whole family will be in jail tonight."

"Graham, calm down," I whispered as people were still staring at us. "We have to be smart about this."

"I am calm!" Graham shouted.

A few more heads turned in our direction as his voice was clearly loud enough for everyone at the restaurant to hear.

I stared at my brother and let a few seconds tick by so that he could collect himself.

"If we want to bring the Kingsleys down, we can't act on emotion. We need an actual plan while keeping in mind that Hannah's wedding is in a few days, and it will bring up a lot of trauma for Avery," I relayed, feeling like the mature sibling in the situation. I already had time to process the information, but it was fresh for Graham.

"I agree. We need to keep this between us until it's necessary for Avery to know," Graham affirmed. "I don't want her worrying."

Finally, Graham was seeing the bigger picture. As much as both of us wanted to alert the authorities and let the police take over, we needed to ensure that the brothers would go down. I had no idea where Kyle was, so I wouldn't know where to lead the police, and I knew that if any whisper about the authorities being called was made known to them, the Kingsleys would flee back to Sacramento. Kyle's exact location was a mystery, but I did know the whereabouts of his brother.

"I know where Michael works," I declared. "We can have him lead us to Kyle."

"Do you think he would actually do that, though?" Graham questioned, not fully on board with my plan. "I surely would never give up someone I love—especially family."

"Good point. You already bailed me out of jail once," I noted. Although the mood was heavy, I managed to get Graham to at least show a slight hint of a grin. "But perhaps Michael's feelings for someone else might trump his sentiments toward his evil brothers."

Graham read the hopeful expression on my face. He understood that I had belief that there was a possibility Michael would betray his own family, but I could tell he didn't know why. Nobody understood the depth of Michael and I's relationship, and honestly, neither did I. I could have been overestimating his feelings for me, but I couldn't come up with another way to find Kyle unless I just waited around and hoped that he would show up to the pool deck again. However, nobody knew how long that could take.

"I mean, it doesn't hurt to at least try," Graham stated, "but you aren't going to his work alone. I am coming with you."

"I wouldn't have it any other way," I exclaimed, grateful that I had my brother by my side.

"It's a dangerous mission, but I think we can execute it," Graham noted.

"Wow, we are really going to do this," I said out of pure realization. "The Jensens are going to take down the Kingsleys."

"My money is on us," Graham shared with a wink. "Do you think we should we go there now?"

"Now?" I shrieked, thrown off by the suddenness.

"A sneak attack," Graham explained.

"A sneak attack is supposed to catch them by surprise, not me," I explained.

"Well, when else are we going to?" Graham questioned. "Hannah's rehearsal dinner is tomorrow, and the wedding is the following day. We could wait until after it's all over, but I don't want to give Kyle any window of opportunity to see you or Avery again. The sooner we take them down, the sooner we get rid of them."

I wasn't prepared for my sibling lunch date to conclude with confronting a Kingsley, but I couldn't think of a better person to go on the journey with.

"Well, then...let's do it," I affirmed.

My brother and I were about to go on an impossible mission, but we were the best duo to derail the evil lurking in Las Vegas—at least I knew there would always be one guy in the world who would never let me down.

24

One Must Go

I had become a frequent visitor to the King Cars parking lot. It had begun as a foreign place, and now I was very familiar with the black pavement that held numerous cars—including Graham's. Although I'd been to Michael's workplace on numerous occasions, that was the first time I had hid outside the building, waiting for my brother to signal that it was clear for me to sneak in and walk through the employee-only door. We wanted a more discreet entrance than last time when I had stormed through the building and walked right up to Michael in front of all his employees. Our mission of persuading him to give up not only himself but also his wretched brothers to the police was a task that called for a more strategic approach. Instead of causing a scene in the garage where everyone worked, Graham and I decided that it would be best if I confronted Michael in a more private setting. It was my brother's job to distract the front-of-house staff while I found his office in order to wait for him there. The plan was simple, really. All I had to do was convince my former lover that he would be better off behind bars with his guilty brothers—easy enough. I thought our idea was pretty foolproof. The only lurking, menacing detail that could potentially lead to the downfall of the total operation was the annoying piece of my shattered soul that still yearned for Michael and wanted nothing more than to protect him. Fortunately for me, there was a long line ahead of him of people who I needed to protect, but for some reason, my heart was trying to get him to skip the line.

I stood outside King Cars, occasionally peering inside through the glass windows to be on the lookout for Graham to obnoxiously yawn—a signal that was his choice. The employees had become more and more familiar to me since I had already been there a few times before, but the usual worker, who was typically positioned at the front desk, was not working today. He was probably tired of seeing my face anyway and would most likely make it harder to carry out the plan since he would know something was off if he saw me lurking around the premises again.

Graham was only supposed to be inside for a few minutes before luring someone to check out his car in order to give him a detailing quote, but the Las Vegas sun was baking me in the summer heat, making me beg for the fall season to come. I assumed Graham was telling the employees every possible detail of his life given how long I was waiting outside, but after a few more glances of the indoors, I finally caught my brother exaggerating a yawn and heading toward the side door while he led an expert to his vehicle. As soon as they left the building, I snuck around the corner and nonchalantly entered the main office space. The key to committing an offense and not getting caught was to act as confidently as possible—which was probably why Kyle Kingsley and his brothers were so cocky—therefore, I proudly held my head up high and headed for the restricted doors as if I knew exactly what I was doing. A part of me was prideful of my ability to quietly make my way into a zone that was strictly off-limits, but another side of me felt dumb for coming up with such a thought-out plan, just to walk through a set of doors undetected with ease. Graham and I thought we were some super-secret spies with how elaborate our plan was, but honestly we probably could have just walked into the shop and into the back without the distraction tactic. Oh well, at least my brother was getting a free quote on how much it would cost to get his car detailed, so it wasn't a complete waste.

I tiptoed down the hall, passing up the pathway that I knew led to the garage and opting to walk in a direction that I had never been before. As a business owner myself, I knew that having an office as far away from all the noise and activity as possible was the key to running a successful operation. There needed to be a physical separation between the owner's private quarters and the rest of the business. Michael and I were pretty like-minded in a business sense, so I aimed my mission toward trying to find the furthest possible area where his office could be. I navigated through the hallway, and although there were numerous doors leading to other areas of the building, it wasn't like it was a maze or anything. There were opportunities to turn left or right, but I kept drifting down the same path until I came to a door enclosing a room that was the furthest away from all the action. I wasn't sure if it was out of habit, or the part of me that still longed for Michael wanted to be as respectful as possible, but I quietly knocked on the door before entering. There wasn't any audible movement coming from the other side of the walls, so I pounded against the wood a little harder. After letting a few more seconds pass, I leaned against the frame and put my ear against the door to see if I could hear anyone coming to open it. It was only a matter of time before an employee would populate the halls and see a random person in a restricted area, so I wasted no more time listening for someone to let me in, and I grabbed the doorknob. It easily gave in to the force of my wrist twisting it. I pushed the door open in a rush since I realized there wasn't a lock preventing my entrance, and I stumbled into a room that appeared to be out of place. The entire building was loud and smelled of gasoline, but the office I found myself in was clean and pristine. Its walls were populated with numerous awards and pictures of employees. The office looked exactly how I would've expected it, and it contained exactly who I was looking for—or better yet, for who I should've initially avoided.

"Welcome to my office, Paige," Michael grumbled behind a large desk. "Take a seat."

He was in the middle of signing some documents when I disturbed him, but he hadn't looked up from his papers to see who had come in.

"Uh, how'd you know it was me?" I stuttered as I nervously sat in the chair across from him.

Without giving me a verbal response, Michael simply turned his computer monitor around to face me. It displayed live surveillance footage of the interior and exterior areas of his business. In the corner of one of the videos, I could see Graham walking around his car with one of the employees.

"Oh, right," I replied, feeling like an idiot for sneaking around when he clearly knew I was coming.

"I can't say I'm entirely upset that you are in my office right now," he began, "but I vividly remember you saying that you never wanted to see me again."

Michael maintained the authoritative demeanor that he always carried while at his place of business. I respected his professionalism, but it felt too formal.

"Just trying to keep the spontaneity alive," I said, trying to lighten the mood. "Anyway, I have something important to tell you."

Michael stopped signing his documents and folded his hands on his desk to await my next words. It was all too business-like. I wished Graham and

I had agreed to carry out our plan during a time where Michael wasn't working so that he would drop his corporate persona.

"We are in a position that I am sure neither of us like, and I know I shouldn't even be talking to you right now," I started. "I mean, you completely hid a giant part of your life from me, and who knows what else you are hiding. I don't think I could ever trust you again. You lied to me." I was deviating slightly from the planned conversation that Graham and I had previously discussed, but I was across from the man who I had strong feelings for, and I couldn't stop my emotions from taking over. "I liked you. I really liked you. And you ruined everything."

Michael was trying to stick to his professional behavior. He kept a straight face, and he was sitting upright in his chair, but his pupils were softened and the corners of his eyes were beginning to dampen.

"I don't know what your reasoning was for completely crushing what we had, but honestly, it doesn't matter at this point. I know a way where you can fix things, and it's going to be up to you whether you follow through with it or not," I explained, going back to the script that Graham and I had talked about.

He raised an eyebrow in curiosity, obviously wanting to know how there was a way to try and mend the brokenness. Michael continued to refrain from speaking, but I knew him too well to know that it wasn't because he was at a loss for words—it was because his armored exterior was severely cracked, and trying to express his feelings into words would cast the final blow to the confident front he was putting up.

"If you truly want to put this all in the past, you're going to give me the information of where you and your brothers are currently staying. I'm going to have the police show up to that address and finally make you all pay for what you did to my best friend. No more running from your problems, Mike Kingsley," I declared, empowered by how I was able to deliver my speech without crying.

Michael still didn't say anything, and I was starting to become frustrated with his silence. The one-sided conversation was not getting us anywhere.

"Do you have anything to say to that?" I asked.

He simply shook his head, and although it was a response to that question, it didn't help give me any answers to the real issue at hand.

"I'll give you some time to think about it then," I said, standing up from the chair.

I headed for the door, turning my back to the man who had betrayed me.

"Paige," he croaked from behind his desk, finally deciding to speak up. "Do you still need a date to Hannah's wedding?"

"Seriously?" I snapped, abandoning my journey for the door and turning back around to face him. "That is where your head is at right now?"

"I just want my last day as a free man to be memorable..." he cautiously pointed out.

I blankly stared at him, giving him a chance to clarify his answer or take back what he had just said.

"If you agree to bring me as your plus-one, I'll take you to my brothers afterward," he clarified.

I briefly contemplated the arrangement, but I didn't ponder it too long as I didn't want him to retract the offer.

"Fine, you can go with me," I agreed. "But don't wear anything too crazy. No tropical prints."

"What about animal prints?" he asked.

I tried to stay serious in that moment because of the severity of our situation, but I couldn't help crack a tiny smile.

"I'll see you at the wedding," I noted.

For the second time, I attempted to leave his office, but I still had a nagging question on my mind.

"Are there others?" I quietly asked Michael, still facing the door that I had half-opened. "Is Avery not the only victim?"

I believed the real reason why I kept my back to him while asking my question was because I had a feeling what the answer would be, and I knew Michael's face would give it away before his words would.

"There will be justice for them all," Michael muttered.

I left Michael's office, gently closing the door behind me. I didn't know how many other girls had fallen victim to Kyle's mischievous ways, but I felt saddened for all of them.

I navigated through the hallway until I was back in the lobby, and I continued to head out of the building and through the parking lot until I reached my brother's car. Graham had the music blaring through the radio and the air conditioning on full blast. I opened the passenger door, and it was obvious that the abrupt noise had startled him.

"You scared me. I didn't see you coming," Graham said, turning down the music. "How'd it go?"

"Good, I guess. He's accompanying me to Hannah's wedding and is going to lead us to his brothers after," I solemnly stated even though I had completed my mission.

"He's going to the wedding?" Graham shouted. "We can't have that. Avery will obviously recognize him. Let's go back inside and tell him he can't go."

"No, that's the deal," I frustratingly let out. "We are fighting for more than just Avery now."

Graham stared at me confused, but he didn't insist on going back inside anymore.

"I trust you, but I don't trust him," my brother explained. "What if he doesn't lead us to Kyle after the wedding?"

"Well, then, at least one Kingsley will go down," I said.

Satisfied with my reasoning, Graham put his car in reverse and backed out of the parking lot of King Cars. With the rehearsal dinner being tomorrow, there wasn't enough time to argue a new plan—Michael was my plus-one, and it was the only way to take down the evil trio. I needed to give a voice to the ones who came before Avery, who were still hiding in the shadows and fearful to start their life again because of what the Kingsleys had done to them. Hannah's wedding was surely going to be a night that nobody would forget.

25

Sisters Before Misters

It felt like yesterday that Hannah, Avery, and I were standing in the long line for the bathroom at Lucky's Tavern, trying to estimate how long it would be until it was our turn, and hoping that our bladders could contain themselves for just a few more minutes. The number of stalls in the establishment had not caught up to the increasing popularity of the bar, which often led to winding queues. With how often we spent our weekends there, they should have reserved a special bathroom just for us. However, the bathroom fiasco was simply a part of the overall experience, and I wouldn't trade my memories at Lucky's Tavern for the world. Granted, Hannah, Avery, and I found ourselves currently waiting in line for the bathroom at Lucky's Tavern again, but things were different. We had never gone to the bars on the night before one of us was getting married. We'd have work, important meetings, and significant events the following morning, but nothing as big as a wedding.

Lucky's was the chosen destination for the after-party following the rehearsal dinner. The term "party" was used loosely in that scenario, as the only people who actually went out that night were us three girls, plus Graham and Reid. I was pretty sure that was all Hannah really wanted in attendance, anyway. Avery and I were her best friends, Graham was overprotective and always wiggled his way into our plans, and Reid just wanted to feel included. We could've ended up at a gas station and he would've enjoyed every second of the adventure.

In Hannah's defense, she didn't go into the day thinking that she would end up at a grungy bar the night before her wedding day, but when the groom decided to have a meltdown during the rehearsal dinner and pick a fight with everyone in his path, including his future bride, she needed a place to escape from the earlier events and clear her mind. If I were in her shoes, I would have immediately canceled everything if my fiancé had embarrassed the waiter in front of the entire group by claiming he was flirting with Hannah when he clearly was simply doing his job and trying to help her decide what she wanted off the menu. If that wasn't the final straw, I would have definitely called off the wedding after he revealed that his promised plans to not travel for work as much once they were married was no longer on the table, and therefore, he decided that having kids was no longer in the future for them. I respected anyone's decision who opted to live a child-free life, but telling your future bride that at the rehearsal dinner was cause enough to break up. Hannah wanted to be more than just a cat mom, and I wasn't sure how she would cope with being on a different page than her future husband. I could tell she was hurt, but she kept a brave face throughout the entire event. Hannah was a lot more forgiving than I was, and although it wasn't ideal to have to go to Lucky's so that she could clear her mind from Elliot's recent behavior, she was still as excited as ever to marry him.

"You guys have been in line for twenty minutes and haven't even moved yet," Graham pointed out as he approached us with Reid closely by his side.

"Thanks, Captain Obvious," I griped, annoyed with how long the line was but taking it out on my brother.

"I'm sure the line will die down soon enough," Hannah shared, trying to add some positivity.

"We could use the men's room," I offered as I observed the few people in the other line.

"Ew, gross," Avery commented. "I'd rather wait here for another hour."

"Well, that's how long we will probably be waiting," I assured.

I counted the number of girls in front of us, but I couldn't see them all because of how far back we were.

"Do you want us to just wait with you guys?" Reid proposed.

"No, you and Graham should go have fun," Hannah relayed. "There's two spots on the dance floor calling your guys' names."

"Actually, there is something else I'd rather do," Reid announced. "Hannah, as your last night of being single, can I buy you a drink?"

Avery, Graham, and I exchanged surprised looks as we had never seen Reid so confident before.

"I'd love that!" she squealed.

Reid held out his hand to lead her to the bar.

"Wait, right now?" she said, observing our position in line.

"We'll probably still be in the same place by the time you get back," I exclaimed.

"We can hold your spot," Avery clarified.

Hannah looked back and forth between Reid, us, the bar, and the line for the bathroom, presumably weighing her options.

"Sure, why not? Let's go!" she eventually decided.

Hannah skipped off to the bar to get her final drink as an unmarried woman with Reid proudly walking beside her. That was most likely the first time someone had ever let him buy them a drink. He was such an awkward person that girls probably walked away before he finished his sentence, if he was even confident enough to ask.

"I can't wait for her wedding tomorrow," Avery confessed. "She has been working so hard to plan it, and I know everything is going to be perfect."

"Right, about that..." Graham began.

"Graham, not here," I interrupted. "Not now."

"The wedding is tomorrow, Paige," he fired back at me. "There is no more time."

"There's no more time for what?" Avery hesitantly asked.

"Babe, there's something you need to know," Graham uttered, his face giving away the fact that he was about to deliver awful news. "...Kyle is back."

Avery slightly stumbled as she took a step backward. The blow of Graham's confession had knocked her off her feet.

"What do you mean he's back?" she stuttered. "What are you trying to say?"

Graham looked in my direction, silently urging me to fill in the backstory that really only I had the full details on.

"I'm sorry, Avery. It's all my fault," I apologized before getting into the story.

"What happened? What did you do?" Avery asked, confused.

"I...uh...sort of was dating Kyle's brother," I slowly revealed. "But I promise I had no idea, and I cut it off right when I found out."

"Your mystery man is Kyle's brother?" she inquired, trying to piece the puzzle together.

"Mike Kingsley," I said, trying to clarify everything for her.

"You don't need to worry, though," Graham assured. "Paige confronted him, and he's going to turn himself and his brothers over to the police."

We were trying to fill Avery in on everything that was going on, but I didn't think our words were coming out in the form of English to her. Everything we said appeared as if it wasn't registering in her brain.

"I'll be by your side the entire day tomorrow, and I've hired extra security," Graham promised. "I will make sure you are safe."

"He's coming to the wedding?" Avery shrieked.

"It's just a part of the deal," I assured her. "Then he is going to lead the police to his brothers, and the Kingsleys will be gone for good."

I was surprised Avery was able to formulate a sentence as I could see her heart beating out of her chest and sweat dripping down her forehead.

"Does Hannah know?" she asked.

"No, we figured it was best to not stress her out even more during her wedding," I followed up. "We can fill her in after her honeymoon."

"I am going to have the police waiting outside the reception, so she won't have to know that anything is out of the ordinary," Graham explained. "Once it's over, either Mike is going to lead the authorities to his brothers or the cops will move in on him, but either way, a Kingsley is going down."

"I can't believe all this is happening," Avery breathlessly noted, looking as if she was still trying to process everything.

Although we were surrounded by the sounds of music blaring and people screaming, it still felt quiet as Avery, Graham, and I stared at each other for a bit, letting everything sink in.

"You aren't going to protect a Kingsley brother this time, are you?" I asked her, remembering that she refused to give Kyle up to the police last time.

"I won't if you won't," she replied.

Avery was my best friend. Starting in high school, we pretty much grew up together, especially when she moved in our senior year. After spending that much time together, it was just a matter of time before our personalities, hobbies, and interests started to merge. Over time, she started acting a little bit more like me, and I began to pick up some of her tendencies, too. However, if there was one thing that I would never acquire from Avery, it was her decision to put a man before herself. Therefore, no matter how much I still had feelings for Michael, I would never go down in history as someone who protected a Kingsley.

26

Wedding Bells

I was standing at the front of the venue along with Avery and the rest of the bridesmaids, waiting for the bride to walk down the aisle. The space was decorated perfectly, and Hannah's desired color scheme of various shades of red was on clear display. She had mentioned previously that most of her budget had gone to the decor, and that was clearly true. Every inch of the room contained either an arrangement of roses or handfuls of petals. It provided an overwhelming floral scent, but it accurately represented Hannah's blooming personality. Her day was finally here, and I was grateful to be a part of it. Although I wasn't the biggest fan of Elliot's recent behavior, he looked extremely enamored with being at the altar, waiting for his future wife to walk through the doors. I couldn't imagine how Hannah would react to seeing all her closest friends and family gathered in one space to celebrate her. It was hard to contain the excitement that I was feeling on her behalf, but I kept a calm demeanor as the groom and the accompanying wedding party were the center of attention while everyone waited for Hannah to enter. Unfortunately, Avery did not match my poised stature. She kept fidgeting and swaying from side to side.

"Are you okay?" I whispered to her, hoping that she would put a stop to her frantic behavior.

"I'm trying to enjoy this day as much as possible for Hannah's sake, but I can't get over the fact that Kyle's brother is here," Avery confessed.

I peered toward the back of the venue where Michael was seated. It was a bittersweet moment having him there. I was relieved that our deal was being carried out by him being in attendance, but I knew the beautiful day would have an ugly ending. Ironically, the wedding was what initially brought Michael and I closer together. However, it was also going to be the day that sparked the beginning to the end of the Kingsley era.

"I know, I'm sorry. But it will all be over after this," I apologized. "I feel bad that I brought someone who hit you in such close proximity to you again."

"Well, to be fair, Mike never touched me," Avery shared, still acting jumpy. "Their other brother, Eli, was the one who punched me."

"Oh," I muttered at the new information. "Well I'm still sorry for bringing someone so evil to the wedding. I know your skin is probably crawling by simply looking at him."

"I wouldn't really say Mike is evil," Avery stated. "He was there, but I could tell he didn't want to be. In fact, I swore he was about to pee his pants during the whole thing."

"But Michael can't be entirely innocent, right?" I stammered. "I mean he's related to Kyle."

"Kyle and Mike are completely different," Avery confirmed.

"Yeah, but there's no way that he didn't know what was happening that night," I interjected.

I was half-hoping that he truly hadn't done anything violent and that I had been right about him from the start, but a part of me needed a reason for why I had cut someone who I cared about out of my life.

"Actually, even Mike hates Kyle. Their parents aren't alive anymore, and I'm pretty sure Kyle had everything to do with it," Avery admitted.

I should have let Michael tell me his side of the story instead of jumping to conclusions. There was an army of cops waiting outside to take him and his brothers down after the reception, assuming that all three of them were equally responsible. Kyle and Eli should really be the ones going down, but in order to get to them, Michael had to sacrifice his own freedom. It was either all of them or none of them, and it was too late to back out now.

In the middle of my mini panic attack about leading Michael to his doom, the doors of the venue suddenly opened, revealing the most beautiful bride being walked down the aisle by her father. The violins and piano began to play, and everyone in the room stood out of respect. Hannah gracefully floated past all of her guests as her white gown hugged her body just right.

"She's gorgeous," Avery pointed out, finally standing still.

I totally agreed with Avery's comment, but my mind was still processing the recent conversation.

Hannah and Elliot came together at the end of the aisle, and a rumble occurred as everyone sat back in their seats to witness the joining of two people. Obviously, the main reason I was there was to watch one of my best friends get married, but my sights were set on Michael. Even in the midst of it being his last day as a free man, he still seemed to be able to let himself enjoy the ceremony. He seemed enamored by the idea of love, and fascinated by the sight of marriage. I should've been fuming with anger over his participation in my friend's attack, but after hearing Avery place all of the blame on Eli and Kyle, there was nothing holding my mind back from imagining myself walking down the aisle with Michael being at the end of it. I only eventually snapped out of my fantasy world when Michael's eyes met mine, and I quickly refocused my thoughts toward the officiant and hoped that he hadn't realized how long I had been staring at him. However, knowing him, he was fully aware of my gaze the entire time.

"We are gathered here today to witness the union of Hannah Livingston and Elliot Stockton," the officiant bellowed. "Before we officially begin, I must ask that if anyone objects to this marriage or has any reason that these two should not be married today, speak now or forever hold your peace."

Since the officiant was looking into the crowd, awaiting an improbable objection, I used that as another opportunity to stare back at the wedding guests and noticed that Michael was still looking at me. I hoped he was also envisioning our own wedding day so I wouldn't feel as crazy for doing so.

"I object!" a voice boomed.

Reid stood up from his chair, and all eyes turned to him. There were numerous gasps sounding throughout the space, the loudest one being Hannah's.

"Hannah, I never believed in love at first sight until you entered my life. Ever since we worked at the restaurant together, my heart abandoned its own rhythm and its only desire was to beat for you. I was too afraid to ever confess my feelings for you, as I didn't think you would ever be with a guy like me. But after starting my new job and working for the most go-getter boss woman in the world, it made me realize that it's better to just say what is on my heart and my mind," Reid announced.

I tried to make myself shrink as much as possible, hoping that nobody would realize I was the boss he was referring to.

Reid scooted through the rows of seats and made his way toward the aisle. He was walking down it, continuing to profess his love for Hannah.

"Hannah Livingston, you are the most beautiful person in the world. It pains me to watch you get married, but if there is even an ounce of your heart that has love for me, I'm asking you to give me one chance to show you how I truly feel about you," Reid confessed.

The audience continued to gasp. Most were so focused on the objection that nobody noticed the groom who appeared as if he was about to punch Reid in the face—good thing we had the extra police presence around. However, to me, the most surprising thing was Hannah's reaction. I would have been livid if someone had objected to my wedding, yet she seemed somewhat...relieved.

"Hannah, please offer me the opportunity to love you," Reid blurted as he outstretched his hand toward her.

Everyone was too stunned to speak, or maybe they were silent in anticipation of Hannah's response. Elliot attempted to grumble some inappropriate words, but even he seemed too in shock to lash out at Reid.

I thought the initial gasps to Reid's speech were loud, but the noise that escaped everyone's mouth when Hannah began to reach for his hand and accept his attempt at stealing the bride away was even louder. Time felt like it had ceased, and I was watching in slow motion as Hannah interlocked her fingers with Reid's and let him lead her back down the aisle. She honestly seemed elated that someone had come to rescue her from the prison sentence of being with Elliot Stockton.

"Are you serious, Hannah?" Elliot shouted after her.

Hannah didn't even glance back as she happily skipped away with her new lover.

"You'll never find someone as good as me!" Elliot shouted after. "I'm the best thing that has ever happened to you!"

Usually in cases like that, the wedding guests' sympathy would have been with the groom who was left at the altar. However, after Elliot's outburst, I didn't think anyone was on his side. Although some of his close family members ran up to him to calm him down and console his crushed heart, I assumed they were just trying to prevent him from making himself look even more horrid instead of actually trying to make him feel better.

Hannah's parents and immediate family also felt the need to chase after their loved one. Once the bride had runaway with Reid, they headed toward the exit, probably trying to get answers and make sense of the unexpected ending.

Avery and I exchanged awkward glances. We were covered by the blanket of silence along with the rest of the wedding guests who still remained in the venue, but as soon as the shock wore off, the place erupted with chatter.

"What do we do now?" Avery asked.

We were both at a loss for words, and we were longing for some sort of direction.

I grabbed Avery's hand and pulled her away from the altar as I bolted toward my brother. In a state of confusion, I was hoping Graham would have the solution. He seemed to always know what to do.

"Did either of you two know that would happen?" Graham asked as soon as we reached him.

Avery and I ferociously shook our heads, confirming that neither one of us could have predicted the rejection.

"I still can't believe it," Avery shared. "It didn't seem real."

"I mean, we all saw how Elliot was acting," I announced

"Yeah, but I didn't think she would actually leave him at the altar—let alone leave him for someone else," Graham said.

"I really underestimated Reid," I added. "Even I would never have the courage to do something like that."

We were all stunned with how Hannah's wedding had turned out, but watching as Michael made his way toward us made me realize that the night was probably going to be full of even more shocking events.

"Well, that's a wedding I'll never forget," Michael said as he joined Avery, Graham, and I. "Thank you for allowing me to be your plus-one, Paige."

I nodded my head in acknowledgment of his praise, but I could hear the fear slipping through the cracks of his forced optimism.

My arms were folded across my chest in a defensive pose, but I felt my body attempt to uncross them in order to latch onto Michael. My mind was telling my body to stay still, but it was a losing battle. As soon as I felt my body about to win, Graham stepped in between us.

"It's time to take us to your brothers," he demanded.

I fully expected Michael to go against his commitment as turning against your own family was asking a lot from him, but he simply nodded his head in defeat.

"We had a deal, and I will honor it," Michael agreed.

"Lead the way then," my brother uttered. "And don't even think about running. There's plenty of cops outside who would happily arrest you right now."

Graham gestured toward the door, but Michael paused before starting his journey to the exit.

"Paige, thank you for giving life meaning again," he confessed, showing me his vulnerable side one last time. "And Avery...I'm sorry that I didn't stop my brothers. On that night, I was as afraid of Kyle as you were, but that's not an excuse. I hope you can forgive me."

Before either of us could respond, Michael followed Graham's direction and began to head out of the venue.

Graham closely trailed behind Michael, and I started to walk behind my brother. However, he wasn't too happy that I wanted to go along on the journey.

"You need to stay behind," Graham ordered. "Both of you should go back to the apartment. I will keep you updated."

Avery acted as if she was about to comply with her boyfriend's request, but this was too big of a deal to not be a part of.

"No, we are coming with you," I stated, holding on to Avery's hand to ensure Graham knew she was also included in this.

"It's too dangerous," Graham explained, slowly walking backward to keep up with Michael who was making his way toward the exit.

"We started this journey together, and we are going to end it all together," I argued. "Avery and I need to witness the Kingsleys go down."

Graham appeared to contemplate my argument, but eventually he gave in—most likely because Michael was already halfway out the door, and we didn't have time to continue to go back and forth.

"Fine, but you both need to stay far behind," Graham insisted. "Do not get too close."

"Okay," I agreed, happy to know that we were going to be able to come along for the ride.

Graham turned to run after Michael, who had now left the venue.

"Come on," I directed toward Avery. "I'll drive."

"Are you sure it's safe to go?" she asked. "Maybe we should just listen to Graham and go back to the apartment."

I walked right up to Avery and put my hands on either side of her head, focusing her attention toward my next words.

"It's time to take down the man who stole way too much from you," I uttered. "The police will protect us."

"The police will be too focused on Kyle," Avery justified.

"Graham will have our backs," I promised.

"There are still two other brothers," Avery noted. "Graham can't take both of them down."

"Michael won't do anything," I shared. "He won't hurt anyone."

"Yeah...well...I thought the same thing about Kyle, and now look where we are. You promised you wouldn't protect a Kingsley," Avery divulged.

After watching Hannah run away into the sunset with someone who truly loved her, it made me realize that life was too short to waste it on being surrounded by those who didn't have my best interest at heart. In another life, I would have kept Michael by my side until the end, but unfortunately, fate wasn't on our side that time.

"We will keep a safe distance away from everything. I want you to finally see the end to this all and get some closure," I shared. "I'm not trying to protect a Kingsley...I am trying to protect you."

I released Avery's head from my hands and took a few steps back to let her make her decision.

"...I mean, I guess you're right," she hesitantly agreed.

After her half-hearted answer, I immediately grabbed her hand, and we raced toward my car in order to not miss out on the action. Today was the day Kyle was going down, Avery would get closure, and the pieces of my heart that still belonged to Michael would most likely crumble away—but at least justice would be served for anyone else who had also been victimized by the Kingsleys. Hopefully that would be worth watching the man I fell for be taken away...

27

Gone for Good

From a young age, I was taught that red and blue made purple. I probably first encountered that lesson in elementary school art class, where the concept seemed simple enough. I could still picture myself as a curious child, hearing about the color theory and immediately setting out to test it. I mixed red and blue paint together and watched as a muddy purple-brown hue emerged. Technically, I supposed the theory was correct, but I always preferred the colors in their pure, separate forms. Purple might have been pretty, but to me, it was just a blend of red and blue. I understood why the two colors were often seen as opposites—one representing warmth, the other coldness. Their unique identities were lost in the haze of purple, yet I never forgot what they were on their own. I remained loyal to them, honoring their distinction. But now, as the flashing red and blue lights of police cars lit up the street in front of the Kingsley's temporary home, that loyalty faltered. I wished, more than ever, that red and blue would come together and create something beautiful—something other than the harsh reality of flashing sirens.

"I can't believe Kyle has been staying here for all this time," Avery announced, her voice a mix of disbelief and curiosity. "How long do you think they've been living here?"

"Too long," I muttered, my voice laced with unease.

We observed the modest house tucked away in a quiet, seemingly average neighborhood. It was the kind of place nobody would ever expect to house evil individuals. The scariest part was that it was only a few minutes away from Exe Apartments.

I felt the knot in my stomach tighten. Part of me was relieved, even elated, to finally close the chapter on Kyle Kingsley once and for all. He had entered our lives years ago, working as the Exe pool security guard. The story had a seemingly innocent start, but it had definitely morphed into something far more twisted. But there was another part of me that felt the sting of bittersweet loss. Closing the chapter on Kyle meant also closing the chapter on Michael and I—right when our story had been getting to the good part.

I had parked my car a few blocks down the street, far enough that we wouldn't draw attention to ourselves, but close enough to witness it all unfold before us. It was surreal—watching the scene from the comfort of my own car. I had only ever seen that type of chaos on the news, but now it was my reality. I could feel the pulse of the moment, the rush of adrenaline in the air, and my heart trying to decide whether it should race or completely stop.

Police lights were flashing, illuminating the otherwise dark and quiet neighborhood. At least half a dozen cop cars were surrounding the Kingsley residence, their sirens still wailing in the background and drowning out everything else. I was surprised there weren't any nosy neighbors coming to check out all the noise, but they probably also wanted to keep their distance out of fear of what all the cops were there for.

The chaotic events continued as the officers crouched behind their vehicles with their weapons drawn as they took their defensive positions, waiting for something to happen. One officer was shouting orders at the house through a bullhorn. If the neighbors weren't aware of the police presence, they definitely were now.

"Kyle Kingsley! Eli Kingsley! Step out of the house with your hands visible!" the policeman bellowed with a firm and commanding tone.

Despite all the flashing lights and shouts through the bullhorn, none of that was the part that held my attention. My eyes were fixed on Michael. He had recently pulled into the driveway and was attempting to give himself up—the ultimate sacrifice for the victims of his brothers. I hated every part of it. It was like watching a movie in slow motion. Michael's body was stiff as he opened the door and stepped out onto the driveway. His hands shot up instinctively.

The moment Michael fully faced the police, it felt like the world paused for just a beat. It was the calm before the storm, as that was the last moment of so-called peace before the world came crumbling down. Officers rushed toward him, their movements swift and sharp. They shoved him to the ground, his body hitting the pavement with a sickening thud. It was like something out of a nightmare. Michael's expression was emotionless, almost as if he had disconnected from the reality around him. Big, burly officers gripped his arms and pulled him toward their squad car as if they didn't view him as a human. I couldn't help but wince at the sight, my heart sinking with every passing second. Michael had always been confident and poised. To see him so helpless was almost too much to bear. My chest tightened as I watched the officers drag him across the gravel and into the back of the patrol car, the door slamming shut behind him—a sign that his freedom was truly gone.

I could feel the tears welling up in my eyes before I even realized it. The flashes of blue and red reflected off the glass of my car window, distorting my view of Michael's empty stare. I blinked rapidly, but it didn't stop them from falling. Avery didn't notice. She was too focused on the action unfolding in front of her. Her gaze was fixated on the house, her eyes darting back and forth between the windows as if she were waiting for Kyle or Eli to step into view.

I wiped the tears away hastily, as I needed to see what would happen next. However, the night wasn't what I had imagined. It didn't feel like justice. It felt like we were all pawns in some twisted game, and Kyle Kingsley was the mastermind behind it all. The confrontation wasn't over. It was just beginning.

The cop with the bullhorn eventually gave up on his thunderous commands, as it was evident his words were not compelling enough to get the brothers to leave the residence. He made some sort of signal to the surrounding officers, and before I could try to guess what it meant, a front line of cops marched straight toward the front door. A tiny gasp escaped Avery's lips as we both realized that was a huge shift in strategy. Neither of us knew how Kyle or Eli would handle a forced entrance—if they were even inside.

A few more verbal commands, demanding that the brothers show themselves, were attempted again, but after another round of silence, the uniformed men lining the front porch of the house had enough of standing and waiting. Perhaps the door was made of paper or was extremely old, but it was abruptly kicked in as if it were made of feathers. It easily gave in to the force of the cop's foot, creating an opening for a bunch of armed men to flood into the home.

Avery and I braced ourselves for the result of the officers' actions. We heard a lot of shouting and crashing, but not knowing what was happening inside made every noise sound even worse. She continued to stare at the gap where the door once was, while I exchanged glances back and forth between

Michael sitting defeated in the back of the car and Graham who was trying to inch himself closer to the scene.

The officers had been inside longer than I anticipated, and I was starting to doubt Michael's ability to hold up his end of the deal. Maybe his loyalty to his brothers outweighed the damage that had been done to the victims. I felt my sympathy toward him turn into anger as I was already waiting for the police to declare the house empty. My tears were probably wasted over a man who had lied to me again. He most likely deserved to be sitting in the back of the police car.

"Paige, look!" Avery shouted, pointing to the movement at the house.

An officer exited the door frame first, but closely following behind was Eli and Kyle handcuffed.

"Michael didn't betray me," I whispered to myself.

I heard the click of the seat belt unlocking, and my passenger side door flung open as Avery had decided to race out of my car.

"Avery stop!" I yelled, quickly letting myself out of my car. However, she already had a head start. "Graham stop her!"

Graham's attention was quickly snapped from the scene unfolding in front of him to his girlfriend, who was currently running toward the man who had traumatized her.

Thankfully, Graham was able to intercept her mission and wrap Avery up in a bear hug before she could reach her attacker. She was kicking and screaming, yelling obscenities at Kyle. She was cursing his name, threatening things I would only say to my worst enemy. By the time I had made it over them, I was only able to catch a few words of Kyle's response to her.

"I knew you'd come back for me," he smirked with his hands behind his back.

Avery continued to yell profanities at him until Graham carried her away. He took her far enough to where she couldn't engage in conversation with Kyle anymore, but close enough to where they could both watch the Kingsley brothers' final demise. I retreated back toward my best friend and my brother, and we watched as they were all handcuffed and finally in custody.

"It's over now," Graham announced. "We did it. It's finally over."

Each brother was driven away in a separate car, and we watched as each one was taken away. They would face the consequences of their crimes, but there was one name still stuck in my mind—Michael. Maybe he didn't deserve the punishment he would face. In fact, maybe he didn't deserve any of it. But I had made a promise to Avery, a promise to not protect a Kingsley, and I had kept it to the very end. And still, as I watched the last car disappear down the street, I couldn't shake the nagging feeling that maybe, just maybe, I should have.

28

Separate Ways

"And now, for breaking news," the anchor announced. "Three individuals were taken into custody facing a wide array of charges, ranging from petty theft to first-degree murder. The suspects were discovered in a quiet neighborhood just outside the downtown area. In the latest update, authorities reported that each of the men has secured legal representation and will be prosecuted separately, based on their individual roles in the crimes. At this time, their attorneys have declined to provide any further comment."

Mugshots of Eli, Kyle, and Michael flashed across the screen as the anchor continued to depict them all as equally heinous.

"Turn it off," I declared, not wanting to hear the rest of the news story.

Nobody argued with my demand, and the television quickly went blank as Hannah abruptly clicked the power button on the remote. I was seated on the couch between my best friends, yet I still felt completely alone.

"At least we know they are in custody," Avery said. "We won't have to look over our shoulder anymore."

"And maybe Michael got a really good lawyer," Hannah added.

She had been more involved in my relationship than Avery was, as Hannah viewed Michael as the guy who made me smile and Avery simply viewed him as Kyle's brother. I didn't blame Avery's perspective, as I may have had the same one if I were in her shoes, but I wished she was better at being able to separate Michael from the crimes of his brother.

There was a sorrowful tension that filled the room. However, arguably the person who was supposed to be the most devastated after running away with a different man after her wedding, was surprisingly the most positive.

"Group hug?" Hannah offered.

Before I could even answer, I was sandwiched between my best friends. It felt like each one of us was giving and receiving a pity hug as all three of our lives had gone awry in some kind of way. The only method I knew to help ease the hurt was to laugh, so in the midst of the tight embrace, I began to giggle. It must have been contagious, as Avery and Hannah echoed my sounds with laughter of their own, and suddenly, the living room was filled with the voices of three chuckling girls laughing their pain away.

"I love that I have forever sisters," Hannah commented.

"Me too," Avery agreed.

"Speaking of forever," I muttered. "Our lease is about to end. It feels like we have lived at this complex our entire lives. Should we re-sign for another year or try out a different apartment? I personally am open to something new, but I also hate moving my stuff."

Bringing up our leasing agreement was like a knife that severed the hug I was encapsulated in. Avery and Hannah abruptly returned to their respective sides of the couch. The initial tension that was squashed from our hug and laughter was now replaced by another awkward air.

"Did I say something wrong?" I asked, observing their timid faces.

"Well, um, there was never really a good time to bring this up, but since we are on the subject of it," Avery started, "I wanted to officially let you know that Graham and I will be moving in together. We found a place closer to the restaurant."

"Oh my gosh," I cried out, "I am sad and happy for you at the same time."

I was hurt to know that my best friend in the entire world and my only brother were moving across town to live on their own. Those two had been by my side for years, and it felt too much of a sudden change for them to be leaving. The restaurant was no more than twenty minutes away so I knew their next residence wouldn't be too far away, but I was so used to having them both at least in the same building as me. I was proud of them for taking the next step in their relationship, but I already missed them, and they hadn't even left yet.

"Hannah and I are definitely going to miss you as a roommate," I shared with a tear welling in the corner of my eye. I just wanted to go one day without crying, but evidently, today was not going to be the day to end the streak.

"Actually," Hannah muttered, "I am also moving out."

"What?" I screamed.

I knew it was only a matter of time before Avery moved in with Graham. She already spent a majority of her nights at his unit anyway, but I didn't expect Hannah to leave in the foreseeable future. I wanted our cats to continue growing up together.

"To others, my wedding came across as a disaster, but to me, it was honestly such a relief. I knew there was something off about Elliot, but I just couldn't put my finger on it," she reasoned.

"He was rude, jealous, overprotective, disrespectful," I listed off for her.

"Anyway," Hannah continued on. "After Reid and I left the venue, we discussed our feelings for each other over a few milkshakes, and I believe he truly is my person. I've never felt this way about anyone."

Hannah and Elliot had gotten engaged shortly after they officially started dating, so I knew that Hannah tended to move fast. However, I couldn't deny the spark in her eyes when Reid was around.

"Wow, my best friends are growing up," I noted. "I don't know what I am going to do without you guys."

"We will still be around," Avery promised. "We are forever sisters."

I was quickly smothered in another group hug, but I embraced that one more than before as I didn't know if it was going to be our last one for a while.

"Avery and I can help you find another apartment, too," Hannah offered.

"Absolutely," Avery agreed.

"Actually," I began, "I think I am going to re-sign the lease and keep the unit. Having three bedrooms is a lot of space, but the cats deserve it."

Toby, Leo, and Benny would truly enjoy the ability to roam through three bedrooms, but I believed the real reason I wanted to keep the apartment was because there was already enough change going on around me. I needed at least one thing to stay the same.

"You know what I just realized?" Hannah announced. "It's the Sunday before Labor Day."

"Last day the pool is open," I clarified.

"Should we attend our final Exe Apartment pool party of the year for old time's sake?" Avery asked.

We all exchanged anticipatory glances.

"I'll race you guys," I said with a smirk. "Last one there has to make friends with the pool security guard."

"No more pool security guards!" Avery shouted.

"Never again!" Hannah exclaimed.

"Then you better not be last," I shared, racing to my room to get dressed.

I heard thumps of footsteps as Avery and Hannah bolted to their rooms to quickly get ready and evade the punishment.

I loved that we were all speeding to attend the final pool party of the year as that was exactly how Avery and I had spent our first weekend at the Exe Apartments. Although years apart, I was still as uneasy as the initial one. When we first moved in, I was excited but nervous about what life had in store. We had moved from our hometown of East Tawas, Michigan, to Las Vegas, Nevada, on a whim. It was actually just an elaborate coping mechanism for Avery to escape her ex-boyfriend, but nobody knew what the effects of that one decision entailed. There were extreme highs and terrible lows, but we made it through to the other side, both as better people. Heading to the final pool party years after our initial move, I still had apprehensions about the future. Big changes were ahead of me, and I felt myself in the same place of wondering where my next adventure would take me. Hopefully, the next few phases of life would also shape me into a better version of myself.

I was going to miss seeing Avery, Graham, and Hannah every day, but the adjustment was going to offer me the ability to really get to know the one person who I'd been dying to further uncover—myself. I was definitely closing a significant chapter in my life, a chapter that may as well have been its own book, but I was excited to be my own main character in my next story.

29

A Fresh Start

The clacking sounds of the computer keyboard rang in my ears as Reid scaled across the keys. I admired the sounds, as they signified work being accomplished. His fingers were flying back and forth, quickly punching in letters and numbers. Reid was clearly in the middle of a very important task as his hands seemed to have a mind of their own. It didn't even seem like he was focused on what he was writing. However, his elite keyboard and multitasking skills were just a part of his personality at that point.

"What are you typing?" I eventually asked in awe of his quick fingers, though I was confused since there wasn't too much work to be done. With Labor Day weekend abruptly turning into winter break, we were on the brink of another slow period.

"I'm building an app for the business," he explained nonchalantly.

"You're building an app? How do you even know how to do that?" I asked, baffled.

Reid turned his computer screen around, and all I saw were a bunch of symbols and codes that I didn't understand.

"On second thought, don't explain it to me," I began. "I wouldn't understand what you're saying."

Reid chuckled at my lack of technological knowledge and returned to being a mad scientist over his keyboard. It was crazy to think that a few months ago I couldn't stand having a conversation with him. I thought his awkwardness was too painful to be around, and now, we were working side-by-side and running a business together.

"Just don't make the app pink," I firmly instructed.

"Why not?" Reid questioned. "I like pink."

"I feel like it's not professional," I reasoned. "And it might get confused as a dating app."

"Are you on a pink dating app or something and are afraid you might mistake the two?" Reid asked.

"No," I said defensively. I hadn't had the urge to meet someone in a while—especially through an app. "I'm just saying other people might mistake them."

Reid began punching at a particular part of his keyboard where I knew the backspace button was located.

"Suit yourself," Reid stated, seemingly disappointed that the app was going to have to be another color.

"Actually, fine. Just make it pink," I said, caving in.

A smile glimmered across his face, and he began ferociously typing away again.

One thing I learned over the few months of working with Reid was that he was usually right.

It was nice to enjoy my job again. Reid was a breeze to work with, and I had an actual office space I could utilize now. Although the lease ending still pained me, it came at a perfect time since I was able to separate my bedroom from my work area. Technically, Hannah and Avery had a few more weeks left on the lease, but I barely saw them as they were busy moving their stuff and getting their new places ready before the holidays. At that point, I saw Reid more than I did either one of them. Avery, Hannah, and I still hung out as much as we could, but Reid was over for eight hours a day, Monday through Friday. Now that he had gained a new roommate, his own dwelling situation wasn't as peaceful as it once was, so he preferred to work in the office—which was formerly Hannah's room.

I kept the integrity of Avery's bedroom in case any guests wanted to spend the night, but until then, it was the cat's new playroom. Toby and Leo often utilized the extra space as their oasis away from Benny. The older cats enjoyed the peace and quiet while letting the younger one go crazy in the living room. Now, there were plenty of spots where the sun spilled into the apartment, providing ample opportunity for all of them to sunbathe and stretch out while doing so. I still would have rather given up the cat's room and the office for Hannah and Avery to move back in, but it was important for me to find the silver lining in it all—or else I'd probably go insane.

It was easier to stay positive when I was constantly busy. After the strange events of Hannah's wedding and the stress of watching the Kingsleys get arrested had died down, I threw myself back into my career. The business soared as Reid and I were tag-teaming the operations, which made things run a lot more smoothly. Work was a good distraction from the prior traumatic events, and it was something to keep my mind off the dwindling number of roommates.

"Are you and Avery coming over for dinner again?" Reid asked. "I'll be working late on this app, so I'll probably just pick up a pizza on the way home."

"No, not tonight," I answered. "It's probably best that I actually eat alone for once and give you and Hannah your space."

"You are always welcome," Reid assured.

He flashed a kind expression at me before zoning back in on his project.

"Hey Reid," I called softly. "Can you do me a favor?"

"Sure, anything!" he eagerly responded, pausing his aggressive typing.

"Go home," I uttered.

He looked at me, confused.

"You have been working so hard these past few months, and I really appreciate it," I began, "but we are caught up on work. In fact, we are ahead of where we need to be. The business is in a great place right now, and we are heading into winter break. Families are going on vacation and spending more time with their children. They won't need our services nearly as much."

Reid appeared to contemplate my comment.

"You're right..." he said. "So we should offer virtual nannies as part of our services! I can add it to the app—it will only take me a few days to integrate. I can start creating a job posting and setting up interviews for the new positions. We will be able to care for children from anywhere!"

"Reid!" I shouted, interrupting his train of thought. "We can revisit the idea after winter break. Go home to your girlfriend."

One of the few things in life that Reid enjoyed more than working was Hannah. It didn't take much more convincing after bringing up her name. Therefore, instead of further developing his app, he packed up his stuff in order to head back to his apartment for the day. He methodically gathered his belongings and began to make his way out of the office.

"Quick question, boss," Reid began as he was leaning against the door frame with his backpack over his shoulder. "Do you think it is too early to propose to Hannah?"

My eyes grew to the size of my head, and I sat frozen at my desk.

"Just kidding," Reid followed up with a slight chuckle and obnoxious wink. "I'm still working on my sense of humor."

"Go home!" I playfully fired, crumpling up a piece of paper and throwing it at him so he would finally leave. "You work too much."

"So I can take the rest of the week off?" he sarcastically asked.

"Bye Reid!" I yelled, laughing at his awkward joke.

He had finally left the apartment to make his way back home, but I could have guaranteed that as soon as he made it back, he was going to open up his laptop and return to working on his app.

Reid was a strange man, but he definitely didn't lack passion. He cared deeply about his job, friends, family, and of course, his girlfriend. Despite the world telling Hannah that she should end up with Elliot—the former veteran turned successful pilot—she followed her heart and ended up with a man who truly showed her what love was.

Avery and Hannah's love lives used to scare me into a deep hibernation. I hid from the world, and I especially hid from the idea of dating again. However, seeing where both of them were now, I knew that all the hurt and pain was worth it. Heartbreak wasn't some life event that had to prevent the feeling of love to ever be experienced again. I believed it signified something great, and something far more positive. I truly felt that a heart breaks so that it can sever itself from a person that is not right—a person that is not meant to be—in order to prepare for a better connection that is coming down the line. It took me a while, but I finally was able to come to the conclusion that heartbreak doesn't stop someone from having a happily ever after, it's simply a small chapter to the greater love story at hand.

30

Got Milk?

I actually enjoyed living by myself more than I would have thought. Although the first couple of months were really rough, I had started to get used to the peace and quiet of my apartment. I still frequently visited Hannah and Avery at their own places, and Reid was constantly working at the apartment, which really helped with the transition from two roommates to none.

I enjoyed the extra helping hand, but it felt like I had traded Hannah for Reid. It had been months since Hannah had taken a break from being a nanny. At first, it was supposed to be a temporary hiatus while she focused on planning her wedding and attending her honeymoon, but since that evidently didn't fall into place, I figured she would have returned to work earlier. It had been months since she was last employed. I figured she needed a few more weeks after her planned wedding to recuperate from all that had happened. After that, I assumed she needed a bit more time in order to focus on her move. When she still didn't return after getting settled in, I gave her the benefit of the doubt, thinking that she was just trying to navigate going from being just friends with Reid to living and working together. Yet, with sufficient time passing by, giving her ample opportunity to return to the business, she still refrained from picking up any more shifts. Her absence wasn't a detriment to the business, as we had plenty of staff to take over her former duties. I just wanted her to get back to her usual routine.

Hannah's life seemed to magically improve after a matter of switching partners. She spent more time enjoying the company of her friends, family, and cats, and growing the relationship with her new boyfriend. I was very confused as to what exactly had brought on the shift from constantly doing something to slowing her life down. Initially, I continued to blame her change in behavior on Elliot's treatment of her. Anyone would have suffered post-traumatic stress after dealing with him. But when Avery and I managed to drag her to Lucky's Tavern one weekend and she refused a drink, my suspicions were raised—and that wasn't the only thing I saw that raised an eyebrow. She always had to use the restroom, which was not convenient when at Lucky's, and she always shielded her stomach when walking through the crowded bar. After witnessing that, I knew there was more to the story about why she wasn't returning to work.

I didn't share my suspicions with Avery, who I believed didn't notice anything off with Hannah as her own life had a lot going on. She and Graham were prepping for a cooking competition show that Graham had been selected to participate in. It was a series that had been airing for a few seasons now. The premise of the show was to have various top chefs across the country participating in cooking competitions against each other, resulting in the elimination of the worst dish after each challenge. Graham would be gone for over two months filming the television show, and even though Avery and I were going to miss him when he left for it, it was definitely going to be worth it. Being broadcast on a popular food channel and representing his restaurant was really good marketing for the business—an aspect that Avery was most looking forward to. Graham was hopeful that he would make it to the end to earn the title of one of the top chefs in America, but I wanted him to win in order to get the prize money. A quarter of a million dollars was life-changing money, and my brother was easily the best chef in the country. He was spending the last few weeks before filming cooking and challenging himself nonstop, but I already knew he was more than ready.

It was nice to witness our trio still remain close while also branching out on our own. Our gossip sessions were a lot more entertaining now that everyone's lives were filled with new updates and fun revelations. However, one of the things I gravely missed about living with roommates was a stocked refrigerator. If I had run out of an ingredient or forgotten to grab it at the store, chances were that Avery or Hannah already had it back at the apartment. Unfortunately, I couldn't rely on their groceries to solve my forgetfulness anymore. Therefore, I ended up at the grocery store late in the afternoon. It was my third time going...that day. However, another perk of living alone was that nobody had to know that I couldn't remember everything I needed. It was only after I got back to the apartment that I would realize I had forgotten to grab something. Reid easily organized my business ventures, but maybe I needed him to organize my personal life, as well.

Reid should have also put his organizational skills to the test and worked with the owner of the grocery store to help create a better checkout system. There was a line for people who only grabbed twenty-five items or less, but there also needed to be a section for shoppers who only came to the store for a few purchases. I only had a tub of butter in my hands, which would have only taken me two minutes at the self-checkout register, but I ended up spending five minutes grabbing the item and ten minutes waiting in line to pay for it. It was as if I was back at Lucky's Tavern, waiting in line for the bathroom. However, the store's structure ended up working out in their favor as by the time it was my turn to pay for my groceries, I now possessed not only just the butter, but three packs of gum, two chocolate bars, and a magazine. The extra items lined the aisles that led to the register, and since I was staring at them for so long, I ended up grabbing them, as well. The gum and chocolate bars would make for a nice sugar intake when I was craving something sweet, but the magazine was something I intended to purchase as memorabilia. Years ago, Avery, Hannah, and I had taken pictures of ourselves in matching red bikinis. In her former job, Avery was a social media manager for a modeling agency, and she ended up submitting the picture of us to a contest on behalf of the agency. The submitted photo was supposed to accurately encompass the brand, but since the agency was lacking in their creativity during photoshoots, Avery decided on choosing the red bikini photo. Her company ended up winning the contest, and in return, the photo was plastered on the front page of a magazine. I assumed the editor really liked the photo, or maybe it was a natural practice to recycle old photos, but somehow the picture of all three of us had resurfaced to the cover a few years later. Therefore, I obviously had to grab a copy.

"I didn't know you modeled," a voice behind me announced.

"Oh, I don't, it was just a—" I turned around to properly address the person who had realized that I was admiring a photo of my two friends and I on a magazine that was being sold at the local grocery store, but the sight of the man made me lose my train of thought, and I ultimately ended up dropping the magazine on the floor. My jaw, and my jaw on the cover, were now on the floor.

"Hi, Paige," Michael said as he picked it up off the floor and handed it to me.

"Hey...Michael," I stuttered, taking back the magazine.

The last time I saw him was when he was being thrown into the back of a cop car, and now we were just casually running into each other at the grocery store.

"What are you doing here?" I shakily asked. "I mean, how are you not in jail? How are you here?"

"Well, it's good to see you too," he joked awkwardly. "Turns out it pays off to hire a really good lawyer. I cut a deal with the police."

"What kind of deal?" I questioned.

"In return for confessing to a bunch of stuff that Kyle had gotten me involved with in the past, I got a lesser punishment," he shared.

"So...you're a free man?" I inquired.

"I wouldn't say I'm totally off the hook," he relayed, raising his pant leg which revealed an ankle monitor. "But at least I'm not behind bars."

I stared at the blinking technology that was strapped around his leg, and I couldn't help but feel somewhat responsible for it.

"How long do you have to wear that?" I asked.

"A year in total," he explained, "so about ten more months."

"You've been walking around free for two months and you didn't think to tell me?" I shrieked.

I wasn't expecting to pick up exactly where we had left off and run into the sunset, but I figured he would have at least reached out to update me on his current situation. Granted, I hadn't reached out to him, either, but it was because I thought he was in prison.

"I figured I'd leave it up to fate. I thought if we were truly meant to be together we'd cross paths again. Besides things usually unfold better between us when we don't plan our meetups," he uttered with a wink.

I wasn't in the most humorous mood, but his sarcasm reminded me of the old times. I was able to release a tiny smile while I scanned my items at the register.

"I've been to Lucky's almost every weekend trying to run into you," Michael confessed.

"I don't really go out that much anymore," I replied, honestly. "And, trying to find me is not called 'fate'—that's called stalking."

"I am open to actually planning to see each other again," Michael expressed. "We could do lunch tomorrow?"

"Well, how will we know if we are meant to be in each other's lives if we give up on fate?" I playfully questioned, using his own logic against him.

I finished checking out my items, throwing them into a plastic bag and leaving the machine in order for the next shopper to use it.

"So, is that a no?" Michael asked, chasing after me.

"How about if we run into each other again, then we can talk about planning something?" I offered.

"Oh, okay. Sure," Michael said.

I continued my journey toward the exit, but after taking a few steps away from Michael, I paused.

"Oops, looks like I forgot to grab milk," I announced loud enough for Michael to hear while I dug into my grocery bag. "I guess I'll have to return back to the store at exactly 2 p.m. tomorrow. Hm...I wonder if I will run into anyone there..."

I gave Michael a sly wink before galloping out the door with my recent purchases in hand.

He returned my gesture with a relieved sigh and a flirtatious smirk.

Of course, the universe would end up bringing Michael and I together again, even if he couldn't exactly run off. The ankle monitor was a reminder of what we had gone through, but at least I also knew he wasn't going anywhere. With all the change that was happening in my life, I appreciated that I knew I had at least one constant. Besides...it was finally his turn to be stalked for once.

A Note From The Author

Thank you for reading my novel, *Until We Meet Again*. Make sure you follow my social media accounts and subscribe to my newsletter for information about upcoming releases. My self-publishing journey would not be able to continue without you, so I appreciate your amazing support!

Subscribe to my newsletter:
https://linktr.ee/authorbaileythomas